Lucy March is a pseudonym of *New York Times* and *USA Today* bestselling author Lani Diane Rich. Lucy lives in southern Ohio with her husband, two daughters, two cats, five dogs, and one best friend.

Visit Lucy March online:
ww.lucymarch.com

By Lucy March

A Little Night Magic
That Touch of Magic

LUCY MARCH

piatkus

PIATKUS

First published in the US in 2014 by St Martin's Press
First published in Great Britain in 2014 by Piatkus
A CIP catalogue record for this book
is available from the British Library.

ISBN 978-0-349-40288-8

Printed and bound in Great Britain by Clays Ltd, St Ives plc

Papers used by Piatkus are from well-managed forests
and other responsible sources.

MIX
Paper from
responsible sources
FSC
www.fsc.org FSC® C104740

Piatkus
An imprint of
Little, Brown Book Group
100 Victoria Embankment
London EC4Y 0DY

An Hachette UK Company
www.hachette.co.uk

www.piatkus.co.uk

For Alastair

Acknowledgments

Thank you to Mary Stella, Eileen Cook, Sue Danic, and Toni McGee Causey for running this book through the grinder and making it better than I ever could have on my own.

Thanks to my incredible agent, Stephanie Kip Rostan, and my legendary editor, Jennifer Enderlin, for their patience, support, and brilliance at what they do. I'm the luckiest writer in the world, and I know it.

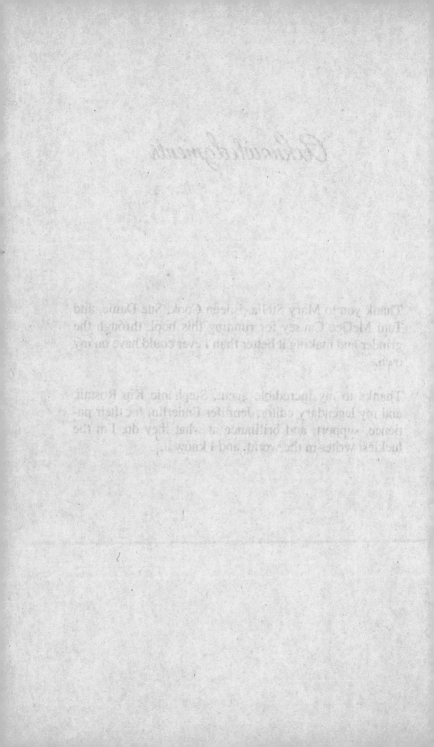

Acknowledgments

Thank you to Mary Stella, Helen Cook, Sue Dame, and Toni McGee Causey for running this book through the grinder and making it better than I ever could have on my own.

Thanks to my incredible agent, Stephanie Kip Rostan, and my legendary editor, Jennifer Enderlin, for their patience, support, and brilliance — that they do I off for the luckiest writer in the world, and I know it.

Chapter 1

"Magic's kind of high-maintenance," I said in low tones to Deidre Troudt as we huddled over the tiny purple potion vial that sat between us on the booth table in Crazy Cousin Betty's Waffle House. "If you don't want this to bite you in the ass, you've gotta follow a few rules."

Ms. Troudt waved her hand at me impatiently. "Give me the disclaimers, Easter, but be quick about it. My lunch hour's only an hour."

"Okay. Well, one, you've gotta really believe in one true love."

Ms. Troudt had been lifting her coffee cup, and halted it in midair to stare at me with those piercing brown eyes, and in a heartbeat, I felt like I was back in her high school English class. Her anger issues were legendary, but she was smart and kickass and she'd had all us kids in her class scared to death of her, which made me kind of love her. I almost started spouting a stream of crap about the themes of passion and transgression in *Ethan Frome*.

"Of course I do," she said. "Why? Don't you?"

I gave her a flat look. "I don't see how that's relevant."

She lowered her coffee cup and tilted her head to the side a bit. "But you made the potion—"

"Homeopathic solution," I said over her, raising my voice just enough to drown her out as I glanced at the tables around us. While the magic element in Nodaway Falls was fairly mundane, we made an effort to keep it under wraps as much as possible. No need spooking the locals.

To the untrained eye, Nodaway seemed like any other small, backward, and economically failing upstate New York town, and I guessed in most respects it was. We had a small grocery, a waffle house/diner, and a bed-and-breakfast. The magic, in all honesty, wasn't that big a deal most of the time. Power in most magicals manifested as quirks more than serious mojo. Take Betty, for instance, the septuagenarian owner of CCB's: She could make baked goods out of thin air. It was kinda neat when you really needed a brownie, but it wasn't anything truly mind-blowing. Olivia Kiskey, one of my best friends and a waitress at CCB's, could make living creatures out of random household objects. Her boyfriend, Tobias Shoop, had some darker powers, but he never used them if he could avoid it.

And then there was me. I'd taken up conjuring to keep the lights on when I got laid off from my job as a county librarian last fall. For the most part, even when the magic got hot, most of the people in town tended to accept our rational explanations, like when I insisted in public that the low-level magical potions I made were homeopathic solutions. Honestly, I didn't care what we called it, so long as I got my bills paid.

"No, wait a minute." Ms. Troudt set her cup down, her expression a mix of annoyance and confusion. "How can you make the po—I mean, *solution*—if you don't believe in it yourself?"

"My job is to mix the stuff," I said, keeping my voice low. "It's perception magic, so it's about *your* perception. It really has nothing to do with me."

"Oh." She shrugged. "I still don't get it, but if you say so, I guess I'll take your word on it."

That was as big a gesture of trust as Ms. Troudt ever gave, so I took it. "What's important is that *you* believe in one true love. Do you?"

She nudged her glasses up on the bridge of her nose. "Absolutely."

I sighed, a little disappointed. No one in the free world had been dumped on by love more than Deidre Troudt. She'd been left at the altar three times, two of those times by the same guy. If I was a better person, I'd talk her out of spending her hard-earned money on a potion that would only confirm that yet another man wasn't worthy of her time.

But I wasn't a better person, and I had car payments.

"The other thing," I went on. "No messing with free will."

She gave me a surprised look. "How would I mess with free will?"

"You can't dump this in anyone's coffee and make him love you. Doesn't work like that, and there are consequences for using magic to manipulate people."

"Consequences?" Her brows quirked under her wild fringe of mud-brown hair, a non-style she'd been using to telegraph that she didn't give a crap since as far back as I could remember. "What kind of consequences?"

I hesitated. The truth was . . . I wasn't sure. It was just what I'd been told, and it meshed well with my personal sense of right and wrong, so I made sure all my clients were clear that they were not to dump potions intended for them into someone else's drink.

I met Ms. Troudt's eye, gave her a dark look, and lowered my voice. "You don't want to know. Just don't do it."

Whatever foreboding I'd put into my voice seemed to miss the target, because Ms. Troudt waved a hand in the air. "Fine. Whatever."

I craned my head to look around her, hoping Liv would be available to bring me a refresh on my coffee, but she was by the front door, talking to two men who had just come in. The first one, I could tell from the shiny back of his bald-ass head, was my older brother, Nick. I wondered what he was doing here. Bernadette Peach, the third in the best-friend triumvirate with Liv and me, had my brother running all over the place preparing for their wedding this coming Saturday. So why was he hanging out in CCB's with some random guy? From the back, I couldn't even recognize who the random guy was, which was weird. I'd been born and raised in Nodaway and I could identify most of our tiny population at a hundred paces. The random guy was taller than any of the guys in the wedding party, with dark brown hair that looked like it had been cut with a weed whacker. There was something familiar about him, though, and my gut did a roller-coaster lunge as if it knew something I didn't . . .

"Hey. Easter." Ms. Troudt snapped her fingers to get my attention, much as she'd done whenever I'd drifted off in English class.

"Yeah," I said. "Sorry, what?"

She reached into her bag and pulled out her wallet. "Is that it?"

"No." I set my cold coffee mug down and turned my attention to the matter at hand. "When you're ready, drink it all at once, like a shot. Then you've got twenty-four hours to get into the same room with your guy."

"Simple enough. Anything else?" Ms. Troudt stared at

the vial with this weird look on her face. It made me uncomfortable seeing her like that, almost vulnerable and everything.

"Look, Ms. Troudt—"

"Knock it off with the *Ms. Troudt* stuff, Easter," she said, her eyes still locked on the vial. "You're selling me a magic potion so I can deal with my love life. Call me Deidre."

"Fine . . . *Deidre*." That felt weird. I hesitated, then pushed it. "You can call me Stacy, you know."

She snorted rudely, but that was a big part of why I liked her so much. She'd never spent a day being polite in her life. She was my hero, and I loved her, and I didn't want her to get hurt over some stupid guy.

"It's not too late," I said, annoyed with myself for being such a soft touch. Soft touches get their new yellow VW Bugs repossessed. But it was Ms. Troudt, so I forced the words out. "You can back out. I don't have to sell this to you today."

She shook her head, determination on her face. "Oh, no. I'm buying it."

I leaned forward. "Look, if you don't know if a man loves you, then your problem is the man, not the knowledge."

She gave me the same dead-eyed look she used to save for the dumb kids. "You think I don't know that?"

"I don't know what you know," I said, feeling a touch of professional indignation, "but you're buying a potion—"

"Homeopathic solution," she corrected automatically.

"—from me, and it's part of my ethics to be sure you know what you're doing before I hand it over. This is powerful stuff, and I want to know you're going to use it right."

I sat back, damn proud of myself. Ms. Troudt eyed me with a look of grudging respect.

"Good for you." She hesitated a moment, then leaned forward. "Look, I believe in The One, but I don't have the time or the energy for him. Whoever my One is, he waited too goddamned long, and now I'm forty-eight years old and I'm pissed off and I'm tired. I've got a few good years left to have a mediocre time in bed, and I have no intention of letting Real True Love screw with that."

"I'm sorry," I said. "I'm not following."

She sighed. "You know the guy I've been seeing? Wally Frankel?"

"Sure. The new pharmacist at the CVS, right?"

"Right. So, he's smart. He makes me laugh. He's above average in the sack. He has this one move where he—"

"Yeah, that's enough."

"People over fifty have sex. Deal with it. Anyway, it's all starting to make me a little nervous. If he's The One and he made me wait this long, I need to beat him to death with my Dyson, and I really like my Dyson. If I know he's not anything too special, then I can keep him."

"So you want him to *not* be The One?"

She grimaced. "For fuck's sake, Easter, don't split your infinitives." She sipped her coffee, then sighed. "I'm sorry. That was rude. My therapist tells me I should take responsibility when I'm rude, so . . . I apologize. Sometimes I forget you're an adult now. You still look like you did when you were in my class."

"I do not," I said. "That was ten years ago."

"Oh, please," she said. "You've got a rack that kicks ass and an ass that takes names. It's unnatural and you know it, which is why you dress like that."

"What's wrong with the way I dress?" I glanced down at my outfit: jeans, a blue cotton buttondown shirt some guy had left in my dorm room back in the day, a white tank underneath, and work boots.

"You've always been one of *those* girls," she went on. "The girls who roll out of bed with perfectly tousled hair and have men waiting in a line just on the slim chance you might deign to kick 'em in the balls. You're not like the rest of us, Easter. You snap your fingers, you can have any man you want. The rest of us have to work for it, and even then, more often than not, what we work for still drips on the toilet seat."

"They all drip," I said.

Ms. Troudt put her hands up. "Hey, don't get defensive."

"Then don't be offensive. Christ. If I had a nickel for every woman who told me I wasn't like the rest of you, I'd have all the nickels. Speaking of which"—I nudged the vial toward her—"that'll be fifty bucks."

Ms. Troudt picked up her purse. "Look, I'm sorry if I was rude. Again. But women like you don't understand what it's like to get your heart smashed in a million pieces."

Right, I thought, but then decided it wasn't worth it. Deidre had done me a favor by pissing me off; I was going to enjoy taking her money now, no guilt.

"So," she said, motioning to the vial, "I drink this on Friday, and the next time I see Wally . . . ?"

"You have to see him physically in person within twenty-four hours, and if he's The One, then you'll see a glow around him, like an aura."

She snorted, then her eyes widened as she looked at me. "Oh, you're serious. And what if I see nothing?"

"Then he's not The One."

She stared at the vial, deep in thought. I raised my hand to wave for Liv to come refresh the coffee, but she was still talking to Nick and the other guy. Just at that moment, she shifted her gaze around the room until her eyes landed on mine, and that was when I saw the tense look on her face. Liv had been through a lot in the last year, and she wasn't set off easily.

Something was going on.

"Well, what the hell, right?" Ms. Troudt said, opening her wallet. "You only live once."

"Yeah," I said absently, my eyes still on Liv, who was focused again on my brother and Random Guy.

Then Random Guy turned to glance around the restaurant, and everything else faded out of existence.

There, existing in my world as if he had the goddamn right, was Leo North.

He looked different. Older. The last time I'd seen him, he'd been tall and lanky; he'd filled out a bit, his shoulders broader and his posture straighter. But as different as he looked, he also looked exactly the same, that slightly dopey smile and permanent five o'clock shadow and that long, stupid nose. I had kissed that nose, a thousand times. Marked it.

It was my goddamned nose and he had taken it with him, the bastard.

My lungs froze in my chest and I couldn't take any air in. My stomach muscles clenched tight, sending waves of pain straight through to my back. I had an instinct to both laugh and cry at the same time. I snatched one of the menus from the holder behind the napkin dispenser and held it up in front of my face.

"Crap, crap, crap, crap," I said, peering up over the menu.

"Well, I'll be damned," Ms. Troudt said, following my line of sight. "Is that Leo North? You know, he's one of the few students I ever actually liked. Hey, North!" She waved in the air.

I let the menu flop down and stared at her. "What the hell is wrong with you? Why would you do that?"

Her eyes widened. "What?"

I released a breath, pushing the panic away. If I couldn't escape, I had to be cool. I put both hands lazily on either side of my coffee mug as Leo walked over. He was smiling at Ms. Troudt, his affable, unassuming manner unchanged, even after all this time. He was the kind of guy no one looked at twice, so incredibly ordinary and average in every way except . . .

. . . except that he was my Leo, and I knew better.

He let out a shout of genuine delight. "Ms. Troudt? Hey! Good to see you."

Ms. Troudt got up from her side of the booth and shook his hand, and she happened to angle herself away from me, which happened to angle him to face me, and our eyes met and he froze. I was trapped, unable to melt into the floor and unable to climb over the booth and run, so I gave a quick wave. He seemed to choke a little on nothing, the air I guess, which I found kind of gratifying. Ms. Troudt released his hand and he took a moment to pull his focus off me and make eye contact with her again. It was enough time for her to look at me, then at him, then back at me.

"Oh, you've got to be kidding me." She nudged Leo on the shoulder. "We know. She's pretty. Stop staring." She turned to me and gave a cocky quirk of her brow, as if to say, *Told you so.* I couldn't work up a reaction; she turned back to Leo.

"Hey, didn't you run off to become a Tibetan monk or something?"

"Catholic priest, actually," Leo said, his voice still a little choked.

"Same difference. And you're not the first of my former students to turn to God. I'm trying not to take it personally. Where the hell have you been?"

"South Dakota," I said, unable to keep the edge out of my voice.

Ms. Troudt looked at me, and she seemed to finally pick up on the fact that something was going on here.

"South Dakota. Wow." She shifted her focus to Leo. "What brings you back here?"

Leo cleared his throat. "Um, Nick and Peach's wedding, actually," he said, not taking his eyes off me. I don't know how long we froze there, just staring at each other, but it was long enough for Ms. Troudt to become visibly uncomfortable.

"Yeah. This is weird. I'm done here." She put a fifty-dollar bill in my hand, swiped the vial off the table, and tucked it into her purse. "I've got to get going. Those mouth-breathers in summer school aren't going to terrify themselves. See you kids later."

It took a moment for Leo to respond, but then he smiled at Ms. Troudt and nodded. "Right. Later."

She shot one last look at me, rolled her eyes, and left. Leo stood where he was.

"Hi," he said.

"Hi," I said.

He sank into the seat across from me. I wanted to kick him in the shins under the table and throw myself into his arms and cry. At the same time.

"So, Father Leo," I said, keeping my voice as cool and light as I could. "Nick said you weren't coming in for the wedding. Did you change your mind? Are you officiating now or something?"

"You don't need to call me Father," he said.

"You're not wearing your collar."

He released a deep breath. "Yeah, I'm aware of that."

"Are you allowed to not wear it? Isn't that against the rules or something?"

"Stacy—"

"Seems like the kind of thing that would be against the

rules. It's been a long time since I've been to mass, but as I recall, they've got rules for pretty much everything. I hear they're frowning on the whole Jesus-in-the-potato-chip thing now."

"Stacy." He reached across the table, then hesitated, his fingertips close enough to mine that I could feel the warmth coming from them. That's probably scientifically impossible, but I used to be able to feel him when he was around the corner in the high school hallway, and I could feel him now, damnit. Still.

Then, on their own power, our fingers intertwined, so naturally, as if ten years hadn't gone by without a word between us.

As if none of it had ever happened.

Leo smiled. "I had no idea it would be this good to see you again."

"Yeah," I said quietly. My heart was pounding and my legs felt wobbly and I kinda wanted to throw up, but I couldn't let go. It felt too good to be connected to him again, like water after so many years in the desert I'd forgotten what water was, let alone how much I needed it.

"Well, don't let it be *too* good to see me," I said, trying to recover my usual swagger and succeeding only the tiniest bit. "I'm very sure *that's* against the rules."

One side of his mouth quirked up a bit; his eyes focused on our hands. "Actually . . . that's not my life anymore."

I didn't feel a response to that at all, although I knew I would later. I would feel all of this later, it was going to haunt me for days if not weeks if not months if not forever, but for the moment, a strange calm was settling over me. The wave of the tsunami was huge and hovering over my head, but for the moment I was dry in the curl of it, although it was inevitably going to crash on me. The only question was when.

"You left the priesthood?" I asked, almost choking on the words.

"No," he said. "I left before it got that far."

"You were gone ten years."

"I left the church before I took my vows, about three years ago. I've been working in construction, actually."

"Construction?" I nodded, trying to process it all. "Well, that explains the shoulders."

He gave me a confused look. "I'm sorry?"

"You should be," I said, the words coming out more biting than I had intended, but what the hell? Leo was back and he wasn't a priest.

Jesus.

His expression softened, and he leaned forward a little, his hold on my hand tightening. "Look, Stacy—"

I held up a hand to stop him from talking. "Not yet. Can't do that yet. If ever."

He nodded, and sat back again. "Okay."

"So," I said, forcing a brittle laugh. "Construction. That's kind of a jump from being all Man of God and whatnot, huh?"

The words were coming out. Were they making sense? I had no idea. I was holding Leo North's hand in CCB's. Nothing made sense.

"I needed to do something else for a while," he said. "I had a lot of stuff to figure out."

"I bet. Why'd you leave?"

He released a breath. "It's . . . complicated."

"Everything's complicated," I said. "Don't think. Just answer. Why'd you leave?"

He met my eyes and smiled, but it was a small, sad smile. "I guess I . . . kind of lost my faith."

I laughed. I couldn't help it. It had been ridiculous, because I knew Leo hadn't left me for the church. The church was just something he did after leaving me, but I'd always felt like the church was the other woman. All these years, every time I walked past St. Sebastian's, I kind of wanted to throw a drink at it and call it a whore.

"I'm sorry," I said. "I didn't mean to laugh. It's not funny."

"Sure it is, a little." That was my Leo. Always kind. Always understanding. Always forgiving. Such a good man.

The bastard.

"Still." I took a breath. "I'm sorry. I really am." I meant it, mostly.

He met my eyes, and put his other hand over our joined ones. "Stacy, the shock of this is going to wear off in a minute, and once that happens, I don't know if we're going to be able to speak to each other."

"Why wouldn't we be able to speak to each other?"

He shrugged. "You're going to be mad. And you get . . . you know. Kind of hard to reach when you're mad."

I let out the most awkward and unconvincing laugh of my twenty-nine years. "Dude, don't flatter yourself. I'm over it. What's your name again?"

He kept his eyes on mine, that small, sad smile still on his face. My throat felt tight and my vision was going dark at the edges; he was the only thing in the world all of a sudden, just my Leo looking at me, and for that split second, everything was like it used to be.

And then Liv showed up and refilled my coffee mug and Leo released my hand and a brick wall of pain hit me hard. It was almost funny. I hadn't seen him in ten years, and suddenly *not* touching him hurt. What the hell was that about?

"Hey," Liv said, watching me carefully. "I'm sorry. It's been really busy. Is your coffee cold?"

I didn't say anything. My heart had stopped dead in my chest, and I couldn't breathe, and I had maybe thirty seconds before I passed out.

"Leo, so good to see you again," Liv said quickly. "I think maybe you should go now."

Liv's protectiveness was so stark, it almost made me laugh. Of course she would be protective; she had been the one to peel me up off the floor when Leo left, and she'd had to practically nurse me through that first year. She had invested a lot of energy in gluing me back together, and there was no way in hell she was going to let Leo North shatter me into a million jagged pieces again. She stood at my side of the booth, her arms crossed and her stance wide, her long dark curls flowing over her shoulders, making her look like a warrior goddess, and her message was clear: *Get out or die trying to stay.*

"Okay," Leo said, and he seemed barely able to get the word out. "I'll, um . . . I'll see you guys later."

A few moments, and the bells on the door chimed; he was gone. I tried to take in a deep breath, but I couldn't. My heart was beating again, though, so that was good.

Leo North. Leo goddamned North.

Liv slid into the seat he'd vacated and leaned over the table. "I called Brenda. She'll be here to cover for me in fifteen minutes, then I'm taking you home and we'll talk, okay?" She reached out and touched my hands. "Are you okay?"

"What?" I made a dismissive gesture with one numbed arm. "I'm fine." I felt my left eyelid twitch, but Liv didn't seem to see it; she was glancing at her watch.

She turned back to face me. "Fifteen minutes. I swear, and then I'm coming for you."

"Sure, great," I said.

The bells on the front door chimed again, followed by some gasps in the dining room, so I looked up. Peach was in her wedding dress, looking like Bridezilla Barbie, down to the platinum-blond hair and the blue eye shadow.

Eleanor Cotton, Nodaway Falls's seamstress laureate, trailed behind Peach, cursing and holding up armfuls of tulle and satin as best she could. Peach glanced around, one hand holding her veil to her poufy coif, the other clutched around her phone. She saw us, and headed over, dragging Eleanor in her wake.

"Oh, thank God!" Peach said. "I was at my fitting when I got a text from Nick!"

"No kidding," Liv said flatly, and I would have laughed if I had it in me. I was still, for the moment, huddled up dry in the curl of a tsunami wave, awaiting the moment when it would inevitably crash down on me.

Peach put her hand flat on the table, leaned over toward me, and stage-whispered, "Leo's in town!"

"We know," Liv said, but Peach didn't acknowledge her. It was a dramatic moment, and those didn't happen too often around here. This was Peach's horse, and she was gonna goddamn ride it.

Peach stood up straight and put her hand to her forehead. "He just showed up. He RSVP'd that he wasn't coming, then he called Nick this morning from the airport. Totally out of the blue. I swear, I didn't know until just now, or I would have told you."

"Fuck!" Eleanor stuck her thumb in her mouth, apparently bitten by one of the thousand pins in Peach's dress. She glared at Peach. "I'm adding hazard pay to your invoice," she said around her thumb.

Peach pulled Eleanor's hand out, looked at the thumb, and gave it back. "Oh, please. I'm an obstetrics nurse. Don't complain to me until you're seven centimeters dilated." She turned to me. "Did you hear me? *Leo's in town.*"

"We know," Liv said again, a little louder this time. "He was just here."

Peach's eyes locked on me in alarm. "Oh. God. Stace! Are you okay? Do you need a drink? Happy Larry's opens at noon."

"I'm fine." I forced a laugh that sounded hollow even to my own ears.

Liv pushed up from the table, looking wretched. "I really have to go. Brenda will be here soon and we'll go back to my place, okay?"

"No, guys, really. I think I just want to be alone," I said, but no one was listening.

"Okay," Peach said to Liv. "I'll stay here with you until Liv's ready, and we'll all go."

"You're not going anywhere in that goddamned dress," Eleanor said, amping up the Brooklyn in her accent.

Peach turned on her. "Can't you see we're in crisis here?"

Eleanor narrowed her eyes. For a seamstress, she was pretty scary. "You wanna be in crisis? Try going somewhere in that dress."

"Really," I said. "Guys, I'm fine. It was ten years ago. Stop making such a big deal out of it."

Liv looked at me, nibbling her lip, and Peach crossed her arms over her middle. They glanced at each other doubtfully, and I managed to get up from the table all by myself, which I thought was pretty impressive.

"I have a load of work to do," I said, stepping around Peach's huge dress. "And I'm tired. I think I might nap."

I kissed Peach on the cheek. "Thanks for coming so fast."

I patted Eleanor on the shoulder. "Sorry for the inconvenience."

I reached out and squeezed Liv's hand, pressing the money from Deidre Troudt into her palm. It was a hell of a tip, but I didn't care. I just needed to get out of there, fast. I didn't have time to do the math on two cups of coffee and personal bodyguard services. "I'll call you later."

They might have responded to me; I don't know. As I walked out of Crazy Cousin Betty's, I couldn't hear anything but a big, crashing wave.

Chapter 2

I drove home on autopilot, finding my way to my trusty Winnebago on the dusty outskirts of town without realizing I had done it until I was pulling the rickety screen door away from the rickety regular door. It wasn't much, but it was mine, and it had been free; my aunt Ruthie had given it to me before she ran off to South America with husband number four.

"I think you might need a place to get away from your mother sometimes," she'd said, stuffing the keys and the papers at me with one hand while the other lifted a frozen margarita. I was only twenty at the time, but even then I knew how right she was. The 'Bago didn't drive; Ruthie had blown a gasket on it while driving it around town for her fourth bachelorette party. I'd had it towed to the four-acre lot I'd purchased with the intent of building a real house someday. The thing was, someday never came, because I never wanted a real house. The permanency of a real house gave me the twitches, whereas the 'Bago always felt comfortably temporary, even after nine years of sitting in the same spot.

I crawled inside, lay down flat on the bed, and stared at

my ceiling. Ceilings in general are boring things to stare at, but try staring at the ceiling in a Winnebago for three hours. It'll make you want to stick a fork in your eye, just for the variety. Of course, if I closed my eyes, all I saw was Leo's expression of mixed shock and elation when he first saw me, and I felt all over again that wonderful, terrifying happiness quickening in my chest, only to be beaten to death by the *How stupid are you?* two-by-four.

"Arrrrgh!" I yelled finally, grabbing a pillow and pressing it over my face before tossing it aside and sitting up. This was no way to spend my time. I had to do something, distract myself, think about something else for a while.

I stuffed my feet into my work boots and headed outside into sunlight that was a little too bright for my taste. I mentally cursed it and squinted, trudging my way down the path through the woods to my sanctuary.

It was just an old garden shed, but it was one of the few things in the world I loved. It had been on Millie Banning's grandmother's farm outside of town, and when we were kids, she, Liv, Peach, and I used to have sleepovers in that old shed. It was pretty big, even for a shed, and we pretended it was our apartment and that we lived there together while we each pursued our dreams. Liv wanted to be a television journalist, tracking down bad guys and getting them to confess on tape; Peach wanted to be a fashion model; Millie wanted to be an astrophysicist; and I wanted to be independently wealthy. The three of them would run around, pursuing their dreams, and I would laze on the sofa (a big piece of foam we'd covered with sleeping bags) and eat Doritos while watching Liv pretend to interview someone while hunched inside the huge fake television we'd made out of the box her mom's new oven had come in.

I never expressed to any of them how much I loved that shed. Sometimes I would go visit Millie just so we could sit together in the doorway of the shed, drinking Diet Cokes and singing bad duets. We were too old to pretend by then, but I still would. I'd pretend that Millie and I were sisters, and that I had also been raised by someone who baked cookies and showed up for school plays and high school graduations.

And then last year happened. Magic came to town in the form of a badass conjurer named Davina Granville, who had set her sights on taking Liv's power. Millie, easily the most fragile out of the four of us, had stupidly let Davina use her to get to Liv, all in an attempt to steal my brother from Peach. Just thinking about it made me furious, even now. Millie had loved Nick for all those years, but had never said a thing, and then when Peach and Nick got together, instead of turning to us and letting us help her, she lost her shit and gave herself over to the most dangerous person who'd ever stepped foot in Nodaway. In the end, Liv had survived, but Millie had not. Our foursome was cut down to three, and I still hadn't forgiven Millie for letting that happen.

Anyway, when the bank sold off Millie's property, I bought the shed from the new owners. I didn't have any particular plans for it at the time, but then the county library downsized and I got laid off and it turned out to be damn near perfect for my new career making magical potions. I wasn't sure if Millie would be happy about me finally having a direction in life, or sad that I was profiting from the very thing that killed her. I liked to believe she was happy for me, and if she wasn't, then it was her own stupid fault. If she hadn't gotten herself killed she could yell at me.

I continued down the wooded path, the sunshine a little more bearable now that I was shaded partially by the trees. I followed the bend in the path to the small clearing where I'd placed the shed. The trees were full with summer leaves, dappling the sunlight into the open space, making it feel more magical than anything I'd ever accomplished with potions. This was the magic of hope, of potential, of dreams. The regular world was no place for that kind of nonsense, but here, in this one space, I could believe in that kind of magic again.

I went around to the side of the shed and yanked the generator cord one, two, three times . . . and it finally took. I'd need to get a new one before winter hit, but that wasn't today's problem, so I wasn't going to worry about it.

I took my keys out of my pocket, popped open the padlock, and stepped inside, feeling peace wash over me as I did. The floor was packed dirt, which gave it a wonderful, earthy smell; clear Christmas string lights lined the doorway and the windows, as well as the ceiling and some of the shelves. I'd painted the wooden walls a bright yellow; the shelves, cloud white. My workbench, which lined the back wall, I'd painted a periwinkle blue. Holding up either side of the workbench were a series of shallow drawers, each with a ceramic drawer pull on it, all of them bright, cheerful, and mismatched. Mason jars in varied sizes lined the shelves, all containing the magical herbs I'd collected over the last year. I'd printed out pretty, swirly labels for the jars in cheerful pastels, and tied ribbons around the mouths of the jars to color-code them by intention. Most ribbons were blue, indicating perception magic, but a few were in dangerous red, indicating some of the rarer and more interesting samples I'd gotten my hands on and set aside for the days to come when I'd be able to do more hard-core stuff. It was my haven, my happy place, and my secret shame. If anyone knew I had gone all Martha Stewart out here, I'd never be able to hold my head up in town again.

I sat on one of the pair of leather-cushioned, twirly bar

stools I'd appropriated from Happy Larry's, started up my little MacBook, and got to work.

I don't know how long I'd been working in my garden shed, but by the time I looked up from my workbench, the sun was close to setting and with a sudden *whap!* of consciousness, I realized I was starving. It was like that sometimes. They say you're doing what you're supposed to be doing when you lose time like that, when the world spins quickly around you and you stay in one space. If that's true, then I'm supposed to be making magical potions, I guess. Or maybe it was just how much I loved the shed. Either way, happy was happy, and I wasn't looking a gift horse in the mouth. It wasn't going to last, I knew. Even in that flash of reconnection to the world at large, I could feel the reality of Leo's return like a punch to the gut.

I pushed him away and focused on the work.

I glanced at the Erlenmeyer flask full of steaming amber liquid over the Bunsen burner and checked my watch. Three hours and forty-five minutes; it was almost done. I had no real hopes of success. Most of my work had been perception magic, beginner stuff. Creating something physical with potions was varsity-level shit even for the most highly trained conjurers. For a rogue conjurer like myself, who didn't have any official training, it was both stupid and improbable. Which, of course, was exactly why I was trying it.

Truthfully, according to the strictest of conjurer's codes, I wasn't supposed to be doing even the low-level perception magic unsupervised, let alone attempting physical magic. That was the kind of thing people went to special schools in Europe or Japan to learn, apprenticing for years before they could even try it under supervision, but the Internet was a beautiful, if dangerous, thing. I'd found the formula on a website last winter, and had downloaded it out immediately, which was a good thing, since the entire website where I'd found it had disappeared by the time I went back to it again after dinner.

The formula hadn't worked yet, but I wasn't giving up. The magical community was only about 1 percent of the population at large, but where there was power, there were people watching. The people watching this particular power took the form of two shadowy magical agencies, and I had no desire to get their attention. So even if I managed to create physical magic, I couldn't tell anyone. *I* would know, though, and that would be enough.

I could tell Leo, a sinister thought broke in. *He'd be happy for me, and he'd never tell anyone else.*

I shrugged the thought away and pulled out an Edison vial, named for its likeness to a tiny lightbulb and made of super-thin glass that flattened just enough on the bottom to give it stability. I glanced at the screen on my MacBook and read the instructions out loud.

"Wait until a single bubble has emerged from amber liquid and surfaced at the top, remove from heat source and allow to cool for ninety seconds."

I watched the liquid carefully, waiting for the single bubble to form at the bottom and then move slowly to the surface. This part always went just fine, so when the bubble disappeared on the surface of the solution, I wasn't nervous. I removed the vial from the burner with my tongs and carefully set it on the workbench, then hit my timer and looked back at the glowing screen on my computer.

This is where I got nervous, the part where it always went wrong in the past: the transfer from flask to bulb. Sometimes the potion turned black when I moved it, which was bad, or it was too hot and it cracked the Edison vial, or it was too cool and turned to honey-colored sludge. Every time, I made a note in my notebook to figure out where it had gone wrong, and tried something different the next time.

Conjurers are kind of an odd group. They're not naturally magical; their magic comes from potions and centuries of secrecy. But in the age of the Internet, where information wants to roam free, it's hard to have power like that and not show it off. To prevent the magical agencies from catching her sharing rogue formulas on the 'Net, a conjurer would usually put in one or two wrong details; if you followed the directions exactly as written, you'd never get it to work, and that was the loophole they would try to use to get out of trouble if it found them.

I'd made it as far as I had by uncovering one obviously wrong step in this formula—she called for purified rather than distilled water when making the base, which is a rookie goof and any conjurer with half a brain would catch it—but I couldn't be sure how many more errors were in the formula, not until I'd tried everything. I knew there was something at this point that wasn't right, but who the hell knew what? And there was always the possibility that the formula was right, and I was just too green to be able to pull it off.

I looked at my remaining instructions.

Pick up flask and swirl 2x counterclockwise. I'd already tried one and three swirls, both counterclockwise and clockwise, and two counterclockwise was definitely the ticket.

The timer dinged, and I picked up the flask and swirled it two times, watching as the now-blue liquid cleared the steam from the sides.

I glanced again at the instructions.

Remain calm. Breathe twice. I always found this part stupid. What my emotional state had to do with conjuring was beyond me, and it always sounded like old wives' tales. Still, when a formula reminded me of this—and they all did—I followed the instructions as laid out. The ingredients were expensive, and humoring superstition was free. But of course, tonight, as soon as I read the words *Remain calm,* I saw Leo's face in my head again, and my heart skipped a painful beat.

I closed my eyes, pushed visions of Leo away, and breathed in and out, twice. Then I opened my eyes and glanced back at the formula.

Pour exactly 1 ounce into Edison vial. I knelt down and looked at the Edison vial, with 1oz etched over a line in the side. This was where it always went wrong, which made me tense, which violated the *Remain calm* rule, which made me think of Leo again.

"Go away," I said through gritted teeth, as though he were a fly. I tilted the flask slowly, and as soon as the liquid hit the narrowed neck of the flask, it turned to thick sludge and wouldn't budge.

"Damnit," I said, and tossed the flask and contents into the trash. There was no point in trying to wash the honey-gunk out; it would solidify within minutes and make everything it touched unusable.

I looked at the stupid recipe in the stupid MacBook, and scrolled down to the section where I'd been putting in my notes.

I typed, *What went wrong this time?* Then I waited a moment and answered my own question.

Leo North, I typed, then shut the computer down.

It was almost dark when I emerged from the path to the 'Bago. I came around the front to find Liv and Peach sitting on the hood of my brother Nick's old forest-green Ford F-150, with the ridiculous EASTER LANDSCAPING logo and phone number on the side. Dude had been too cheap to pay a professional, and had painted it himself. It looked god-awful, and it made me laugh every time I saw it. Well, almost every time; at the moment, it wasn't doing much for me. I walked toward them, wondering if I could sneak in to the 'Bago without them seeing me. Peach was fussing with her phone, but Liv saw me almost immediately. She hopped off the hood of the truck and headed right for me as I walked toward them.

Liv was wearing her usual, a pair of ill-fitting jeans and a quirky T-shirt; this one had a dinosaur on it and a caption that read, ALL MY FRIENDS ARE DEAD. Peach, on the other hand, wore painted-on capri jeans, a red-and-white polka-dotted buttondown shirt tied around the waist, and red patent-leather shoes with heels that would have killed a mortal woman. Her hair was bound in a red bandanna, and her lipstick was a perfect match to the shoes.

"Hey," I said, motioning to Peach. "It's Rosie the Riveter, the spank-me version."

"Yay!" Peach said, hopping off the truck's hood. "She's being mean. She's okay."

"Of course I'm okay." I managed a brittle laugh. "Why wouldn't I be okay?"

Liv and Peach exchanged looks, and then focused on me.

"We were worried," Liv said. "You haven't been answering your phone. Where were you?"

"Oh, sorry." I motioned lamely behind me in the direction of the shed. "I was working. I must have left my phone in the 'Bago."

Liv looked at me, her eyes narrowing. "You haven't . . . taken anything, have you?"

It took me a moment to realize what she was talking about, but I shook my head. "No. I don't self-medicate. Against the rules."

Peach hopped off the hood of the truck and held up a bottle of Jameson Irish Whiskey. "That's okay, baby. The doctor is in."

They smiled and I smiled back, and for a moment of total insanity, I felt like bursting into tears. I can handle people being jerks to me on rough days, but the second someone shows me kindness, it kills me. I collected myself while focusing on my keys and unlocking the door, then we all went inside.

Peach put the bottle down on the counter and wrenched the cap off while Liv opened my cabinets, pulling out one glass from my mismatched menagerie of drinkware. I sat down at my little dinette table, and they crowded together on the tiny bench seat on the other side.

"How are you doing?" Liv asked, her expression a little too sympathetic for my taste.

"I'm fine." I lifted my glass. "How are you?"

Liv and Peach exchanged another glance.

"Stop doing that," I said, motioning between them. "You know I hate that. You have something to say, say it."

"All right," Peach said. "We think you're going to try to pretend this thing with Leo isn't a big deal when it's obviously a big deal, and with these conjuring powers that you have now, we're afraid you might blow up the town if you don't deal with it properly."

Liv shot Peach a look, and Peach gave her a defiant stare. "What? That was one of the possibilities we discussed."

"Don't worry," I said. "I'm fine. There's no *thing* with Leo." I felt a sharp stab in my gut as I said his name and took a drink. "He's back in town. Big deal. It's a free country. He can go where he wants. It's all fine." I drank again. Work had saved me from having to deal with Leo, and my best friends were going to force the issue. Something about that seemed wrong.

"How silly of us to worry," Liv said flatly.

"It was a long time ago," I said. "Really. No big deal."

"It was a big deal at the time," Liv said.

"Of course it was. My boyfriend slept with a girl at college then ran off on a guilt-bender and became a damn priest. Are you kidding? Teenage girls live for that kind of drama. *Dawson's Creek* had nothing on me."

Liv looked at me, vague disappointment on her face, then shook her head. "Enough of the bullshit. I think I should turn him into a squirrel."

"Oh, I like that idea," Peach said.

"Right?" Liv said. "I mean, what's the use of having magical powers if you can't make things the way you think they should be, right?"

We all went quiet and looked at one another. The magic was thrilling at times, but it had also come at a high cost. Had things been the way they were supposed to be, Millie would be sitting on one side of me, offering to make hot tea and telling me everything was going to be okay. Instead, her ashes were in an urn in Liv's backyard garden, and her ruthless willingness to use magic to change things she didn't like had put her there.

"I was just kidding," Liv said quietly. "I can't turn living things into squirrels, anyway."

Liv reached over, grabbed the bottle off the counter—something you can do while still seated at the dinette, God bless the 'Bago—and refilled my glass. I lifted it up to take a sip, and then I crumbled. I let my head lower to the table, and I just started crying. It wasn't the big ugly cry, just the steady stream of tears that happens when it's all just too damn much.

Liv got up and scooted into the bench next to me and put her arm around me. Peach got the Kleenex and set them on the table. I just cried, and cried some more, and then when I thought I didn't have any left in me, I kept on crying. At least I didn't have to explain anything; they had been there for it, both for the experience of me and Leo together, and for the devastating aftermath.

After a little while, I managed to pull my head up from the table. I grabbed a Kleenex, swiped and sniffled, then sat up straight and downed the last of the whiskey in my glass.

"No," I said, my voice croaky. "I'm not doing this. He's not doing this to me." I swiped at my face and said, "No," again, as though through sheer force of will I could stop it from hurting.

"Okay, that's it." Peach reached into her purse and pulled out her phone.

"What are you doing?" Liv asked.

"I'm calling Nick," Peach said. "I'm gonna tell him Leo can't come to the wedding."

"No." I took the phone from her, canceled the call, and handed it back. "Don't do that."

"But it'll ruin the wedding for you," Peach said.

"That's okay," I said. "It's not my wedding."

"It's on Saturday," Peach said. "You can't live like this for four days until he leaves."

I sighed. "Nick and Leo have been friends since grade school. I'm not going to be the reason my brother's best friend isn't at his wedding."

Peach and Liv exchanged doubtful glances, then Liv gave me a thoughtful look. I swiped the tissue under my nose and said, "What?"

"Nothing, it's just . . . why is it that you can't self-medicate again?"

I sighed and rubbed my eyes, grateful to not be talking about Leo for a minute. "It's kind of like an audio feed-back loop; the magic turns back in on itself and gets exaggerated. I don't know. Something like that. They say that's what made van Gogh cut off his ear."

Peach's eyes widened. "Is that true?"

I managed a half smile. "Probably not. You know conjurers. They always claim every crazy person in history was a conjurer who went wrong. They're sick of the natural magicals getting all the ink."

Liv smiled. "Okay, so you can't make anything for yourself, but maybe I can get ahold of something someone else makes and—"

I held up one hand. "I don't use magic. I profit from it. Very different relationship."

"But if someone else can make you something, give you some . . . I don't know. Emotional distance. Just until Leo leaves."

I patted her hand. "I'm fine, really. I had too much to drink on an empty stomach and it's Leo. Bad combination. I just need to sleep it off."

Liv didn't move, and neither did Peach.

"That's your cue to leave," I said.

Still. Nothing.

"Okay," I said. "I've got a guy in Niagara Falls who supplies me with my magical ingredients. Hey, have you heard from Cain lately, Liv? Is he still conjuring?"

"He's back in Tennessee, and I have no idea what he's doing. He's not terribly chatty. And don't change the subject."

I looked at Peach. "Is he coming in for the wedding?"

Peach's eyes widened. "Oh, crap." She looked at Liv, panic on her face. "Should I have invited him?"

Liv kept her focus on me. "I know what you're doing."

"He's the closest thing Liv has to family," I said, "and Liv is like family to you . . ."

Peach pulled out her phone. "I have to call him. Maybe it's not too late."

Liv took the phone away and patted Peach on the hand. "He doesn't want to come to the wedding, and he's not going to be offended. Stacy's just trying to get us off her back."

Peach looked at me, shaking her head in disappointment. "Using my wedding paranoia against me. That's low."

"Fine," I said. "If things get bad, I'll go see Desmond and get a potion or something."

Peach gave me her very serious look. "You promise?"

I took my index finger and crossed it over my heart. "Now you two have to get out of here. I'm dead on my feet. I need some sleep."

Liv and Peach exchanged glances, and then both nodded, deciding between the two of them that I was okay to be left alone. It took three weeks for them to get to that point when Leo first left; that was progress, I guessed. I almost had them out the door when Liv turned to face me.

"I don't like you being alone all the way out here," she said. "I know you won't call if you need me."

"I will totally call," I lied.

She eyed me, her eyes narrowing in thought. I had a moment's unease, wondering what she was thinking—Liv is exactly the kind of woman who would cuff our ankles together if she felt I needed it—but then her face cleared, and I let out a breath. She reached into her purse and pulled out her enormous set of keys, an array of every key she'd apparently ever needed, along with every keychain that had ever caught her eye. She stuffed them in my hand, then nudged past me to walk over to my sink.

I looked down at the keys in my hand, then down at her as she knelt and pulled a small, clear glass mixing bowl out of the cabinet under the sink.

"Am I supposed to know what she's doing?" I asked Peach.

Peach shrugged. "Don't look at me."

"Hang on and shut up for a minute." She put the bowl in the sink and turned on the water, then took the keys from me. She singled out one keychain and showed it to me.

"Oh, crap," I said, and laughed. "You still have this?"

It was one of four strip pictures of us we'd had taken at a picture booth at the Chautauqua County Fair sometime in high school: me and Liv squeezing in on the bottom, with Peach and Millie behind us. Millie held a puff of pink cotton candy as big as her head and stuck her tongue out to lick it. Peach was crossing her eyes. I was practicing my ironic sexy eyes, apparently, and Liv was playing it straight, her grin so big and so wide you could practically count all her teeth. For graduation, Liv had cut the strip up into four squares, and had them each encased in clear plastic and made into keychains. I'd lost mine at the beach the following summer; we'd put Millie's in the urn with her ashes last year. I had no idea where Peach's was. Liv's had apparently been part of her key ring from hell all this time, and it looked it.

"Oh," Peach said, her voice cracking with emotion. "Millie."

We were silent for a moment. We didn't talk about Millie much, mostly because I was still pissed off about it, Liv still felt like it was all her fault, and Peach was too much of an open nerve about Millie for either of us to handle.

"I can't believe you kept this," I finally said to Liv.

"Of course I kept it." She grasped the plastic square in her palm and ripped it cleanly from the Gordian knot of keys, then gave the mass back to me.

"Okay." I said. "I didn't see that coming."

She cupped her hands around the square and closed her eyes. For a moment, there was silence, nothing, and then I saw a thread of yellow light swirl out from her cupped palm and zip around the back of her hand, curling inside again. Then another, then another; little snakes of light racing around her hands.

Magic.

"Really?" I glanced at the clear bowl of water in my sink. "You're making me a keychain fish?"

She opened her eyes and grinned at me. "Yep." She walked over to the fishbowl and dumped the thing in.

When Liv's powers had first come in, this sort of thing happened accidentally, in moments of heightened emotion. She'd get scared and make a bunny out of a mug, that kind of thing. The accidental menagerie she'd accumulated when all this was going on always looked more like the original object than what they'd been turned into. That mug-bunny, Gibson, didn't even have a full back. He looked like a red ceramic bunny with the top hump of his back sliced off and open, and while Liv adored him and treated him like a real pet, I never quite got used to it.

The fish, however, was a different story. Liv didn't use her magic often, at least not that I knew about, but her game had definitely gone up in the past year. He looked like a real fish, as if Liv had just blown him up like a little oblong, clear plastic balloon. He had fins and big, bulgy eyes, and gills that moved in and out as he flitted from side to side in the bowl. His little nose sported the one last link of the metal chain Liv had wrenched him from, and through his sides, the picture of the four of us, encased in protective plastic, showed through.

"Oh." Peach swiped at her eyes, then tucked her hand through Liv's elbow and rested her head against Liv's.

"I know you're not a pet person. I just don't want you to be alone." Liv looked at me, a little anxious. "Do you like it?"

I leaned over and stared at the fish. It was strange; he was essentially a living picture frame, and that felt odd, but there was something about him that was still weirdly comforting.

"Yeah," I said. "I do."

I walked them outside and waved from my cement

stoop as they drove off in my brother's stupid hand-painted truck. I sighed heavily, mushy with love for them and my dumb brother, and continued waving until they were out of sight. Then I went back inside, took a swig of Jameson's directly from the bottle, and stared down at the fish.

"Bet you didn't see this coming." I took another swig as I headed toward my bed. "Trust me, Nemo. None of us ever do."

Chapter 3

It was three in the morning by the time I'd navigated the quaint streets of downtown Niagara, and my hand hesitated over the buzzer marked LAMB by the glass door next to the art gallery. I could turn around, go home, and no one would ever know any better. I could suck it up and push through the rehearsal dinner and the wedding, and then everything would go back to normal and I'd be fine.

Until Leo left. Again.

I hit the buzzer. I waited a few minutes and hit it again. There were a few more moments of silence, but then the light in the stairwell came on, and I could see a pair of elegant male legs glide soundlessly down the steps. Forget the voice; if you want to know a Brit at first sight, look at the way he moves.

Also, if you wake him up at three in the morning and he dresses in a pair of slacks and a buttondown shirt before coming to answer the door, that's a clue, too.

Des peered through the glass for a moment, all bright eyes and cheekbones, and then he recognized me and his face brightened.

"Well, if it isn't the lovely Ms. Easter," he said as he

opened the door, his demeanor so bright and cheerful that, had it not been for the pillowcase wrinkle on his cheek, I would have thought he'd been up already. "To what do I owe the pleasure?"

I slid into the small space at the base of the stairs and said, "I woke you up in the middle of the night. Stop being so nice. It's creepy." I tried to meet his eye, but couldn't do it and ended up talking to the concrete under my feet. "I need some stuff."

His voice sounded mildly surprised. "Business has picked up, has it?"

"No." I raised my head, hating everything, but especially stupid Leo North. "I need you to make something. For me."

He blinked twice, then understanding washed over his face. "Is everything all right?"

I gave him the dead eyes. "Yes. I'm here at three in the morning because everything's fine."

"Of course." He motioned toward the stairwell, and I went first, moving as quietly as I could until I got to his front door, which I pushed open. I'd been to Desmond's apartment about once every six weeks for the past eight months, although before it had always been during daylight hours. Now it felt uncomfortably intimate.

"Please, sit down." He motioned toward the small dining table next to his tiny kitchen. Although the place was small, he made it work. The furniture matched, all simple wood pieces except for the brown leather couch that seemed to be required of all single men, American or otherwise. His walls were clean white, accented with the occasional piece of artwork, most portraits of some kind. Next to the dining table was a painting of a young woman in a long dress holding a stick out for a greyhound dog. She was laughing, and seemingly unaware of the moment being caught forever by an artist's eye.

"Shall I make some tea? Coffee?" Desmond pulled open his refrigerator. "Bollocks. I need to go shopping."

"No, thanks. I just . . . I need . . ." I sighed. I wasn't sure exactly what I needed. I hadn't researched anything. I'd just tossed and turned in bed for five hours, then gotten in the car.

Desmond shut the fridge door, reached into a cabinet, and pulled out some lemon cookies. He put them on a small plate and set them down in front of me. I looked up at him.

"Please," he said. "I'm British. I have to offer you something or I'll begin to twitch."

He nudged the plate toward me and sat. I took a cookie and played with it in my hands as I spoke.

"I need you to make something for me," I said. "There's someone . . . there's a man . . ." I let out a harsh sigh of frustration and dumped the cookie on the table. "Screw it. *The* man. *The* man of my life has come back after a long time and he's not back for me, he's back for my brother's wedding, and I just need . . . something. Emotional distance. To get me through the next few days." I swallowed. "Maybe the next month or so."

"Ah. I see." Desmond sat back, his brow knitting a bit. "*The* man, really?"

I nodded. "I didn't read up on what I want, exactly, but I figured you would know."

"I have an idea, yes. I'm just rather surprised you didn't try to make it for yourself. Many brash young conjurers do, you know, the first time they need something for themselves."

"I know the rules."

He smiled, showing slightly crooked teeth. "You have never struck me as a follower of rules, Ms. Easter."

"I'm full of surprises," I said. "So, you know what I need?"

"Hmmm?" He seemed distracted for a moment, then said, "Oh, yes. It will take some time, I'm afraid. About . . ." He glanced at the antique clock on the wall, then looked back at me. "Six hours?"

"Oh." I released a breath. "You mean . . . you can do it now? That would be great. I thought it would be a day or so, at least."

"Ms. Easter, in the time I've had you as a client, I have never known you to be excitable. Quite the contrary, in fact. If you are at my doorstep at three in the morning, it's an emergency, and I'm a professional. I take that seriously." He stood up, reaching his hand out to me. I took it and stood as well.

"My workshop is in the basement. I'd invite you down with me, but it's very small and barely comfortable for one. You're welcome to wait up here."

"No, that's okay. I'll get a hotel room and come back."

"Certainly you could do that," he said. "But I have a perfectly good and very empty guest room right down the hall here, and you're welcome to it."

He started down the hallway. I followed him.

"It's the purple vials I've been using for you, isn't it?" he asked casually over his shoulder.

I rubbed one eye with the base of my hand like a four-year-old. Now that my tension about how I was going to survive Leo's visit was draining, I was feeling dog-tired. "Does it matter?"

"No," he said and stopped in front of a door, his hand on the knob. "The vials are new and I'm wondering how they're working out for you."

"Great," I said. "I mean, a vial's a vial, right? The clear ones were good. I've only made one potion in the purples." I shrugged and yawned. "They seem to be fine so far."

"Good." He opened the door, flicked on the light, and stepped aside. I poked my head in. It was small, and only sported a twin bed, but it was made and clean and the duvet was so fluffy that it looked like a big white cloud.

"Lovely," I muttered, and went facedown into the cloud.

It seemed like two seconds later when I felt Desmond's warm hand on my arm, but judging by the full sun streaming through the tiny window in his guest room, at least five hours had passed. I, however, didn't seem to have moved; I was still on my stomach, right leg hanging off the edge, making a Stacy Easter–shaped dent in the world's fluffiest duvet.

"Ms. Easter?"

I rolled over onto my back, then pushed up on my elbows.

"I just spent the night, Des," I said. "Call me Stacy."

He smiled. "All right, Stacy. I've got everything ready for you, although if you'd rather go back to sleep, you're perfectly welcome—"

"No, no." I maneuvered myself into a sitting position and squinted up at him. "I'm good."

"If you'd like to use the bathroom, it's just down the hall to the right. I'll wait for you in the living room."

He left, gently closing the door behind him. I sat there on the edge of the bed for a moment, staring down at my feet, unable to believe where I was and what I was doing. Then I thought about Leo, and my gut clenched, and I believed it. I went to use the facilities and a few moments later I sat down next to Desmond on his couch.

"I could only make you one dose for right now," he said, handing me one of the little purple vials he supplied me with. "It's a somewhat volatile concoction, but it will be good until next Wednesday, give or take. I wouldn't take any after Monday, to be on the safe side."

"Hmmm." I held up the vial. "What do you mean, volatile?"

"It works by suppressing brain chemistry," he said.

"So, it's . . . what? Basically just a drug? I thought this was magic."

He put his hand under mine, lifting it up to bring the vial closer to him. He stared at it like a man in love. *"Any sufficiently advanced technology is indistinguishable from magic."*

I closed my hand around the vial, and pulled it away. "Sorry, what?"

He blinked, as though just waking up, and I felt a light nudge of guilt at keeping him up all night. "It's a quote, from Arthur C. Clarke. All magic is simply brain chemistry. Natural magic is just a switch permanently flicked on in the brain, allowing that person to influence the physical world around them in heightened ways. Conjured magic, what we do, flicks a very specific switch that turns itself off after a few hours. Eventually, science will have all the answers. For now, call it magic if you like, but you could call it science and be just as accurate."

"My best friend made me a living fish out of a keychain," I said. "I'm calling it magic."

Desmond smiled at me. "I accept that." He motioned toward my hand holding the vial. "Back on topic, when this solution is fresh, its effects are specific, and will suppress only the emotions associated with romantic love, both the pleasure and the pain. After a few days, when the chemistry begins to break down, you could accidentally suppress something else: joy, anger, fear."

I shrugged. "That doesn't sound so bad."

"Well, yes, if it suppresses an emotion we can do without for a while. Imagine the damage someone could do in twelve hours under the influence of something that suppressed, say, her empathy."

I took a moment to imagine that. Didn't take much; I just pictured my mother. "Volatile. Got it."

"Don't misunderstand. It's well made, and the risk of real danger is small. I've provided this for a number of clients with no ill effects thus far. This particular formula uses an extract of Saint-John's-wort, a fairly pedestrian ingredient, but combines it with an infusion of a rare weed found only in the Orient—"

"Holy crap," I said. "Are you telling me you've got Anwei Xing in here?"

He straightened and smiled at me, pride in his eyes. "Ah, of course you know about Anwei Xing. Forgive me for forgetting who you are." He kept his eyes on mine, and for a second I had this crazy thought that he was going to try to kiss me, but then he just shook his head. "I apologize. I didn't mean to talk down to you. It's just that most of my clients don't do their homework nearly as thoroughly as you do."

I handed the vial back to him. "I'm sorry. I know what Anwei Xing goes for on the open market. I'm self-employed in a crappy economy, and I've got car payments to make. I can't afford this."

He reached out and curled my fingers around the vial. "Nonsense. I didn't have it imported in. I harvested it myself when I was visiting a colleague in Beijing last year, which reduces the cost dramatically. I've got plenty in my stores, and while I will charge the market value for anyone else wanting it, for you . . ." He released my hands. "Consider it a professional courtesy."

I played with the vial in my fingers, eyeing him. "How much?"

"There's no charge," he said.

I sighed, placed the vial on the coffee table, and stood up. "Look, I'm really sorry I took up your whole night, but I'm out. I don't know what you want from me, but eventually, you're gonna call that marker in for something, and no matter what it is, I'm not gonna like it. The only thing I owe on is my car, and those terms were made out in writing. Thanks anyway."

I started toward the door, but before I got a few steps he said, "In writing? Would that make you feel better?"

I stopped where I was, feeling the pull of emotional distance. *Anwei Xing.* On a professional level, I wanted desperately to know how it worked. And on a personal level . . .

Leo.

Desmond held up his index finger, went to his kitchen, and pulled out a pen and a sheet of paper. On it he scribbled something, signed with a flourish, and handed it to me.

I read out loud. "I willingly give, free of charge, this potion containing Anwei Xing to my friend and colleague, Ms. Stacy Easter, expecting nothing in return. Signed, Desmond Lamb." I looked at him, and he laughed.

"You are the most suspicious person I have ever met. It's quite delightful." He swooped up the vial in his hand and placed it in mine, over the piece of paper.

"Pour the contents of this vial into six ounces of liquid and drink immediately. This is one dose, and the effects should last about twelve hours."

Anwei Xing. *In my hand.* I closed my fingers around the vial, the sheet of notepaper crumpling as I did.

Desmond smiled and held his arm out, walking me to the door. "Drive safely, and don't hesitate to call if you need anything."

"Thanks, Des." I made it to the open door, then suddenly turned to face him. "Hey. What are you doing Saturday?"

He blinked in surprise. "Do you think you'll need more before then? I could make another batch and get it you by tomorrow, if you'd like."

"No, I mean . . ." I let out a breath. "It's my brother's wedding. Peach, my new sister-in-law, is making us wear pink satin halter tops with white polka dots and enough crinoline to lift a zeppelin. I wasn't going to bring a date because it's a really awful dress and being the date of a bridesmaid just sucks. But now Leo's going to be there and I'm gonna be on the volatile stuff and you look like you'd clean up good, and I was just thinking, if you weren't doing anything . . ." I trailed off, feeling like an idiot. "You know what? I'm sorry. Forget it. I'm just being—"

"Tell me where to be and when," he said, smiling. "If for nothing else, how frequently does one get the chance to see a polka-dotted zeppelin?"

Chapter 4

"Well, I guess it's my turn," Leo said, pushing up from one of the red vinyl chairs that made CCB's famous. He looked at Nick and smiled. "Nick . . . wow, I can't believe anyone is actually gonna marry this guy, let alone someone so beautiful."

Everyone laughed.

This is what an alternate universe feels like, I thought as I sat at my table in a cleared-out Crazy Cousin Betty's, Peach's natural choice for her fifties-themed rehearsal dinner. I stared down at my plate, good food prepared by a real caterer but put in those separated triangles in classic metal TV-dinner trays, and I chuckled.

Only Peach would plan an evening like this.

I glanced up just as everyone laughed at something brilliant and charming that Leo had said—I hadn't heard it, I was trying to shut him out because even the sound of his voice wedged into the cracks in my heart and expanded painfully—but it was Leo, so I knew it was brilliant and charming.

He continued talking, and I stared down at my TV-dinner plate, trying to distract myself with wondering where in the hell Peach had found them, although the distraction wasn't working that well. Even not looking at Leo, I could still feel him, and it was like having an itch on your back you couldn't scratch; it was making me crazy. At least Peach had had the foresight to seat him at the table farthest from mine, with the rest of Nick's guys. I was with Liv, Liv's significant other Tobias, and my mother at the table nearest the door, giving me an easy exit if I needed it.

Liv leaned in closer to me, her fork still hovering over the TV-dinner plate. "You okay?"

I smiled in her direction, noticing that Tobias was also watching me with protective eyes. If Liv was a warrior goddess, Tobias was the god of thunder: dark, looming, and quiet until the moment came for you to hear and feel nothing but his wrath. Both of them magic, both of them gentle until pushed, and then watch out. If I said the word, they'd have Leo trussed up like a Sunday pig and on the next bus out of town. I can't say the idea didn't have its appeal, but. . . .

I glanced at the special table facing the rest of us, where my brother sat beaming at Leo, one arm around his bride-to-be's chair, as happy as I'd ever seen him.

"I'm fine. Stand down." I lifted my champagne flute and smiled, and they relaxed. Leo continued his speech, and everyone laughed, and I cursed my stupidity. I should have taken the damn dose that Desmond had given me, and just asked him to bring me more for the wedding. But no; I wanted to test myself in Leo's presence, I wanted to show up tonight only to find that he didn't affect me at all, that I was over it, that it was just the shock of seeing him again that had laid me out flat, and that I would be able to bear his leaving after the wedding without so much as a sigh.

I was delusional.

Everyone laughed at Leo's final joke, and he raised his glass.

"You're the closest thing to a brother I've ever had, Nick," he said. "You're a good man, and Peach is an amazing woman, and I know you two will be very happy."

We all lifted our glasses as he finished up, and I raised mine as well, and then our eyes met for the first time since he'd crashed back into my life, and the cracks in my heart expanded some more.

Bastard, I thought, and sipped my champagne, holding his gaze like some kind of dog scrambling for dominance. I wasn't going to look away first, wasn't going to let him see what he was doing to me. In the end, after a nanosecond that felt like days, he glanced away and I was dominant and you know what?

It didn't make me feel any better.

"I'd like to say something now, if that's okay."

To my left, the Widow Lillith Easter stood up, black silk clinging tight to her bony limbs. I reached to pull her back down—after all, I had one job at tonight's dinner, and keeping my crazy mother quiet was it—but Nick held up his hand to allow it. I almost overruled him; he always gave everyone second, third, eighteenth chances. The triumph of optimism over experience, that was my brother. But then Peach gave me a nod indicating I should give my mother her shot. With great reluctance, I let my hand fall back to my champagne flute and took a hearty sip.

"To my son, my darling firstborn, Nicholas. I am so proud of you . . ."

The Widow began her gushing. I caught movement at the other table out of the corner of my eye; Leo was pushing up from his seat. I gave a quick shake of my head— *I've got it*—but he quietly moved to position himself a few feet behind our table, standing on guard, just in case a tackle was necessary. Even he knew my mother better than Nick did.

Poor, sweet, naive Nick.

"And to Bernadette . . ."

The Widow raised one skinny arm holding the champagne flute a little higher as she locked her eyes on Peach. Even through the black silk of her dress, I could see my mother's muscles tense as though preparing for attack, and for a moment, I thought she was going to throw her champagne flute at her soon-to-be daughter-in-law. I wasn't the only one who saw it, either; at the front table, Peach visibly tensed as my mother spoke, and who could blame her? The Widow spit her name out as though she were saying, *And to the whore of Babylon* . . .

The Widow forced a smile on her pale face. "To Bernadette . . . You are a beautiful woman."

Nick had one arm draped around the back of Peach's chair, and he smiled as, for the moment, his faith in our mother seemed to have been rewarded. Meanwhile, Mr. and Mrs. Peach sat at their table with Grandma Peach, looking happy and oblivious. They'd moved to Florida some years back, and had apparently forgotten the kind of woman my mother was.

The rest of us hadn't been so lucky.

"You have captured my son's heart, and he's a good man, so there must be some great virtue in you."

Nick's smile dimmed and his eyes closed for a moment, then he shifted as though to stand. I stood up and made a subtle motion with one hand; my job was to throw myself on the grenade, and I was happy to do it if it got me out of there without having to be polite and awkward with Leo. Besides, Nick was going to have to defend his wife from our mother for the rest of his life; he should get this one night off. Also, the Widow was all of ninety-eight pounds dripping wet; I could toss her over my shoulder and haul her out if I had to, and Nick knew I would. He relaxed back in his chair, a little.

"I do question some of the choices you two have made. We all know that cohabitating before marriage is a sin before God, but—"

I put my hand on her shoulder, digging my fingers into her flesh, hard. She didn't flinch.

"Wish them the best, Widow," I said quietly into her ear, "and sit the hell down."

The Widow met my eye with steel and raised her voice. "—I believe that God forgives the genuine heart . . ."

I glanced at Peach, who kept a stiff smile on her face, and nodded for me to let the Widow continue. My spidey-sense was telling me to haul the Widow out *now,* but I stepped back and shared a weary look with Liv.

The Widow's eyes glittered with her victory, and she turned her attention back to Peach. "Bernadette, it is my sincere hope that you will find your way back to Jesus, and repent of the poison you have injected into my good boy with your whorish ways—"

"Yeah, I'm calling it," I said, and started toward the Widow.

"—and find a home in the Heaven He has promised us all." The Widow turned to me as I took the flute out of her hand and placed it on the table, her eyes wide with something that couldn't possibly have been surprise.

"What?" she said, blinking innocence. "I'm not done."

"You are so very done." I grabbed my purse in one hand and the Widow's wrist in the other.

She tried to yank herself out of my grip. "You need to let me finish. I was about to get to the part where I talk about how Jesus forgave the whores and loved them anyway!"

"Thanks so much everyone, had a great time." I waved to the Peaches, blew a kiss to Nick and Peach, and yanked on my mother's arm. "Show's over, Tammy Faye." I glanced back at Liv and Tobias. "You're on."

Liv stood up and lifted her glass, clanging her knife against it with fervor to drown out the Widow's objections as I yanked on her arm, dragging her bodily from the premises.

"I am not done!" the Widow said.

"Yeah, you are."

Leo was at the door without missing a beat, holding it open for us. I met his eye quickly, and that stupid pain shot through me again. I was close enough to smell the Ivory soap on his skin, and I cursed myself again for being so cocky about the Anwei Xing.

"Need any help?" he asked sotto voce as I pushed the Widow out the door ahead of me.

"No." I met his eye again, and it hurt again, and then I added, "Thanks," and moved out after her, grateful to hear the ringing bells on the door jingle as it shut behind me.

I dragged the Widow to the street where I'd parked my bright yellow VW Bug, pulled the door open, and pointed to the passenger seat. "Get in."

"I will *not*!" She started back toward CCB's, and I darted in front of her, blocking her. Then she turned on her heel and tried to go the other way; I blocked her again.

"Watch yourself, Widow. I'm younger, faster, and I've got rage issues. I can do this all night."

She stomped one foot. "I wasn't done. If you had just let me finish—!"

"You called the bride a whore," I said. "There's nowhere you can go from there but down, and she's Nick's girl and my best friend. You want to get to Peach? You're gonna have to go through me first, and there's no way that's happening."

"If you think I'm going to be dragged out of my son's first rehearsal dinner—"

"*Only* rehearsal dinner," I said, advancing on her, "and that's exactly what is happening. Nick loves Peach, and I love Peach, and you've already used up what grace you got by giving us life, so if you think that pushing us to make a choice is going to end in your favor, lady, then you're gonna want to take a moment to think again."

The Widow's thin nostrils flared in fury. "*You.* You're no better than she is. Sleeping with anyone and everyone, not caring how it makes *me* look, how it makes *me* feel. I have to go into that confessional every week and unload *your* sins as though they are *my* shame! How do you think that makes me feel?"

"I don't give a crap how you feel. I spend time with you for Nick's sake. He was the one who protected me from your crazy when Dad left—"

"*Died,*" the Widow said.

"Eddie Easter is a drag queen in Brooklyn."

She gasped, her face going white with horror. "Who told you that?"

"No one. He tried to Facebook friend me a few years back," I said. "But don't worry. I haven't told anyone."

She visibly relaxed, her face impassive as she tried to resuscitate her fiction. "The man is dead. You were at his funeral."

"Throwing a party doesn't make it someone's birthday," I said. "He called us two days after that funeral to ask for money."

Her eyes widened, and she pointed her index finger at me. "Well, if he's so alive, why isn't he coming to his only son's wedding?"

"I don't know . . . because he abandoned us to the care of a crazy woman, let us believe he was dead for two days, and then called asking for money?"

The Widow rolled her eyes and shrugged. "Well . . . he's dead to *me.*"

"And the whole world revolves around you," I said. "I know. But to the point: Are you going to behave yourself tomorrow, or am I going to chain you to the radiator in your bedroom?"

She gasped, her eyes wide. "You wouldn't!"

"Wow," I said, shaking my head in mock surprise. "It's like you don't know me at all."

I heard the bells jingle again and tensed, expecting Leo, but when I looked up, Peach was standing at the door of CCB's, arms wrapped around her tiny middle as her pearl-blue dress swayed around her knees. She started down the sidewalk, heels clicking on the cement, and I put my hand on the Widow's puffy blond coiffure.

Her black eyes glittered with fury. "Stacy Imogen Easter, stop this right—"

"You have the right to remain *silent*," I hissed, and pushed down on her head until she collapsed into the open seat. I kicked her legs in, slammed the door, and clicked my key fob to lock it, then turned to face Peach as the Widow cursed at me and banged her fists on my passenger-side window.

Peach had tried to wipe off the mascara trails, but I'd known this girl my whole life, and I knew when she'd been crying.

"I'm so sorry, Peach," I said. "Go back inside and enjoy your night. Don't let her ruin it."

Peach sniffed and nodded, but still looked miserable. "I just need a minute."

"If it helps, she still likes you better than she likes me." I heard movement in the car and looked down just in time to see the Widow trying to unlock the driver's-side door. The second she succeeded, I hit the fob again and re-locked it.

"It's like a game to me, Widow!" I hollered to be heard through the window. "Keep fighting. I enjoy it!"

She threw herself back into the passenger seat and glared at me.

"Maybe I should talk to her," Peach said.

"I'm pretty sure that's a bad idea."

The Widow had managed to unlock the passenger-side door and I felt it push open slightly behind me. I held up one finger for Peach to wait, then turned and wrenched the door open, sticking my index finger into my mother's expertly preserved face.

"Lady, the only thing keeping me from killing you and burying your body where no one will ever find you is Nick, but if you scratch my car, even my love for him won't save you." She recoiled in horror and I slammed the door, getting the skirt of her dress caught in it this time. I leaned against the door and clicked the fob again, ignoring the rocking of the car as she tried to yank her dress free.

"She's a hellbitch, Peach," I said, "and she's never going to change."

Peach's lower lip trembled. "Maybe if we just talked, you know . . . got to know each other a little better . . ."

"There's no good to come from knowing Lillith Easter better. Trust me."

Peach sighed. "I just . . . I don't want my wedding to be ruined because my mother-in-law hates me." Her eyes filled with tears. I leaned forward to put my arms around her, being careful to keep my butt pressed against the door in case the Widow attempted another escape. She had seemed to go quiet, but I knew better than to ever turn my back on her for long.

"Don't worry about the wedding," I said. "I've got a plan."

Peach pulled back a bit, eyeing me suspiciously. "You're not going to do anything . . . magic with her, are you?"

"Don't worry about it," I said. "Just know that I got it covered, and relax. Consider it a wedding gift."

Peach sighed, leaning over to look at my mother in the car, who was yanking fruitlessly on the skirt of her dress. Peach straightened and said, her voice quiet, "She's agreed to take a potion?"

I took a moment too long trying to formulate a non-committal answer to that, and Peach gasped.

"You can't give it to her against her free will! Aren't there consequences for that?"

I shrugged. "There won't be consequences. Pinkie swear. Your only job is to have a wonderful wedding, and to make my brother happy." I hugged her, patting her on the back as I said, "How you make him happy is entirely up to you, just promise you'll never give me the details."

Peach watched me with a worried expression, then sighed and pulled on a wan smile. "Okay."

She stepped back from the car, and I pushed away from the passenger-side door. Within a heartbeat, there was the click of the lock as the Widow made another attempt, and I hit the key fob fast, enjoying the sound of her frustrated scream through the glass.

I put my arm around Peach, turned us both sideways where the Widow could see us clearly, and said loudly, "If it doesn't work out with Nick, give me a call."

And I planted a smack right on her lips. The Widow went still in the car, and I could hear her gasp in horror.

Peach laughed and hit me on the arm. "Geez, Stacy! She already hates me!"

"I just need to stun her enough to keep her in the car until I can get in." I waved Peach away. "Go on. Have fun. Love you."

Peach giggled and said, "Love you, too."

I watched as Peach went back inside CCB's, waiting to take my butt off the passenger-side door until the bells had stopped jangling again. I was about to walk around to the driver's side when I felt eyes on me. I glanced around

and saw Leo watching through the plate-glass window.
Our eyes met, and locked. This time, there was no pain,
just that wild rush as we smiled at each other and all the
years of separation, the hurt, the anger . . . it all just seemed
to melt away. We were on the same side, the way we had
always been, and for that moment, I felt that connection
between us, as strong as it had ever been. It felt good.

Too good. Dangerous good.

I gave a short wave, and he waved back, hesitated a
moment, then disappeared back to the party. My heart
rose, flipped, and dove down into my stomach, where it
whirled playfully around a tightening knot of panic.

Tomorrow's problem, I thought, then walked around
to the driver's side and got in. The Widow gaped at me in
horror. I started the car, putting one arm around her seat
as I reversed out of my parking spot.

"You are going to hell," she spat. "You are absolutely,
beyond the shadow of a reasonable doubt, going to hell."

"It was never gonna end any other way," I said, and
started what I knew would be a very long drive home.

I banged on my mother's door at seven the next morning.
The wedding wasn't until two thirty, but I didn't want to
take the chance of her making contact with either Peach
or Nick before I'd had a chance to work my magic on her.
When she didn't answer, I walked in and shouted, "Hey!
Widow! Coffee time!"

She appeared at the top of the steps dressed, of course,
in black. Considering that she had no other color in her
wardrobe, it wasn't that much of an insult. I had more
than once suspected that she'd faked my father's death
partially for the excuse to always wear her favorite absence of color.

I held up the Starbucks containers. "I brought coffee!"

Her face brightened, her lips already pulled into a

pseudo-smile by the tightness of the blond bun on top of her head. I led the way to her dining room table and set the drink carrier on the table.

"Skinny soy vanilla latte, bitter and fake, just the way you like it." I grinned as I set her cup down in front of her.

"Well, isn't this . . . nice," she said, a heavy note of suspicion in her voice. "What do you want?"

I sat down and took a sip of my full-fat mocha. "I want to talk to you about last night."

Her face shifted into a smile; it wasn't real, she didn't own a real one, but it was what she had, and I appreciated the effort. "Apology accepted."

"Let me know when one is offered," I said. "You acted like a wild animal, and ruined it for everyone."

Her eyes widened with shock. "Oh, please! It was fine, and Peach was so . . ." Her rictus tightened. ". . . lovely."

I had to smile. No matter how many times the woman did the gaslighting thing, it always amazed me. "You don't recall me having to haul you bodily out to my car?"

"I recall you being inappropriately pushy, yes. But as I said, apology accepted. Bygones, et cetera." And with a magnanimous wave of her hand, she absolved me.

"Unbelievable," I muttered, and left it at that. It was still early, but it was going to be a busy day, and I was pressed for time. I reached into my purse and took out two vials with dropper caps in them. One was purple, and the other was a reused clear white one. Technically, you're not supposed to reuse vials, but since it was the only clear one I had handy and there was only harmless green tea inside each of the vials, I wasn't too concerned.

"You know what I do, right?"

She waved a hand at me. "Of course. You're a librarian."

"I *was* a librarian, until they closed it down and I got laid off. Thanks for paying attention."

She waved a dismissive hand in the air. "I remember that, of course."

"Of course. Anyway, I sell magic potions now. You know this. I know you know this. Greta at the salon is one of my biggest customers."

The Widow's right eye twitched, and I could see the darkness shade her eyes. My mother had about five minutes' worth of fake congeniality in her on any given day, and I'd used them up. Which was okay.

I had a plan.

I nudged the purple vial toward her, and she flinched away, and spoke in the kind of low, dangerous tones I remember so well from my childhood. "I don't know what kind of Satan-worshipping nonsense you've gotten yourself involved in, Stacy, but I will have none of it."

"Really? Oh. Okay." I picked up the purple vial and held it in my hand. "That's too bad. It's a beauty potion."

"I don't really care what . . ." She trailed off, right at the point when her mind processed the key word. "Beauty potions aren't real." There was just enough wistfulness in her voice to let me know I had her firmly on the line.

"Oh, sure they are. You know how there's a way you see yourself, and then there's how you really look when you pass by the mirror and you see yourself, *really* see yourself? It's kind of a disappointment, you know?"

She slid her hand along her tight-bunned hair. "I don't know what you're talking about."

I kept my eyes on her face as I talked. "Oh, you know. You remember yourself in your twenties, with bright, clear skin, and then you see yourself in a mirror and there are those wrinkles . . . the papery texture . . . lips kind of no color at all."

I took a moment examining her features, then made eye contact and shrugged. "Well, if you don't know what I mean . . ."

Her posture straightened and she tapped perfectly man-icured nails on the table. "I don't, but I'm sure some other women do."

"Oh. Sure. *Other* women, we know how hard it is for *them*." I laughed.

She didn't laugh, just lasered her eyes in on the vial in my hand.

"So, what does it . . . do?" she asked, making a vague motion.

"Oh? This? Nothing, it just creates a . . . I don't know what they call it. A glamour, I guess, that makes every-one see you the way you see yourself. Younger, prettier, thinner . . ." I shot an appraising look at my mother. "Well, not thinner necessarily. You might put on a few pounds, you know, so people can still see you when you turn sideways."

She rolled her eyes and gave me a disapproving smirk, but then her focus landed back where I wanted it: on the purple vial.

"It all depends on how your beauty manifests for you. I figured with all the pictures that were going to be taken today, you might want it. But silly me, I keep forgetting about how much you love Jesus and hate Satan."

I dropped the purple vial back into my purse, pretend-ing not to notice her talons making an instinctive grab for it before she pulled herself back.

"That's all right," I said. "Maybe I'll just give it to Mrs. Peach. The mother of the bride should be the most beauti-ful at a wedding right? I mean, besides the actual bride herself, but it's not like anyone can give Peach a run for her money in the beauty race anyway, right? Even you in your heyday had nothing on Peach. I mean that girl is . . ." I sighed and stared off a bit into the middle distance, put-ting a dreamy expression on my face. ". . . so beautiful."

"Oh, Stacy." The Widow frowned. "I know you do that just to upset me, and I don't appreciate it."

I dropped the dreamy expression and looked at her, then pointed a finger at the space between her brows. "Wow. You remember when I was a kid, and you said if I made a face, it would stay that way?"

"Yes," she said. A beat passed, then she gasped and flew her fingers to her forehead. She kept her composure for a minute, then got up and went to the kitchen cabinet door she'd installed a mirror inside of, taking inspiration from the lockers of teenage girls. She checked herself out, smoothing the space between her brows, then cursed under her breath and sat down again.

"I suppose . . . ," she said, maintaining an expression of feigned disinterest, "that I wouldn't be a good mother if I didn't look into what you're doing, make absolute sure that it's not devil's work."

"Yeah," I said, and reached into my purse. "Failing to do that is what would make you a bad mother."

She was just reaching out for the vial when I snatched it back.

"There's a catch," I said.

She sighed and rolled her eyes. "Of course there is. I should have known."

"You will behave today," I said. "And don't pretend you don't know what I mean. Don't look for loopholes. You will be actually nice to Peach. You will speak only when spoken to, and then with a smile and as few words as possible. Are we clear?"

She rolled her eyes. "You talk as if I'm such a monster. If I'm such a bad mother, how did Nick turn out so well?"

"Because he's Nick, and he was born a better person than either of us will ever live to be." I leaned forward. "Are we clear?"

She screwed up her lips to the side, thinking, then held her hand out. I set the vial out of her reach, opened her coffee, and dumped the ounce of green tea in. She grabbed the cup and swirled it, then took a sip and ran to the mirror again to examine herself.

"Why . . . wow! I think . . . I think it's working!"

"Of course it is. I'm very good at what I do." I smiled and held up the clear vial. "Don't you want to know what this is for?"

She glanced back at me for a moment, saw the clear vial, and then looked back at herself in the mirror. "Should I care?"

"Yes, you should. This is the antidote."

She pressed her fingers against her face and giggled. "My skin actually feels softer!"

Of course it does, I thought. *Your delusion is more powerful than anything I could have made.*

"You're gonna want to listen to this, Widow. If I hear one word from anyone about you being a bitch to *anyone,* not just Peach . . . if I see one expression on your face that isn't kindness and delight, all I have to do is get a drop of this on your skin, a single drop, and your face will break out in wrinkles they can see from space."

Magically, of course, that was impossible, hence the green tea. But the Widow didn't know that.

She gasped and turned to me, one bony hand going protectively to her face. "What kind of person would even *think* of doing such a thing?"

"Hey, you raised me, lady." I leaned my elbows on the table and played with the clear vial, enjoying the way my mother tensed up every time it moved. "It only works in conjunction with what you've already taken. So if you splash it back on me or anyone else, it won't do anything."

I smiled, appreciating my own genius. No actual magic,

hence no violation of free will and no consequences. Sometimes I really loved me.

Her eyes widened. "I knew it! I knew you couldn't do anything just to be nice!"

"Of course I wasn't doing it just to be nice." I tucked the clear vial into my purse, stood up, and walked over to her. "Behave, or they'll be talking about you in hushed tones at the salon for years."

Her eyes narrowed and her lips thinned and for a moment, I thought she was going to slap me, even though she hadn't done that since I grew taller than her. I waved a finger at her, indicating her face.

"Watch out. Stays that way." I put my purse over my shoulder and blew her a kiss. "Wow. You really do look *amazing*."

She turned her attention back to her mirror, and I made my escape. It was the first of many errands I had to run that day, and time was short.

Chapter 5

I picked up my pink satin polka-dotted halter-topped zeppelin dress (and matching clutch bag) at Eleanor Cotton's and half listened to her many warnings about proper care while trying to inch my foot out the door and take Peach's multiple frantic calls. I picked up my shoes while calling the caterer to double-check the details, and as I pulled up to my Winnebago, I was so involved with my phone call obtaining Addie Hooper-Higgins's solemn vow that she wasn't going to slip tons of flaxseed into the wedding cake that I didn't even notice my brother's truck parked in my usual spot until I almost smashed into it.

"Oh, shit!" I said, and Addie said, "It does not! Everyone at Vonnie Peet's wedding got food poisoning, and that's what caused all that diarrhea. I swear, it wasn't the cake!"

I yanked my car to the left, narrowly missing Nick's truck, and parked the Bug.

"Look, Addie," I said, "I love you, but these are bacon-eating, beer-drinking, trans-fat-loving people. Introducing flax to their systems is gonna clear them out, and we only have two porta-potties rented for the night. Now swear to me on Julia Child that you didn't load that thing up with Roto-Rooter."

Addie sighed. "I'm putting my hand on *Mastering the Art of French Cooking* right now. I swear."

"Great. See you there." I hung up and got out of the car, in no mood to deal with whatever crisis my brother was having.

"Nick, I'm telling you, if you've got cold feet, you came to the wrong girl," I said as I reached into the back of my car and grabbed for my dress bag, which was the size of three women. Peach and her damn crinoline. In the other arm, I balanced my shoe box and the matching clutch, wrapped in plastic by a fastidious and paranoid Eleanor Cotton. "I've got eighteen things to do and three seconds in which to do them, brother, so there's no time for sensitive hand-holding. You're going through with this wedding if I have to hog-tie you to—"

And then I straightened up and saw Leo stepping out of Nick's truck. My throat constricted in surprise, and regret. Since the Anwei Xing only lasted twelve hours and I didn't want to be Cinderella on the clock, I'd planned on taking it right before the ceremony. It didn't even occur to me that Leo might show up at my house first.

Jerk.

"Is Nick okay?" I said, my voice cracking. Damnit, damnit, damnit. He was—had been, I mean—an almost-priest. Didn't he realize how unkind it was to ambush a person?

"Nick's great," he said, tentatively stepping closer, his eyes locked on mine. "I've never seen him so happy."

"Great." I broke the eye contact and started toward my front door. "Then whatever it is can wait until the wedding's over."

"My plane takes off tonight, after the reception."

I worked hard not to look back at him, although I felt his pull on me, and I moved slower than I should have.

"Stacy . . ." I could hear his footsteps as he came up behind me. I had my hand on the screen door handle, my keys were out . . . but I still stopped.

Why did I stop?

"I love you," he said quietly, and I wanted to cry. Instead, I leaned forward and banged my head lightly on the side of the 'Bago. So close. If I had just taken the stupid drops . . . if I had just gotten inside faster . . . if I had just . . .

But it didn't matter, because I hadn't and now the emotion was roiling inside, making me woozy. By the time I turned around to look at him, it was already too late. I was laid open, and getting more and more pissed about it as the seconds ticked by.

"Did you hear me?" he asked.

"Yeah," I said, injecting as much steel into my tone as I could, hoping it would cut him. "I heard you."

"Stacy, I mean it. I still love you. I never stopped."

I narrowed my eyes. "Do you have a death wish or something?"

His Adam's apple shifted as he swallowed, but other than that, there was no sign of fear or weakness in him. He was ready to take whatever I gave him, and even though I wanted to kill him, part of me respected that.

"No," he said simply.

"You left me," I said, advancing down the steps. He didn't move, so I had to move around him, and then I was looking up at him, but it didn't matter. I had the fury. I had the power. *"You* left *me."*

"I know. I'm sorry."

"You're *sorry*? Are you kidding?"

"No." He stood calmly, feet braced, ready to face the storm he'd created.

"You slept with someone else, then left me to become a *priest,* you son of a bitch!"

"I remember," he said. "I was there."

I advanced on him, my hands shaking. "No, you weren't. You ran away like a coward and hid behind the skirts of the church. You knew what we had, what we were, and you threw it away."

He met my eyes solidly. "I did. I know."

"And now, you're back for . . . what? Forgiveness?"

He shook his head. "I'm back for whatever you'll give me. You can hate me if you want, and I won't hold it against you, but I'm here now, and I have to tell you how sorry I am."

I felt like my lungs were caught in a vise. I couldn't breathe. I couldn't speak. And, just like old times, when I couldn't do something, Leo stepped in and did it for me.

"None of it happened because I didn't love you," he said, his voice stiff. "I need you to know that."

"Oh, I knew that," I said bitterly. "One of the classic signs that a man loves you is when he runs off and doesn't speak to you for ten years."

"I didn't think you'd ever forgive me. I didn't think I could ever do anything for you but bring you pain, so . . ."

"So . . . you went into the priesthood?" I shook my head. "That is literally the *worst* reason to become a priest."

"Yeah. Found that out. Thanks."

There was a hint of a rueful smile on his face, and I almost laughed with him for a moment . . . *almost* . . . and then it all hit me again and the anger raged through me. The shoes started to slip out of the crook of my arm, so I just threw them on the ground. Screw it. The clutch and dress bag followed and, freed from my burdens, I advanced on him. I must have looked pretty scary because this time, he stepped back, eyes wide.

"You son of a bitch!" I hollered. "You *left* me!"

"I know."

I put my hand flat on his chest, and felt his heart beating under my fingers, and a wave of pain crashed into me so hard that I thought I was going to fall over. How did he do that to me? Still? Shouldn't that have gone away over the years? But no, there it was, the same as always. I touched him, and my body physically altered. It was like . . . .

. . . *magic.*

"It was *us,*" I said quietly, my voice low and faltering. "You know how many people get this, what we have? No one, that's who. And you threw it away. How could you do that?"

It took him a moment to answer, and then he said, "I hurt you."

"You don't know what I felt. You don't know what you did to me. You were *gone.*"

"No." He placed one hand gently on mine, pressing it against his chest. "*Before* I left."

I stared up at him, my mind reeling. And then, I hit on something that felt like a missing puzzle piece. "What? You left because you slept with that girl?"

He stared at me for a moment, looking confused. "Well . . . yeah. Why did you think I left?"

The memory of that night flashed through my head. I'd thrown things. I'd screamed. I'd cried. I'd been ugly, the way that my mother had always told me I was ugly when I was a kid.

You may be physically beautiful, Stacy, she had said, so many times through my childhood that it became like a chorus in my brain. *But you're vicious and angry and ugly inside, and no one can love that for very long.*

"I thought . . ." My voice cracked and I stared up at him. "I thought you saw me."

He shook his head. "Saw you what?"

I pulled my hand away from his chest at the same moment that he reached out to touch my face. His hand froze in midair, and I took a step back.

"What do you want from me?" I said.

He took a deep breath. "Nothing. I just . . ." He blinked. "I've been thinking a lot lately. Working through things." He let out a short laugh. "I have a therapist."

"About ten years too late," I said, unable to cut the edge in my voice.

"Yeah." He nodded, all seriousness. "I screwed up, bad. And you're right. I hid, and the closer I got to taking my vows, the more I knew I'd screwed up. So I got out, and I got a job, and I worked on things. Now I know who I am again, and I'm not wasting time hiding anymore."

I took a moment to process this, and then I said, "Okay. Well, good for you. I'm glad you . . . found yourself or whatever. But that has nothing to do with me, so—"

"It has everything to do with you."

I looked up at him and shook my head. "What are you talking about?"

"I came back because I thought . . . seeing you . . ." He released a breath. "Dr. Roth said that when I saw you, I'd stop thinking of you as . . . well. Mine. He said you'd be different. He said those feelings would go away, and I'd be able to finally let it go and move on." He let out a bitter laugh. "He was wrong."

"I can't do this," I said, my breath coming in short as my heart rate kicked up. "I have to . . ." I turned around, saw my shoes and clutch and dress on the dusty ground, and was grateful for Eleanor Cotton's plastic-wrapped paranoia. ". . . the wedding," I mumbled.

I numbly went to pick up my things, and Leo talked behind me.

"I love you, Stacy," he said, "and I think you love me, too."

I grabbed the shoes, almost dropping them again, my hand was shaking so much. "Oh, really?" I said, trying to keep my voice strong even as I was unable to look at him. "You're a cocky little man of God, aren't you?"

"I was twenty-one. My father had just died, and I was away at school . . ."

I shook my head. "I told you not to go back for finals."

". . . and I screwed up. I hurt you and I wasn't man enough to face that, so I left. Maybe I don't deserve a second chance, but wearing a hair shirt for the rest of my life isn't going to fix anything, either."

"Nothing's going to fix this," I said. "It's broken."

He stared at me. "You really believe that?"

I lowered my head, unable to meet his eyes. "Yeah."

He went silent for a while, and then he said, "For ten years I've tried to convince myself it was my imagination, this thing between you and me, but it isn't, is it?"

I gathered my stuff in my arms and climbed up the cement stoop to my door. All I had to do was open it and go inside and hide until he went away. But I couldn't pull the door open. I couldn't shut him out. I just stood there, frozen, listening as he moved closer.

"Tell me it's my imagination, Stacy. Tell me there's nothing special between us, and I'll go away. I'll get a better therapist, check myself into some kind of . . . I don't know . . . rehab for delusional people."

I rested my forehead against the door frame, willing myself to go inside. I couldn't move.

"Stacy," he said, his voice low. "Is it my imagination?"

Before I realized what I was saying, I'd already said it.

"No. It's not your imagination."

Even without looking at him, I could feel the tension releasing from him, as though I'd just done him a favor. I hadn't. Lying to him would have been the kindness, but long ago, we'd promised each other we would never lie to each other.

And at least one of us was a man of her word.

I managed to turn myself around and look at him, and my love for him was still so powerful it almost knocked me over. I wanted to throw my arms around him, kiss him until neither of us could see straight. Bring him to my bed and keep him there forever.

But that was weakness, and if loving Leo had made me anything, it wasn't weak.

"It's not your imagination," I said, my voice gaining strength. "If knowing that matters to you, if it makes a difference, then great. Have it. I still love you, and I always will."

His eyes reddened, and my heart cracked at the sight of his pain. I could always handle my own pain, but his just wrecked me. That night when he'd told me about the girl he'd screwed in his dorm room on the last night of finals, just eight weeks after his father's death, half of my misery was in seeing how much he'd been hurting. And then he'd walked away, and I'd wanted to go after him, but I didn't because I thought it would be easier on both of us to give it some time, to tell him I forgave him when he came back.

Except he never came back.

I looked at him now, and he was beautiful and I wanted him for my own again so bad, I felt like I was cracking down the middle. But I couldn't have him. I didn't work that way anymore. The part of me that knew how to be with someone was broken, and there was no point in pretending otherwise. No way was I taking him inside only to have no place for him to stay.

"Loving you isn't something I did for a while, Leo. It's something I *am*. I can't change it any more than I can change the color of my eyes."

His jaw tensed and his lower lip quivered, and I knew what was coming. In two minutes, we'd both be blubbering helplessly like a couple of stupid kids, and this was all going to get to be too much very soon if I didn't put a stop to it now.

"I love you." I felt the relief in the words for just a moment as I said them; then I pulled myself together and pushed through the rest of it. "But that matters so much less than you'd think."

His face froze, and it took a moment, but he nodded.

I swallowed, willing the tears back.

"Go back. Go to the wedding. Get on your plane. Then don't ever darken my fucking door again."

I stood there on my stoop and watched while he slowly walked to Nick's truck. A moment later, he drove away, leaving a trail of dust kicked up in the air behind him. I don't know how long I remained there, staring, but it was long enough for the dust to settle, and for a silver Honda with Canadian plates to pull in and park next to my Bug. A moment later, a long, lean Desmond Lamb stepped out, cutting a fine figure in a classy black suit.

I barely noticed. I was still staring at the dust Leo had left behind.

"Well, Stacy, I must say, I didn't have you pegged as the rustic sort . . ." That must have been when he caught the look on my face, because he stopped talking.

"Stacy? Are you all right?"

The sight of Desmond went hazy through my tears. Without a word, he relieved me of my dress and shoes and matching clutch, and ushered me inside. He sat me at my kitchenette and dispensed the Anwei Xing potion into a glass of Diet Coke.

I drank it down without a word and went to take my shower.

"I don't know what you did to Mom," Nick said as we danced to Harry Connick Jr. on the parquet floor the wedding planner had set up in the middle of the town square, "but thank you."

"Me?" I smiled up at him and batted my eyelashes. "I didn't do a thing."

"Yeah, right. Was it that magic stuff? The stuff you and Liv have?" I'd explained how the magic worked to Nick a few times, but he never really understood. Kind of the way I never understood when he explained to me how a carburetor worked.

"Liv has magic," I said. "I have potions."

"It's all the same to me," he said. "Did you hocus-pocus her or what? She told Peach she was beautiful twice, and didn't follow it up with *for a whore* or anything."

"I didn't do anything magic to her," I said. "I just explained things in a way she could understand."

"Good for you." He tried to twirl me around, and ended up stepping on my toe. My big, bald brother was good at his landscaping business, and he was good at making Peach happy, but he couldn't dance worth a crap.

"Sorry," he said, and I rubbed the top of his head.

"Twinkle lights were a bad idea," I said. "They're all reflecting off the top of your shiny pate."

"Yeah, cut it out," he said, and pushed my hand away. Next to us, Desmond twirled Peach around with perfect grace and she hollered out, "Is it too late for returns? I want this one instead!" and a bunch of nearby guests laughed.

Nick shrugged. "It was only ever a matter of time before she got wise and left me for someone better looking."

"Oh, shut up," I said. "You're a catch and you know it."

Nick shrugged and smiled. "I know." His eyes clouded a bit, and he said, "Hey, you okay?"

I blinked in surprise. Nick had once accidentally knocked me off the monkey bars. I'd landed hard and he'd carried me, bleeding from the head, to the school nurse's office. Not once in that entire fifteen minutes had he asked me if I was okay.

"Yeah, I'm fine. Why?"

He bopped his head back and forth a little, the way guys do when they don't know how to express an emotion-based thought. "Nothing. It's just . . . Leo. I thought by now you'd have stabbed him with a spork or scratched his eyes out or something."

I rolled my eyes. "*One* time. One time you stab someone with a spork, and you never hear the end of it."

"Hey," he said, giving me that big-brother look. "I'm not kidding. I know you let it all go for me, and thanks, but now I want to know. You okay?"

I smiled, and came upon the edge of the strange emotional chasm I'd been feeling since Desmond had shown up that afternoon. Turns out, Des was a crackerjack conjurer, and the Anwei Xing had draped a thick canvas over everything I felt connected with Leo. Our eyes had met a few times during the ceremony and reception and I had felt . . . nothing. It was weird; certainly not unwelcome, but . . . weird. Never in my life had I felt disconnected from Leo North, even in the worst moments. It was the connection that hurt, and I was glad to be rid of that pain for a night, but at the same time, it felt wrong, like a vital piece of me had gone missing.

Well, better missing than hurting. But at the moment, my big brother was staring down at me, wanting an answer.

"That was a long time ago," I said. "Old news."

Nick nodded, and didn't seem to quite believe me, but

he accepted it. He tried to twirl me again and met with more success this time, but it still wasn't great. The music ended and I hugged him.

"Congratulations, butt munch."

"Thanks, sissy girl."

"Hey!" I pulled back and punched him playfully on his shoulder, but before we could get into a real brawl, Desmond walked Peach over, her arms around his neck.

"I love this man!" she said, and leaned back, hands still clasped around Desmond, to offer a kiss to Nick. Nick took her offer while Desmond dipped her a bit for easier access. I laughed, and Desmond met my eye and winked. Then Nick, five inches shorter than Desmond but a good bit heavier, said, "Get your mitts off my woman, limey."

"Alas, fair lady," Desmond said, smiling at Peach, "honor compels me to release you. Honor and fear of your new husband."

Peach shot her arms up in the air and screeched, "My husband!" and then threw herself around Nick and kissed him in a way that I didn't need to see. I tucked my hand in the crook of Desmond's arm and let him lead me back to a table at the far edge of the party, where we could sit and watch the revelry from a distance. He handed me a full champagne flute, and we clinked.

"You seem to be feeling better," he said.

"I am." I sighed. "I'm sorry about all that this morning. It was just—"

He held up one hand. "No explanation required. I'm glad I could help."

I smiled at him. "Thank you. You're a good friend."

He raised a brow. "Are we friends?"

"We're friends," I said. "Yeah."

"Excellent." He sipped his champagne. "I'd like that very much."

I felt a whoosh of cold air on the other side of me, and

turned to see that the Widow had seated herself in the chair next to mine.

"I have had five separate people come up to me tonight to tell me how young I look!" She grinned and held up one hand, all fingers splayed. *"Five."*

"Great." I held up my champagne flute and motioned toward Desmond. "Lillith, this is my date, Desmond. He's a . . . colleague. Desmond, the Widow Lillith Easter. My mother."

The Widow kept her eyes on the dance floor, allowing an absent "Uh-huh" as Desmond held out a hand to shake, which went ignored. I rolled my eyes and he smiled, bringing his hand back gently to rest on my knee. I allowed it. I had ditched the crinoline underskirts after the ceremony, allowing the pink polka-dotted satin to hang naturally, and the warmth of his hand was nice through the sheer fabric. I wasn't sure if there was anything between me and Desmond or not. I hadn't really thought of him that way before, he was just the guy I got my supplies from, but things were different now. Maybe. I wasn't feeling anything at all in the moment, but the chasm was still there, and if I did have any romantic feelings, I wouldn't have felt them anyway. For tonight, I was letting that go, enjoying the peace of the empty space inside.

"See over there?" the Widow said, pointing to the dance floor. "That's Vicki Federman. Her husband Dan just told me I was absolutely glowing, and I swear, she's going to kill him!"

"Ah, homewrecking," I said. "Such a fun pastime."

The Widow turned her eyes on me and huffed. "Sorry, dear. Have I been treading on your territory?"

"Ah, ah, ah." I patted my polka-dotted clutch, a warning tone in my voice.

The Widow's eyes widened. "You said I had to be nice to *Peach.*"

"I said *everyone*. That includes me."

"Why should I be nice to you?"

"I would say *because I'm your daughter,* but I know that wouldn't get me anywhere, so let's go with because I said so."

"Well," Desmond said, standing up. "I would quite like another turn around the dance floor." He stepped past me and offered his elbow to the Widow. "Would you do me the honor, Mrs. Easter?"

Her eyes widened. "Are you . . . English?" She looked at me as though to say, *How did* you *get a classy date?*

He smiled at me briefly, then turned his attention back to the Widow. "I am indeed, and it's my goal as the sole representative of fair Britain to dance with all the beautiful women at this affair today, yet you have somehow evaded me. Might I have the pleasure of a place on your dance card?"

Without so much as a glance at me to see if it was okay, she jumped up and tucked her hand in his arm. Desmond gave me a quick wink before escorting my mother out to the dance floor.

He was a good egg, that Desmond. Way too good for me, probably, but I'd cross that bridge later.

My clutch buzzed on the table behind me, and I reached in to see who was calling.

DEIDRE TROUDT.

I hit the top button twice, sending the call directly to voice mail. She'd left three messages just that afternoon, and I hadn't had the time or energy to call her back. She probably wanted more potions; that happened a lot with first-time customers. One potion works, and suddenly they want potions for everything. That was why I had a new VW Bug.

Well, whatever she wanted, it could wait.

"Is this seat taken?"

I didn't need to look up to know the voice; as soon as I heard it, an empty calm fell over me like velvet, and I knew it was Leo. I glanced at my watch; Desmond had dosed me at eleven that morning, and it was a little past ten now. I was still feeling the peaceful, cozy nothing I'd felt when Leo and I had made eye contact at other times during the day, and it was probably safe enough, for a little while longer at least.

I shrugged and motioned to the chair. "It's a free country."

"My plane leaves in a few hours," he said, taking the seat.

I took a breath, then shifted in my seat to look at him. I was tense for a moment, but then there was nothing.

It was glorious.

I smiled. "Have a nice flight."

There was a hint of confusion in his expression, but he just said, "Thank you."

We sat in awkward silence for a moment, and I just kept looking at him, feeling nothing. It was wonderful. Amazing. Thoughts raced through my head, all of them unencumbered by emotion.

Desmond is a really good conjurer.

I should marry him.

It'll be okay, as long as I never love him.

Which I won't, because I love Leo, and I will never love anyone else.

"Are you okay?" Leo asked, breaking into my thoughts.

"Me?" I lifted my champagne flute and took a drink. "Never been better. Why?"

"You look a little strange." He seemed to realize what he just said, and backtracked. "I mean, you look great, but . . . something's different."

I stared at him for a moment, wondering how he could tell. How could he see it, with just a glance? Liv hadn't said a word, and she'd spent much of the day standing next to me, watching Peach get married. Plus, she knew me better than anyone.

Well, better than anyone other than Leo. Who was getting on a plane and leaving me forever, again, in just moments.

And I didn't feel a thing.

Definitely going to have to marry Desmond, I thought.

"Stacy?" He shifted a bit closer. "What's going on?"

"Nothing. I'm fine." For a moment, I felt a twinge of something unpleasant, and wondered if I'd gotten too cocky, tested the power of the Anwei Xing too much. I forced myself to look at him, felt the twinge again, and said, "Don't let me keep you from socializing with everyone. You've got a flight to catch."

"Okay." He stood up, took a few steps away, then turned back and motioned toward the dance floor. "I just wanted to say . . . he seems like a good guy."

I blinked for a moment, not understanding, and then I looked in the direction Leo had indicated and saw Desmond twirling my mother around the dance floor, heard her laughing even above the music.

"Oh, what? Desmond?" I waved a hand in the air. "We're not—" And then I thought, *Why the hell am I protecting Leo?* and let my hand fall again. "Thanks. He's fabulous in the sack."

Leo smiled. A genuine smile. "Glad to hear it."

I met his eyes. "Really?"

"No. And yes." He took a deep breath and released it slowly. "I didn't realize you were with someone when I came by your place earlier. Nick said you weren't . . ." He shook his head. "Doesn't matter. I want you to be happy. I hope you know that."

"I'm happy," I lied, and damn him, he knew it. I could

see it in his face, that slight raise of the eyebrows that said, *Oh yeah?* How did he always know?

This time it was a jolt, not a twinge, a debilitating lightning bolt of everything I'd ever felt for Leo. Love, anger, hurt, sexual desire. All at once, in one overwhelming blast. *Christ.* I glanced at my watch again. He needed to leave, *now.* I stood up.

"I gotta go. Have a safe flight home, Leo—*augh!*" Saying his name cut through me, and I hunched over a bit and winced. In a moment, Leo was at my side, holding me up, sending more pain, love, and heat shooting through my body at his touch. I pushed away from him, grabbed my clutch, and headed away.

"Stacy!" I could hear his footsteps thudding softly on the grass behind me as I moved into the dark, away from the twinkly party lights and into the empty playground area of the town square.

"Go *home,* Leo."

"What's going on? Are you okay? Are you . . . are you *smoking?*"

That threw me, and I stopped and turned to look at him. He stopped, too, a few feet away, but instead of staring at my face, he was staring at my clutch.

"What the hell is going on here?" he asked, eyes wide.

"What?"

I glanced down, and that's when I saw it. It looked like ropes of glowing red smoke, dancing around my hand, and I caught a whiff of a strange, acrid smell.

Burning satin.

Under my fingers, my clutch was on fire.

Chapter 6

"Jesus!" I threw the clutch to the ground and held up my hand; the glowing red smoke was dissipating, but it was definitely still there. This was not my imagination.

I swallowed, my mind reeling. I'd had that power, fire-starting, only once before, when Liv had transferred magic to me accidentally. Magic manifests differently in everyone, and had manifested in me as fire, and I had burned paper and melted metal without feeling so much as a touch of warmth on my palms. Had Liv somehow . . . ?

I glanced out at the dance floor: Liv and Tobias were drinking champagne and talking quietly at the edge of the crowd, and no one else existed in their world besides each other.

But . . . no. Liv wouldn't have done that. Not without my consent, and not without having a damn good reason.

"Stacy?" Leo's voice was calm, but low and serious.

I looked at Leo. "Give me a minute. I'm not sure what's happening, and I'm super not sure how to explain it to you."

The smoldering clutch started to vibrate at my feet. I bent to reach for it, then looked at my hands; the thin ropes of red smoke were fading away, but they weren't entirely gone yet. Without me saying a word, Leo picked up the clutch, pulled out my phone, swiped at the screen to answer, and held the phone to my ear.

"Um . . . hello?" I said.

"What the *fuck* is going on, Easter?" Deidre Troudt hollered from the other end. "I've been calling you all day!"

"Brother's wedding," I said, my voice weak. Leo was standing next to me, so close, and I just thought, *Screw it,* and leaned into him, letting him hold me up. He put his other arm around me, and this time, maybe because I wasn't fighting it anymore, his touch was comforting, so I allowed it.

"I don't know what the hell you gave me," she said into the phone, her voice low, "but there is some weird-ass shit going on here and I'm *freaking out*!"

What I gave her? The One True Love potion? My mind raced; it had just been simple perception magic. An easy, rookie potion. The same thing I'd tested on Liv earlier in the year with no ill effects.

Then again, Liv was already magic.

But I was so careful, *so careful,* with my potions. I triple-checked them before bottling, and in eight months of active practice, not one of them had gone south. There were agency-trained conjurers who couldn't make that claim.

But still . . . something wasn't right.

"What's going on?" I asked her, my voice eerily calm to my own ears. I flicked my hands a couple of times, and the last bits of glowing, smoky magic disappeared. I took the phone from Leo and stared up at him as I listened to Ms. Troudt.

"I got this weird blue light all over my hands earlier today," she said, her voice low but sharp. "I look like friggin' Electro-Girl!"

"And what happened when the light came?"

Her voice went flat. "Really? Weird blue light doesn't come as a surprise to you?"

"I'm good at rolling with things. What happened?"

There was a heavy sigh on the other end of the line, followed by an embarrassed whisper. "Bluebirds."

What the . . . ? "Bluebirds? How?"

She hesitated, then said, "They popped out of the thin air and started . . . flying around my head. Like . . ." She huffed again, and I could feel her frustration through the line as her voice went into a sharp whisper. *"Like I'm a fucking Disney princess.* Now, what the hell is going on here?" Before I could answer, she said, "Hold on. I gotta pee," and then there was a gentle clunking of the phone being placed on a counter.

Out on the dance floor, there was the sound of the crowd gasping and then the music cut out, but I didn't look over. It was probably just Nick taking off Peach's garter with his teeth, and no way did I want to see that. I had to focus.

Something was wrong with my potions. They were sparking independent magic.

But that was impossible. The only people who could create independent magic were magicals.

Or conduits of magicals.

I swallowed hard, remembering what had happened last year. Millie had made herself a conduit of Davina, allowing Davina to use her life force to fuel darker magic. That one stupid choice had unloaded a lot of hell on us all, and had ended with Millie in an urn. Fear slid cold over my skin, and I took a deep breath.

Calm down.

Even if there was some conduit stuff going on, that was a temporary thing, and a real, genuine magical had to start that process. As far as I knew, all the magicals we had in town—Liv, Tobias, and Betty—knew better. And besides all that, there was no way for the potions I made to spontaneously give someone magical powers. If that were even possible, and I wasn't at all convinced that it was, it was way beyond my pay grade. I was still working first-level potions, simple mixtures that did only what they were made to do, and then wore off, and that was it. There was no way I could accidentally give someone real magic.

It wasn't possible.

Except it was happening.

"All right, I'm back," Ms. Troudt said on a sigh. "Don't take your bladder for granted, Easter. In twenty years, you're gonna have to go every ten minutes and it's gonna suck."

"Thanks for the advice."

"You're welcome. Now let's talk about the fucking bluebirds."

"Ms. Troudt, I don't—"

"You just made me into a cartoon character, Easter," she hissed. "Call me Deidre."

"Whatever. Look, I don't know what happened, but I'm going to figure it out and I'm going to fix it. I'm going to—"

"Hey. Um . . . Stacy?"

I looked up at Leo, who was looking out at the dance floor. I followed his gaze to see what he was seeing, but I couldn't see much of anything except that something was glowing in the middle of the floor, and the party was unnaturally quiet.

Through the phone, Deidre Troudt went on. "Whatever you're going to do, Easter, you'd better do it *fast*! I was at my therapist's and—"

"Yeah, I'm gonna have to call you back, Ms. Troudt."

I hung up, then turned to Leo and said truthfully, "I don't know what's happening."

"That makes two of us," he said.

He took my hand and led me to the reception dance floor. The guests were standing stock-still in a circle around the dance floor. Leo nudged people aside, pulling me behind him, leading me to my mother, who was in the middle of the dance floor, her hands spread out, ropes of green smoke snaking around her hands and lower arms.

And she was glowing. A gentle, soft rainbow of light flowed around her entire body, making her look like she was sitting in an invisible tank of water lit by shifting, multicolored light.

"Stacy!" she called out when she saw me, her eyes wide. "I'm so beautiful! I'm *glowing*!"

My ankles wobbled in my heels as I stepped forward. "Yeah, Widow. I can see that."

"I'm the most beautiful woman here," she said, her face beaming.

And then, she fainted.

Everything after that happened so fast, and I just followed the wave of motion. Within moments, Tobias had my mother in his arms, lifting her as easily as he would a baby bird. He headed straight for Liv's house, which was about two blocks down from the town square on Zipser Lane. Peach and Nick took over with the guests, distracting them and convincing them that they'd just seen an amazing light show that had overwhelmed my mother, who, Nick hinted, had probably had too little to eat and too much to drink. In short order, the music was playing again. Liv, Leo, Desmond, and I followed Tobias back to Liv's place, and before I knew what was happening, Desmond was attending to my mother, who was laid out on the couch in Liv's huge Victorian house.

"Anyone have a torch?" Desmond asked. We all stared at him, and he stared back for a moment, then said, "I apologize. A flashlight, I mean. The smaller the better."

Liv disappeared into the hallway and returned a moment later with a Mini Maglite. Desmond pulled open my mother's eyelids one at a time and flashed the light over them.

"What are you doing?" I asked.

"I'm a doctor," Desmond said simply.

"No you're not," I said, although he was attending to the Widow with such automated deftness that I knew as soon as I said the words that I was wrong.

"I am, actually. Not currently working in that capacity, but . . ." He pushed back from the Widow and stood up. "I don't think she's in any danger. She's rather slight, and I noticed she had a fair bit to drink tonight. Possibly the shock was a little much. Is there a proper bed I can remove her to?"

Liv motioned toward the stairs. "Top of the stairs, first door on the right. And the second door on the right, and the first door on the left . . ." Liv smiled at Desmond, although there was tension in her eyes. "We're lousy with guest rooms here. Would you like me to show you?"

"No, no, it's quite all right." And with that, he delicately lifted the Widow and carried her upstairs, leaving me and Tobias and Liv and Leo to stare at one another in silence for a while.

Liv spoke first. "So . . . anyone know what happened here?"

"I think it's my potions," I said numbly, looking at Tobias who, out of all of us, had the most knowledge of and experience with magic. "They seem to be making normal people magical."

Tobias crossed his arms over his chest. "What do you mean?"

I held up my clutch. Tobias took it, examined it, and handed it to Liv. Liv turned it over in her hands and then stared at me.

"I did that tonight," I said. "I gave Deidre Troudt a potion a few days ago, and she's manifesting bluebirds. And now the Widow is . . ."

Wait, I thought, and the jumbled mess in my head started to sort. *Wait . . .*

"You self-medicated?" Liv asked. "I thought you weren't supposed to do that. Maybe that's what—"

"I didn't." *Wait.* "No. Desmond made that potion for me."

"Made what?" Leo asked.

I opened my mouth to explain, got exhausted at the thought of it, and gave a dismissive wave of my hand. "Long story." I focused back on Liv. "All I gave the Widow was green tea. I told her it was a beauty potion, but I was lying through my teeth. It was just strongly brewed green tea, I swear my life on it. You know how paranoid I am about that stuff."

Liv looked at Tobias, as if working my defense. "She really is super-careful."

"Tobias," I said, "have you ever heard of anything like this?"

"A potion that makes non-magicals magical?" He gave Liv a careful look. "Well . . . yeah. There was that stuff Davina gave you last year." Liv looked tense, and he put his arm around her. "But Davina's dead. She didn't do this."

Liv let out a sharp huff. "Yeah, but if *she* could do it, maybe someone else could, too. Maybe someone slipped me something. I've had contact with both you and your mom today . . ."

I shook my head. "But the Widow and I have night magic . . . and you're . . ."

Liv shook her head. When her powers had first come in, she'd had day magic, which meant her power could only manifest while the sun was up. But in the final battle with Davina, she'd gotten night magic, too. She rarely used her magic now that she had it under control, so it was easy to forget everything she could do, and how unusual and special she was. And around unusual and special people, strange things tended to happen.

"Crap," I said. "Have you had any contact with Deidre Troudt?"

Liv closed her eyes and cursed under her breath. "She came in for dinner last night."

Liv and Tobias and I exchanged worried glances, and then I shook my head. "No. That's not it."

"How do you know?" Liv asked, nibbling one corner of her lip, and I tried to think of a good solid reason why. I couldn't. The last time I'd seen something like this, it had been Liv under the influence. Still, something about that wasn't right . . .

"I'm sorry," Leo said, putting his hand out in the middle of the huddle to get our attention. "Did you guys say *magic*?"

"Yes," I said, and met his eyes. "Magic, real magic, like the kind you heard stories about when you were a kid. Liv can make living creatures out of household objects. Tobias can stop a man's heart with a look."

Liv stiffened at that and gave me a look. Tobias's power was scary-dangerous, he tried never to use it, and it was the source of a lot of tension for both him and Liv.

"Sorry," I said. "I'm trying to be succinct."

Leo looked back and forth from one of us to the other. "Yeah, I still don't know what you're talking about."

I glanced at Liv, and she pulled the polished mahogany Chinese stick that was spiked through her chignon out of her hair and closed her hand around it. As her hair fell around her shoulders, hazy yellow smoke curled around her hand. When she opened her palm for us to see, the stick was a snake, writhing up her wrist.

"Wow," Leo said, and looked closer. Liv closed her hand around the snake and a second later, opened her hand again to reveal the stick. He looked at me, amazement in his eyes, and laughed. For a moment, I wanted to revel in that discovery with him, but there was no time, space, or reason to indulge anything with Leo. I had to stay focused.

I looked at Liv. "My spidey-sense is tingling. Something's weird."

"Ms. Troudt is manifesting bluebirds," Liv said. "We passed 'weird' two exits back."

At that moment, Desmond returned to the living room and moved to my side, inserting himself easily between me and Leo.

"Your mother is going to be okay," he said. "She should wake up just fine in the morning, but it's probably a good idea to keep an eye on her for the night." He looked up at Liv. "With the surfeit of guest rooms, I was wondering if I might impose upon you for the evening? I can check in on her, make sure she's all right."

"Of course," Liv said, then started for the stairs. "I'll go put fresh bedding in the other rooms."

Tobias stood there for a moment, his eyes going from Leo to me to Desmond, then back to me.

"Yeah, I'm going with her," he said, then disappeared after her, leaving the three of us alone together in awkwardness.

"So, wow, you're really a doctor, huh?" I said to break the silence, turning to Desmond.

"Neurologist, by trade. I worked mostly in research, but I did a full residency in a real hospital, and I assure you, your mother is going to be fine."

"Oh, I don't care about that," I said, waving a dismissive hand. "I'm just surprised, that's all. I would think you could do better as a doctor than you are as a . . ." I trailed off, glancing at Leo, who was watching me care-fully.

"I could do better as a doctor, perhaps," Desmond said, "but I couldn't do more."

Cryptic, I thought, but then just said, "Thank you."

Desmond smiled at me. "Of course."

"Well," I said, "if you're staying to keep an eye on her, I guess I'd better stay here tonight, too."

There was another long, awkward silence, and then Leo said, "It looks like you guys have everything under control here. I'm gonna . . ." He motioned toward the door, then, as if on an afterthought, reached his hand out to Desmond. "I'm sorry. We haven't been introduced. I'm Leo North."

Desmond's eyebrows rose a bit, and he glanced at me before accepting Leo's handshake.

"Desmond Lamb."

"Desmond," Leo said, taking Des's hand firmly and meeting his eyes with a respectful if sad smile, like a man who'd just lost a game, fair and square, and had no one to blame but himself. Then he released Desmond's hand, turned to me, and said, "Good-bye, Stacy."

I hesitated a moment. My mind was in a whirl, and I knew I should just let him leave and be grateful he was gone, but instead I said, "I'll walk you out."

I touched Desmond's arm to tell him to wait, and he sat down on the couch. I walked with Leo through the foyer in silence, and shut the door behind us when we stepped out onto Liv's porch. We both froze there, him not moving down the steps, me not going back inside, but neither of us really doing anything else.

"Do you . . . need me to explain . . . all that back there?" I said in a broken, uncertain tempo.

"Yes," he said. "But it seems like an involved thing,

and . . . my plane . . ." He seemed to be having trouble getting words out, too.

"Right. Your plane."

He moved toward the stairs, and I followed him.

"Where are you going?" I asked, not so much wanting an answer as wanting to keep him there, just for a little while longer. The Anwei Xing had worn off entirely, and I was back to the uncomfortable push–pull of both loving him and never wanting to see him again.

He stopped on the top step and turned to face me. "Home."

"And where is that? I knew you were somewhere in South Dakota, but I didn't know where."

"Aberdeen."

"Do you like it there?"

He met my eyes. "Does it matter?"

We went quiet for a little while, and then I said, "We're never going to see each other again, are we?"

He lowered his head, and his voice was thick. "Don't say that."

"Why not?" I asked. "It's the truth, isn't it?"

We stared at each other in silence for a long time, and then Leo looked away.

"I have to go," he said. "Nick's truck is at the reception. I have to get it. I'm driving them in to the airport. Our planes leave at about the same time."

I looked at him in the moonlight, and felt like I was losing a part of myself. Again. The blessed shelter of the Anwei Xing was gone, and here I was, stuck with Leo on the last chair when the music stopped, feeling exactly what I hadn't wanted to feel.

Stay, I thought.

"Fly safe," I said.

He reached out tentatively, his hand seeming to move

almost against his will. I closed my eyes as his fingers glided into the hair at the back of my head, and was hit with a rush of disappointment when his kiss landed on my forehead instead of my lips.

"Be happy," he whispered, and by the time I opened my eyes again, he was turning the corner at the end of the street, heading back to the town square and my brother and wherever the rest of his life would be.

Good-bye, Leo.

I stood there, staring into the night, both relieved and sunken with a sadness I was pretty sure would be with me every day for the rest of my life. Maybe I hadn't done the right thing by sending him away, but I'd done the *only* thing; I was sure of that. I was even uglier and angrier now than I'd been back then, and it was only a matter of time before he saw that and realized I wasn't worth it. Leo leaving now was survivable; if we'd spent any more time together, if I'd indulged in even the tiniest bit of hope for us, I was pretty sure *survivable* would no longer be on the table.

Then I went back inside, took Desmond by the hand without a word, and led him upstairs to Liv's guest bedroom.

Chapter 7

"Psst! Psst! Stacy!"

I started awake as my mother jostled my shoulder. She was still wearing her black dress from last night, the one Desmond had put her to bed in, and somehow, it didn't have a single wrinkle. Her hair was pulled back tight in a bun, and her makeup was perfect.

The woman was a freak.

It took me a moment to realize I was still naked—all the good parts covered by the sheet, thank God—and then it took me another moment to process that Desmond was gone. I pulled the covers up to my neck and sat up.

"What do you want?" My pink satin polka-dotted maid of honor dress was lying in a lump on the floor. My eyes darted around instinctively for Desmond's clothes; there was no sign of him at all. I relaxed. I didn't care much what my mother thought of me, but old habits of hiding everything I did of which she might disapprove—which was pretty much everything—were hardwired into my DNA.

"I need more of that stuff," she said, kneeling by the bed, desperation in her eyes. "I need another dose. Now. Give it."

Great. I turned my mother into a magic junkie. "Is Liv awake?"

"Yes, everyone's up, except for you. It's past nine o'clock."

"For fuck's sake!" I fell back on the bed. "I'm self-employed, Widow. I don't get up before noon unless there's a national emergency or free pancakes."

"Where's your purse? Is it in your purse?" She scrambled across the room to the chair where my singed clutch had landed. She picked it up, taking a moment to visibly disapprove of the charred finger marks on the side. She rolled her eyes, flipped it open, and dumped the contents onto the dresser, giving no apparent heed to the *clunk* my very expensive phone made as she did. I took that time to grab my dress and slide it back on. By the time she turned around, eyes wide, I was decent again. I couldn't find my underwear, but I'd deal with that later.

"Get your bony mitts off my stuff." I went to the dresser, picked up my phone, which was still working no thanks to my mother, and swiped it on. No messages from Deidre Troudt, which I took as a good sign. I would drop by and see her later, try to sort this stuff out, but first, I was going to need coffee. Lots and lots of coffee.

"Where's the purple vial?" the Widow said from behind me.

I stuffed my things back in the purse and turned to look at her. "I threw it out."

Her eyes lit, and her fingers went to her throat in horror. "You *what*?"

"It doesn't matter. It was empty. I had one dose and I gave it to you."

"Well, go home and make me more," she demanded.

"My god," I said. "It's like it would literally kill you to say *please*." I glanced down to see if my underwear was on the floor, and took its disappearance as some kind of judgment on my sleeping with Desmond last night.

She rolled her eyes and huffed. "Fine. *Please.*"

"No." I flipped the sheets back and muttered to myself. "Huh. Oh, well."

The Widow crossed her arms over her chest and tried to look imposing. "Stacy Imogen Easter."

"What?" I rubbed my eyes.

She was staring daggers at me. "You will make me some more of that potion. Now. *Please.*"

I laughed, amused by her interpretation of manners. That always killed me. "Oh, right. No."

"*Excuse* me?" Her eyes narrowed in a way that would have frightened me to death when I was a kid. Every now and again, when she really wanted me to do something for her, she'd pull out that look hoping it would work again. It didn't. I stepped past her and slipped my feet into my shoes.

"Look, Widow, I'm not giving you anything, ever again. Get over it."

"But I need it! I was *beautiful* last night. Everyone said so. I *glowed.*"

"I know," I said, and the memory of last night's series of weirdnesses—*glowing, bluebirds, fire*—made my shoulders tense.

She tapped her fingers impatiently on the dresser. "I need more of that stuff. How fast can you make it for me?"

"Second verse, same as the first. I'm not making you anything. I've got bigger fish to fry today, Widow."

I started toward the door, but her bony fingers grabbed my arm. She wasn't strong enough to hold me against my will, but the shock of her cold touch stopped me anyway.

"Get your hands off me before you lose them," I said

darkly, meaning it. "No one touches me without an invitation, even you."

She let me go, but closed the space between us. "What do you want? Money? I will give you money. But making your mother beg like this is a shameful, ugly thing, which makes you an ugly person. I just want you to know that."

Like you'd ever let me forget. I shook my head and let out a bitter laugh. "You are the most unfathomable piece of work I'd ever met. And, lady, I used to work in a county library."

I moved out the door past her, and she was tight on my heels. I made my way downstairs to the kitchen, where Tobias was cooking up pancakes and bacon. Liv and Desmond were laughing at the table, and when I entered, she raised an eyebrow at me. I gave a casual shrug and sat down.

"Good morning," Liv said, eyes glinting with amusement. "Sleep well?"

"Yes, I did. Thanks." I served myself a pancake while Desmond attended to my mother.

"It's good to see you, Lillith. You look well this morning. How are you feeling?"

The Widow smoothed her hand over her hair and giggled like a little girl. "Just wonderful, thank you."

Desmond smiled, but didn't try to share an intimate look with me or anything, which was very much to his credit considering how intimate we'd been the night before. Although, now that I thought about it . . . *intimate* maybe wasn't the right word for what we'd been. The lights had been off, all relevant parts functioned, and we both made it home and God bless his soul he didn't try to cuddle afterward, but there was nothing intimate about it. At the moment, he was being great: casual, discreet, polite. Despite that, I found myself wishing Liv had the power to make people disappear. The last thing in the world I wanted to deal with now was what had happened with Desmond last night.

"Although I am a *little* embarrassed about last night," the Widow continued. "I still honestly don't know what happened."

"You're ninety-five pounds, you eat like a bird, and you drank two glasses of champagne," I said around a bite of bacon. "You blacked out."

"Stacy," she hissed. "I know I raised you better than to talk with your mouth full."

I took another bite. "Actually, no, you didn't."

"Well, this is certainly turning out to be a lively morning," Desmond said, and Liv laughed.

"This is nothing," Liv said. "You should have been there when we went shopping for prom dresses. Stacy almost strangled Lillith with a sash."

The Widow huffed and rolled her eyes. "I think that's a bit of an exaggeration."

Liv and I both shook our heads, and Desmond smiled. Then Tobias appeared with a fresh plateful of pancakes for us.

"Tobias, you're a god among men," I said and forked one off the plate before it hit the table.

He looked at my mother. "Lillith? Do you want something to eat? Kitchen's open. I can make whatever you like."

"Oh, no, thank you," she said. "I had a half a grapefruit earlier this morning." And she put her hand on her stomach as if it were going to explode.

I reached for a third pancake. I didn't really want another one, but I knew it would drive her crazy, and I wasn't above pettiness at the moment. I was on edge. I needed to jettison my mother, get back to my car parked by the town square, send Desmond back where he came from, and then figure out what the hell was happening.

All while trying not to think about the fact that Leo was gone. Again.

"You know, I have a pair of sweatpants that might not fall off you," Liv said to me. "You're welcome to them if you'd like. I'm sorry I forgot to get you anything for pajamas last night. By the time we came out from making the third bedroom, you were already in bed." She blushed a bit and was putting obvious effort into pretending she didn't know that I'd slept with Desmond. "Do you need fresh clothes?"

"No, thanks," I said. "I've done the walk of shame in worse than this before."

There was a moment of awkward silence, and then Desmond said, "It was a lovely wedding," and we all hopped on how lovely it was, clutching the life raft in a sea full of conversational sharks.

"Okay," Tobias said, when he put the last pan in the sink. "Lillith, how about I give you a ride home?"

"Well . . ." Her posture got inexplicably stiffer, and she looked at me. "I was thinking that Stacy might . . ."

She eyed me; she was nowhere near giving up on this beauty potion thing. I took a deep breath and thought, *It's not worth the fight. It's green tea. Just give it to her.*

"I'd take the ride from Tobias," I said, "because the walk from here to your house is gonna be hell on a hot day."

She gave me a good, solid glare with a clear message— *ugly, Stacy, just ugly*—and then pushed up and slid her bony arm through Tobias's elbow. He held the swinging kitchen door open for her and gave Liv a playful look before leaving. She watched him as he disappeared, a loving light in her eyes that usually made me feel sorry for her.

This morning, however, I wasn't feeling sorry for her. I remembered the touch of Leo's lips on my forehead from last night, and thought, *Gone,* and a rush of emotions hit me. Jealousy. Anger. Resentment. For ten years, I'd been perfectly happy without love, seeing it clearly for the field of disfiguring land mines that it was, and in three days, he'd come in and ruined everything. Now there I was, holding back tears because I was standing on the edge of a field full of guaranteed pain and devastation, heartbroken because I was never, ever going to step foot in it again.

Get it together, Easter.

"Are you okay?"

I felt Liv's hand on my arm, and with a *whoosh* I left my field of land mines and returned to the kitchen with her and Desmond.

"Yeah," I said, and rubbed my eyes. "This is just really early in the morning for me."

"Oh, right," she said, but I could tell by the look in her eyes that she didn't quite buy that excuse. Still, she let it go, because she's Liv, and Liv is Awesome.

"So . . . do we have any theories on what happened last night?" She had an intake of breath and looked from me to Desmond, then back again, her eyes panicked. "I mean, not with you two, I know what happened . . . I mean, I didn't mind . . ." She hid her face behind her hands and spoke through them. "I mean . . . the weird magic."

I patted her on the arm. "It's okay, baby. No. I don't have any theories, yet. I need some time to think about it. I'll figure it out."

"I think I might go upstairs and locate a missing sock," Desmond said, standing. "Leave you two girls to talk."

He smiled at us both, making no special effort to snap up any kind of meaningful eye contact with me, which I appreciated, and then he disappeared, which I appreciated more.

"Okay, now seriously, how are you doing?" Liv said once the last of Desmond's footsteps faded out up the stairs.

"I'm fine."

"You slept with Desmond. You okay with that?"

I shrugged, keeping my eyes on the table. "No big deal."

"What about Leo?"

I felt a stab in my chest, and released a thin breath. "He's gone."

"He *left*?" Liv sounded disappointed, which was weird, because she was the one who most wanted to duct-tape him naked to the belly of the first plane out of town.

I nodded. "Last night."

"Stace . . ."

I looked up at her then. All that sympathy, all that empathy. Liv was a good woman, the best friend a girl could have, and I wanted nothing more than to get out of there, as fast as possible.

"I'm fine," I said, forcing a smile. "Good riddance."

Before Liv could challenge me, Desmond stepped back into the kitchen. "I found my sock." He handed my singed clutch to me. "And I discovered an item or two of yours, which I took the liberty of putting back into what's left of your handbag."

My underwear. I smiled and took the clutch from him. "Yeah? Where'd you find 'em?"

"Ceiling fan," he said delicately, then looked at Liv. "Thank you for your hospitality. I hope it wasn't too much of an imposition."

"Oh, no," Liv said. "We have more space than we'll ever use. This was my mother's house. She left it to me and it's too big, but I can't bring myself to sell it, so . . ." She looked around, that wistful expression she got when she talked about her mother taking over her face. I wondered what that was like, having a mother you'd miss if she were gone.

Liv pulled out of it and smiled at Desmond. "Thank you for taking care of Mrs. Easter. It was really nice of you."

"It was my pleasure."

I snorted out a laugh and they both looked down at me.

"Sorry," I said. "It's just like the Stanley Cup of politeness in here."

Desmond gave me a casual, no-big-meaning smile. "I'm going to be late for an appointment I have this afternoon, and I rode to the wedding with you. Are you about ready to head out? Or, if you'd like, I can call a taxi to bring me to your place to retrieve my car." He glanced around, then let out a stuttered laugh. "I'm sorry . . . does Nodaway Falls have a taxi service?"

"That's cute. I'll take you," I said, pushing up from the table almost fast enough to knock it over. "I've gotta get going, too."

Liv walked us to the door, gave me a hug, and made me promise to call her later, and then Desmond and I were out in the sunshine, walking through my town on a beautiful morning: past Peach and Nick's house next door, with Nick's stupid green pickup in the driveway; past Ginny Boyle, who waved and offered her good wishes for Nick and Peach from her porch where she sat drinking coffee, and would not wait for us to be out of earshot before making her round of calls about me still wearing my maid of honor dress as I shamelessly marched through town with last night's date. Every step we took was one more step through my life that I was making with a man I barely knew, and all I could think of was escape.

"About last night . . . ," he began, and I held up one hand to stop him talking.

"Hey, don't worry about it," I said, pulling out Speech Number One and keeping my eyes on the sidewalk before us. "I'm not that kind of girl. I don't need to cuddle afterward, and I don't need you to pretend you want to see me again, or say you're gonna call. It was an itch. We scratched. You're off the hook."

"Oh." There was a long silence while we walked, and then he said. "Well, this is awkward."

"Don't worry about it," I said. "I'm not playing games. I'm really good with just going our separate ways and re-membering each other fondly."

"No, I mean . . ." He paused for a moment and stopped at the corner just as we were about to hit the town square. I could see the Bug waiting for me, but now I had to stop and look at him and talk to him, because continuing to walk would be too rude, even for me.

"Actually," he began, "I was hoping I might see you again, and now I'm not quite sure how to broach that sub-ject. Could you perhaps clarify your fishing metaphor? Are you letting me off the hook for my benefit, or are you throwing me back for yours?"

Crap.

"I'm sorry. I'm a jerk. I just . . ." I closed my eyes and released a breath, trying to sort it all out in my head. I kept them closed and just talked, getting it all out as quickly as possible. "You've seen me naked. You've seen me cry. You ate breakfast with my mother. I need you for my busi-ness." I opened my eyes. "In about fifteen seconds, you've somehow connected to every area of my life. It's too close. Nothing personal, but I don't want anyone that close. Last night, I was . . ." I stopped, unable to finish the thought, because it led back to Leo, and I didn't have the strength to think about him yet. "I had a lapse in judgment and you're footing the bill for that, and I'm sorry."

He stood there for a moment, just looking at me, and then smiled. "I understand completely."

"Thank you."

We started walking again, and I felt better with every step that brought us closer to the Bug. Soon, we'd be at my place and he'd be gone and I could go inside and then I'd be able to think. Figure out what the hell happened last night. Stare at my keychain fish and maybe, just maybe, process what had happened with—

I stopped where I was. Something was ticking in my brain. Something I'd seen. Something that didn't quite compute.

"Ms. Easter!"

A girl's voice called my name, and it threw me from my train of thought. I blinked and looked toward the corner of Zipser Lane, the street where Liv and Peach and Nick lived, and something connected in my head.

Nick's truck was in the driveway.

Which meant that after dropping Nick and Peach at the airport, someone drove it back.

Goddamnit, Leo, I thought with equal parts anger and elation.

And that's when I noticed a short, awkward red-headed girl heading toward me, crossing at Zipser Lane.

"Who is that?" Desmond asked.

"Um," I said, trying to place her while my mind was still reeling around that damn truck. Then I focused, and remembered where I knew the kid from. *Damnit.* She seemed like a sweet kid, but telling her no again was not what I wanted to be doing right now. "It's the checkout girl from Treacher's IGA. Cleo. Chloe. Kelly. Something like that. Give me a minute, okay?"

I started back toward Zipser Lane, wanting to put my eyes on that truck again so I could be sure I wasn't imagining things, but the checkout girl stood in my path. She had her long, scraggly red hair pulled into a ponytail, and her eyes welled up huge behind her thick glasses, making her look like one of those cartoon kittens.

"Ms. Easter, I really need to talk to—" She stopped as I walked right past her, and then I heard her footsteps plodding after mine.

"Ms. Easter is my father," I said, focusing my eyes in

the direction of Peach and Nick's place, even though I couldn't see the driveway yet from where I was. "Call me Stacy."

"I need to talk to you . . . about . . . you know."

I sighed, stopped, and turned to face her.

"What did I tell you the last time I talked to you, Chloe?"

She pushed her glasses up on her nose and looked up at me, clearly nervous, which was smart, because I was in a scary state at the moment. "It's Clementine, actually. Clementine Klosterman?"

"Sorry. Clementine. What did I tell you the last time we spoke, Clementine?"

She pulled one edge of her lip under her teeth. Most girls did that to look unassuming and vulnerable, so whoever they were talking to would ease up on them. This kid was doing it because she was genuinely unassuming and vulnerable. It was like watching a live nerve walk through a thicket of brambles, and it made me tense just looking at her.

"You said . . . ," she began, but her throat caught, so she cleared it and started again. "You said that you couldn't help me?"

"That's a statement, Clementine," I said. "When you make a statement, don't say it like a question. It'll make people think you're weak, unsure of yourself, an easy mark, and they'll take advantage of you. Let's take another run at it. What did I tell you the last time we spoke, Clementine?"

She swallowed visibly. "Um . . . you said that you couldn't help me."

"Right," I said. "And why can't I help you?"

"Because I'm too young," she said, and then started talking in double-speed desperation, "but I'm seventeen, and I'll be eighteen next spring and—"

"What *else* did I tell you, Clementine?"

She sighed and her shoulders slumped downward.

"You said that you don't make magic potions, you make homeo—"

"Homeopathic solutions," I said over her, finishing the sentence. "Right. Which means that I can't make the quarterback love you, so beat it."

"Oh, it's not the quarterback," she said quickly.

"Linebacker, then. Either way, I can't help you, and I've got stuff to do."

I started down the street again, and damned if her stubborn little footsteps didn't follow me. "But I heard some stuff about things happening at the wedding last night, your brother's wedding, and—"

I turned on her. "What did you hear?"

She skidded to a stop, visibly drummed up all her courage and said, "I heard that your mother was glowing. You know. Like magic and stuff?"

Crap. Of course, I knew it would be all over town eventually, but that was pretty fast, even by the fiber-optic standards of the Nodaway Falls grapevine. But before I could deal with that, I had to get this kid off my leg, so I turned my attention to the task at hand.

"Yeah? In the seventh grade, people said that I had sex with Matt Grieb in the back of the bus on the way home from the class trip. That didn't make it true." I sighed and put my hands on her shoulders. "Listen to me, because this is the last time I'm going to tell you this. If the boy doesn't love you without a potion, you don't want him."

"But it's not just about a boy," she said. "It's because my—"

"Stop arguing with me, Clementine. I gave you my answer. It's no. I respect your determination, but now is not the time, okay?"

She looked up at me with those big kitten eyes, and God help me, they started to well with tears. I let out a huff of frustration, grabbed her elbow, and dragged her

down Zipser Lane with me until we were close enough to
see that I hadn't been imagining things: Nick's truck was
definitely parked in the driveway. Of course, it was possible that Nick and Peach had postponed their honeymoon
to check on my mother, but . . . no. In my gut, I just knew,
the way I always just knew about things where Leo was
concerned.

Leo was still here.

I pointed. "See that fugly green truck? That truck means
that the man I've loved since before I was your age is still
in town, and the fact that I'm here looking at that truck isn't
saying much for me, either. He ripped my heart out ten
years ago, and now he's back, and I'm twenty-nine years
old, and he can still level me with a touch." I put my hands
on her shoulders and turned her to face me. "I'm angry, I'm
tired, and it hurts just to look at him. Is that what you want
for your future?"

Clementine slowly shook her head, looking a little
scared.

"Don't fall in love now, Clementine, because when you
fall in love at your age, you don't know enough to hold
anything back for yourself, and that means that for the
rest of your life, he'll be able to get in, whenever he de-
cides he wants to, and you won't be able to do a damn
thing about it."

That's when I saw Desmond out of the corner of my
eye, standing patiently at the end of the road, respecting
our space as he waited. I met his eye briefly, got hit by a
metric ton of guilt, and looked back at Clementine.

"Consider me your cautionary tale," I said. "Now get
the hell out of here."

She nodded, then darted away with her head down,
giving Desmond a wide berth as she approached him on
the sidewalk. Desmond waited for me to meet him at the
end of the street, and I stopped and stood there for a

while, just looking at him. He seemed like a good guy: straightforward, uncomplicated, maybe a little cool but I'd had heat, and I was still nursing the burns. There was a lot to be said for cool.

"Sorry about that," I said finally, not sure if I meant the delay with Clementine, or the fact that I'd used him to shake Leo off my skin, or if I was apologizing for me just being me. Gun to my head, I'd say all of the above.

"Not to worry." He held his hand out in invitation for us to continue our walk, and get on our own separate ways. With gratitude, I started down the street, anxious to drive him back to the 'Bago and send him away.

If he was a good man, he'd stay gone.

Chapter 8

Two hours later, I drove to Deidre Troudt's house, my mind still in a jumble.

That morning after Desmond left, I had gone out to my garden shed and looked through all of my supplies, trying to see if some detail there might explain what had happened. Nothing was weird, nothing was out of place. All the ingredients I'd used in Deidre Troudt's potion were pretty standard, and none of it looked as if it had been tampered with. Of course, I hadn't made the Anwei Xing potion, but Desmond hadn't touched Deidre Troudt's potion, or my mother's fauxtion; those had been mine from start to finish.

I'd held my hand out in front of me; there had been no sign of the magic since last night, and right now, it looked like an ordinary hand. No ropes of smoky light, nothing unusual at all, aside from that wonky pinkie finger I'd broken in the third grade. Then again, day magic manifested as electric light, and night magic, as light-filled smoke. I had spent some time that morning testing to see if I could light a candle, with no joy, but the real test would be after the sun went down.

I tried to remember back to last summer, how I'd burned paper and melted my car keys. They had both been surprises to me, but I couldn't recall any specific trigger. Except I wasn't running on my own steam then; it had been Liv's day magic that had fueled mine, and her magic had been triggered by strong emotion. She'd gotten freaked out, and I'd melted my keys.

The night before, when I'd burned my clutch, I'd been with Leo, and the magic had been night magic, and it had been all mine.

That was when I'd felt the nudge of intuition, and I tried to follow it. I had taken a potion to keep me from feeling anything for Leo, and then when the potion wore off, I'd sparked some magic.

My mother had taken a potion—okay, not really, but she *thought* she had—that had made her more beautiful, and just when she was feeling at the height of her beauty, *her* magic had sparked.

Deidre Troudt had taken a potion to show her The One, and her magic had sparked . . . she said she'd been at her therapist's, hadn't she? Which didn't make sense, because she'd taken the potion to learn about Wally Frankel, the pharmacist. If this theory had ever held any water, it was leaking fast now.

It was a start, though. I turned the corner to Ms. Troudt's house and almost swerved into what would have been oncoming traffic if she hadn't lived on a cul-de-sac.

Nick's green truck was in her driveway.

I carefully pulled over to the curb and parked the Bug, then took a deep breath and closed my eyes. Any doubt I might have had about what Nick's truck in the driveway meant was now gone. Unless Deidre Troudt was having some landscaping done, Nick wasn't at her house. And even if she was, no way would he be working the day after his wedding. No, Nick was definitely on a beach in

Spain right now, sipping cocktails with his wife, the way he should be.

It was Leo. Of *course* it was Leo. He was still here. Not only that, he was still here *and* sticking his nose into my trouble.

I got out of my car and headed toward the front door, but before I could knock, I heard laughter coming from the backyard. I went to the wooden fence and unlatched it, walking through until I found Leo and Deidre Troudt laughing at the picnic table set in the middle of her garden.

"Oh, man," Deidre said, wiping her eyes. "I'd forgotten about that."

"Nick still says it's one of his proudest moments," Leo said. "Although I don't think you can say as much for the chicken."

They both busted out laughing again, and that's when Leo saw me, his laughter fading as our eyes met. Ms. Troudt followed his gaze back to me and said, "Hey! Easter!" and that's when I realized she was drunk.

"Hey, Ms. Troudt."

"It's Deidre, damnit." She pushed up from the picnic table and staggered inside without bothering to tell us where she was going or when she'd be back.

I sat down opposite Leo and whispered, "What the hell are you doing here?"

"Same as you, probably," he said, meeting my eye coolly. "Trying to figure out what's going on."

"You don't need to figure out anything. This isn't any of your business."

"Maybe not," he said, challenge in his eyes, "but you're in trouble, and I'm not leaving until you're not in trouble anymore."

"When did you decide that?" I asked, leaning forward. "Did you know you weren't getting on that plane when you left me last night?"

He shook his head and gave me a small, sad smile. "I went through security and everything."

Before I could respond, Ms. Troudt stumbled back out of the house, a carafe of hot coffee in her hands. Leo was up like a shot, taking it and the empty mug she carried. She gave it all up to him and came back to sit down next to me. Leo poured coffee into the mug, put the mug in front of Ms. Troudt, set the carafe on the table and sat down, his intention clear: He was going to stay and listen to everything. I started to say something to him to get him to leave, but Ms. Troudt patted my arm to get my attention.

"Glad you're here, Easter. You're gonna fix this, right?"

"I'm gonna try. What happened?"

She leaned both her arms against the picnic table, hung her head in dejection, and said, "He had the aura."

I glanced at Leo, who was watching us with sharp eyes, taking everything in. I let it go and focused on Ms. Troudt. "So, Wally is The One?"

She shook her head slowly from side to side, reminding me of an elephant. "No. Dr. Feelgood."

I stayed silent for a moment, hoping she would elaborate on her own, but when she didn't, I said, "Who?"

She raised her head and looked at me. "Dr. Darius Wood, Ph-friggin'-D. My *therapist*. You know, the therapist I've had for *twelve freaking years*?"

I nodded, even though I hadn't known, but it didn't matter.

"Oh, wow," I said.

She pushed herself up higher, but when she talked, she talked to the coffee mug. "I had an appointment on Friday, and I took the potion first because I was meeting Wally for dinner right afterward, and there wouldn't be time. But then . . . Dr. Wood had the aura." She finally looked at me.

"It was blue. Well, blue-ish. Kinda green, maybe. A little purple at the edges."

I glanced at Leo, who was paying very close attention to everything Ms. Troudt was saying. "Leo, I could really use some coffee . . . ," I said.

He met my eyes, clearly on to the fact that I was trying to get rid of him. "Later."

Dammit.

"For the entire forty-five minutes," Ms. Troudt went on, oblivious to the tension between me and Leo, "I stared at him and mumbled. He must have thought I'd had a stroke. Then after the appointment I went into the bathroom down the hall to cry, and the next thing I know, four bluebirds are racing around my head. By that time, *I* thought I was having a stroke. Then I hid in the stall for an hour until they went away." She laughed for a moment, then thunked her forehead against the picnic table. "Fuck my life."

"Ms. Troudt . . ." She raised her head and gave me a flat look, so I said, "I mean, Deidre . . ."

She sighed. "What?"

"I'm trying to figure out what happened, so I can fix it. What were you feeling, exactly, when the bluebirds appeared?"

She gave me a blank look. "What do you think I was feeling? I was *pissed.* I waited my whole life for that bastard to show up, and when he does, he's my goddamn *therapist*? I mean, come on!"

"I know," I said. "That's really unfair. But I need you to tell me about the bluebirds. Were they solid, or kind of transparent, like a hologram? Did they disappear into thin air, or fly off? Did they look real, or cartoony?"

"Hologram, disappeared, cartoony," she said miserably.

"Does that mean something?" Leo asked quietly.

"Yes," I said. "I don't have to go chasing down escaped

cartoon bluebirds, for one, and if it happens in public, Ms. Troudt can say it's a high-tech Japanese . . . I don't know. Hologram hat."

Ms. Troudt snorted. "Japanese hologram hat. I'll give you one thing, Easter, you have always been creative with the bullshit."

"Ooh!" I said, my heart pounding with a cheerful thought. "Or maybe it's just perception magic. You know, maybe you're the only one who can see them. I mean, the potion I gave you was perception-based; maybe you just saw something only you could see. Did anyone else see them?"

She gave me one of her patented your-stupidity-disappoints-me looks. "In the bathroom stall? No."

I sighed. "Okay . . . well, still. It's a maybe, and if you're the only one who saw them, maybe it'll just . . . I don't know. Wear off." I tried to inject a hopeful note in my voice.

"You're being chipper. I don't like it. Cut it out." Then she groaned and put her face in her hands. "Oh, hell. My head is gonna explode."

I looked at Leo. "Maybe you should get her some water."

"Sure." He got up and disappeared silently into the house.

"And the thing was, I *knew*," Ms. Troudt said to me after Leo left. "I knew when I started seeing him twelve years ago, but I rationalized. I thought, *Of course you love him, Deidre. He's the only man who's ever listened to you.* And I just let it go. I wasted *twelve years*."

"Well, you could just tell him how you feel," I said. "Go on a date, see where it goes."

She gave me a look. "He knows that I think my g-spot is traveling, because Wally can't seem to find it in the same place twice. How am I going to make small talk with this man?"

Leo came back out with a large glass of ice water. He slid the door shut, walked noiselessly back to the table, and set it down in front of Ms. Troudt.

"Deidre?" he said, his voice soft and comforting.

She shot me a look. "See? *He* calls me Deidre."

He motioned to the water in front of her. "You need to drink this, or you're going to feel terrible when you wake up later."

She pushed herself to a full upright position. "Right. Right." We stayed silent until she finished the water, at which point, she looked at me with a hazy expression.

"If he's The One, he feels the same way, right? I mean, can someone be your One if you're not theirs?"

I exchanged a look with Leo, and then we spoke over each other.

"No," Leo said.

"Maybe," I said. "It's complicated."

She looked back and forth between us. "Fat lot of help you guys are." Tears sprang to her eyes, and she covered them with her hands. "Twelve *years*."

I reached out to pat her on the arm, and that's when I saw them. At first, they showed up like a strange blue blur around her head, looking a little bit like a blurry sideways Ferris wheel. Then they took form, looking cartoonish and slightly transparent, but I could see the breeze from their flapping wings shifting some of Ms. Troudt's mussed hair. So much for my it's-just-perception-magic theory. This was full-blown, 100 percent, kick-you-in-the-balls magic.

"Oh, crap," Ms. Troudt whined. "They're back, aren't they?" She kept her hands over her eyes, ignoring the electric blue light that was snaking over her fingers. Circling her head, the birds began to chirp.

"So help me God," she said, still frozen with her hands over her eyes, "if they start braiding my hair, I'm going to have to kill someone."

"Stop thinking about Dr. Feelgood," I said. "Think about something else."

"How does that help?" she said. "If you tell me *not* to think about something, of course I'm going to think about it. It's basic psychology, Easter."

"Okay, okay," I said, and moved back a bit to give the birds a wider berth. "Think about . . ." I flailed for a moment, then said, "Ferris wheels."

She pulled her hands down and looked at me. "Ferris wheels? Really?" Then her eyes crossed as her focus went up above her forehead, watching the bluebirds in orbit. "Fuck. My. Life."

"You know, I've always kind of liked the end of *The Taming of the Shrew*," Leo said, and Ms. Troudt's focus snapped to.

"What?" she said, her voice suddenly sharp.

Leo smiled. "I don't think it's anti-feminist at all."

Ms. Troudt blinked twice. "Are you *kidding* me?"

"No." He met my eyes. "I think it's about give-and-take in a relationship. Sometimes, the man has to give, sometimes the woman."

"Yeah, except he starved and tortured her first," I said. "He made her say the *sun* is the *moon,* just to put her in her place."

"And when she did, he gave her everything," Leo said. "He gave her himself, everything he owned, everything he was. He did everything in his power to make her happy. Wouldn't you say the sun is the moon if the trade-off was happiness? Give an inch to gain a mile?"

"Are you kidding?" Ms. Troudt sputtered, throwing her arms out. "The big deal is that he made her sacrifice her integrity, her personality, who she was at her core. He tortures her to make her change, and she *does* it! That whole speech at the end? Just be pretty and give him whatever he wants? *Place your hands below your husband's foot*? You seriously think that's a pro-feminist message?"

"Kate's happy in the end, though, isn't she?" Leo said.

"Yeah, because she was written by a *man*!" Ms. Troudt and I said in unison, and then we looked at each other, equally incensed.

And that's when I noticed that the birds had gone. Ms. Troudt saw my eyes flicker upward, and hers did the same. Then she sighed and gave Leo a small, tired smile.

"Well done, North. Glad you learned something in my class, even if it was just how to piss me off." She finished the rest of her water and pushed up from the table. "I'm going to bed."

I stood up and walked a little bit with her. "One quick thing," I said quietly, when we were almost at the back door. "I'm not sure, but I think it's emotion that triggers the birds. I don't think it's anger, though."

She looked at me, her focus fuzzy. "It isn't?"

"No, I think . . . I'm not sure, but I think it's sadness."

"Oh." She nodded. "Okay. I'll just try to stay good and pissed off until you get this worked out, then. Shouldn't be too hard. It's my default setting."

She reached out, and for a moment I thought she was going to slap my face, but instead she just placed her warm palm on my cheek.

"Please be as smart as you are beautiful." Then she slipped into the house, slid the door closed behind her, and pulled the vertical blinds, leaving me and Leo alone in the garden.

I walked over to him and crossed my arms over my stomach as I stared down at him.

"Go home, Leo," I said. "This isn't your business and it has nothing to do with you."

He looked up at me, his expression serious. "I think I am home."

I tensed. "What?"

"I still own my dad's house," he said. "Ben and Suzy Berger have been renting it, and they're moving to Atlanta in August. I was going to find another tenant but . . . maybe I'll just stay."

My throat constricted. "Can't kick Ben and Suzy on timing, can you?"

He stood up, locking his eyes with mine. "I'm taking it as a sign."

"I thought you lost your faith," I said.

"Not all of it."

He kept up with the eye contact, and I knew that looking away was losing, but I wasn't entirely sure I wanted to win whatever the prize was at the other end of the staring contest, so I turned and started down the gravel garden path to the side door in the fence. "Okay. Fine. You want to stay, stay. But stay out of my way, out of my life, and out of my business."

I could hear his footsteps crunching on the gravel behind me. I slammed the wooden fence door shut, but it didn't have time to catch on the latch before he grabbed it.

"What's going on here, Stacy?"

"Nothing that concerns you, Leo."

I was almost to my car door when he caught me by the arm and turned me to face him.

"You know what this is. I'm just asking you to tell me."

"Fine." I let out a heavy sigh. "It's magic. You saw it. Remember Liv and the stick-snake? That's magic. There's magic in the world, Leo, and I'm hip-deep in it. Will you go now?"

He blinked once slowly, as though mentally swallowing the information. "Magic." He nodded. "Okay."

"Okay? What do you mean, *okay*?"

"I mean . . . okay. Look, I was almost a priest. I've taken crazier stuff than this on faith, and if you tell me magic is real, then magic is real. Okay."

A wave of affection rolled over to me, but I knew a world of hurt would follow if I allowed it, so I clamped it down. "It's wonderful that you're so open-minded. Now go away."

He stood his ground. "I think you're in trouble, and if that's the case, then I want to help."

"First of all, whatever trouble I may or may not be in, I'll handle it. Second of all, if my theory is right, you'll just make things worse."

His brows knit. "What do you mean?"

I let out a hefty sigh, debating over how much I wanted to share with him. But the reality was, it didn't matter what I shared and what I didn't. He was Leo, and I couldn't hold anything back from him, which was a big reason why I needed him to leave.

"The potion I gave Ms. Troudt was so she could see if her boyfriend, Wally, is her One True Love, but she saw the aura around her therapist, and that's when the birds erupted. Then, when she got upset about him today . . . birds. My mother's potion was . . . well, she thought it was about being beautiful, and when she felt beautiful, she glowed."

I stopped there, trying to figure out how to explain what that all had to do with me. But it was Leo, so I didn't have to. Something in his expression cleared, as if a sudden understanding had just washed over him.

"You took a potion because of me. That's why you were so strange at Nick's wedding."

I lowered my eyes. "Strangling you at the wedding would have taken the spotlight off Peach, so I took something to make me feel nothing when I saw you. And then, when it wore off . . ." I swallowed, unable to finish.

So he did. "When it wore off, I was there, and you scorched your bag."

"I don't know how it all works yet. And I may be making connections where there aren't any. When Liv's magic came in, it happened when things were emotionally heightened, and all of those situations are emotionally heightened, so . . ." I stopped and looked up at him. "I think it's the emotion that does it, but not just any emotion. It has to be related to something . . . really important to that person."

"And I'm important to you." It was a statement, not a question, but it had such a strong tone of longing that it made my heart hurt just to hear it.

"Don't play dumb," I said, my voice soft. "You know how I feel about you."

"No," he said. "I don't."

Our eyes locked, and it was like he entered me somehow. The eyes are the windows to the soul, right? I always thought that was crap, but when Leo looked into my eyes, there he was, in my soul, warming the cold, empty space he'd left there, making me whole again. I had missed him so much for so long that I'd stopped feeling it, but now that he'd settled back inside me, I realized that I had never started living again after he left. I'd just kept breathing, and that was something entirely different.

I couldn't help myself. I moved closer. It was the pull he had on me; I couldn't have resisted him any more than the moon can resist orbiting the earth. It's nature, and it was my nature and his to be together. His hand went to my chin and nudged me to look up at him. Our faces were inches apart, and his breath was warm and sweet on my lips. He hesitated a moment, and I was waiting for him to ask to kiss me, because if he spoke, if something solid passed between us, I might be able to latch on to it and resist.

But he didn't ask. His lips met mine and I closed my eyes and wrapped my arms around his neck, my last bit of resistance overpowered by my need for him. It was zero to sixty in a white heat; his arms went tight and hard around my waist, and my hands went to his shoulders, down his arms, as if I were drinking him in through touch. He felt like happiness and hope, the first day you smell a new season on the air, that first exhilarating plunge on a roller coaster. He was sincerity and truth; love, kindness, and vulnerability; the thrill and danger of being alive in the world—all things I'd been avoiding since the day he left, because they reminded me of how this felt, and remembering was too painful to endure.

He lifted me onto the Bug's hood and pressed against me, his hands running down my back, to my waist, the feel of his strong touch so familiar and yet so strange at the same time. His mouth opened and his tongue slid against mine, and he still tasted the same: dark and sweet and deep, like chocolate and coffee. Every touch felt like pieces of a puzzle clicking into place. *Click, click, click,* and the world was back to the way it should always have been.

We pulled apart after I don't know how many minutes, both of us breathing heavily and clinging for dear life, our fingers digging into each other as though we were afraid to let go. At least I had an excuse: I was sitting on the sloped hood of a VW Bug. If I let go, I'd topple to the ground.

"If that was supposed to be a test," I said, digging my fingers into his shoulders as I tried to catch my breath, "then I should probably tell you that my power only works at night."

"It wasn't a test," he said. "It was an inevitability."

I nodded; he was right. As long as the two of us were within touching distance of each other, this was an inevitability, which was why I'd spent the better part of my adult life buying insurance against it. I pushed him away and slid off the car, then stood on wobbly legs by the driver's-side door.

It was time to pull the trigger.

"Leo," I said, my voice scratchy, "things have changed."

He raised one hand and touched my face, smiling. "They haven't changed that much."

I closed my eyes and blurted it out. "I slept with Desmond last night."

Leo froze; I could feel his hands go taut, still on my waist, at the same instant that his shoulders went to stone under my fingers. A moment later, he released me.

"I'm sorry," he said, and gave a short, shocked laugh. "I forgot about you and Desmond. There's been so much going on I must have just . . . I'm so sorry. I didn't mean to disrespect—"

"There is no me and Desmond," I said stiffly. "He's is just a guy I work with."

Leo looked at me, his head quirked to the side like a dog who couldn't make sense of the sound he'd just heard.

"You don't want me, Leo," I said, trying to keep my voice even. "I'm not the same girl you left behind."

He released a breath. "How do you know what I want?"

"Please, you were a priest—"

"*Almost* a priest. I'm still a man."

"Yeah? How many women have you slept with in the past ten years?"

He went quiet. "To be fair, for most of those years, I had taken a vow of chastity and was living in a monastery with a bunch of guys."

"I've slept with twenty-two men." I shook my head and held up one hand. "Wait. Sorry. I forgot Des. Twenty-*three*. All of them outside of the sanctity of marriage." I let out a bitter laugh. "Hell, one of them was Tobias."

And there it was, exactly what I'd been looking for: a hint of distaste, just a quick flash on his face, but it was there, and I saw it. I didn't mention that the thing with Tobias was years ago, when he first came to town, way before he and Liv ever got involved, but it didn't matter. The girl who had saved her virginity for marriage to him had given it up for pretty much everyone else in town, including her best friend's true love. Surely that would be enough to make him understand that whatever we'd had didn't matter. Things were different now.

I'd made sure of it.

Except then, his face cleared and he shook his head. "I don't care."

I pushed myself away from the car in frustration, moving closer to him, making sure that every word made it through his thick skull, so he could finally understand what a waste of energy this thing between us would be.

"That's just the number of guys I've screwed. Don't even make me count the number of guys I've fooled around with. Remember Frankie Biggs, from high school? I made out with him on the pool table at Happy Larry's last year, and crazy Amber Dorsey almost killed him over it."

Leo blinked. "Wait. You used to hate Frankie Biggs."

"I still do. He's an ass. This is what I'm trying to tell you. Get it through your head, Leo. You're the good boy, the almost-priest, and I'm the town slut. You still want me now?"

He stared at me for a moment, and then understanding washed over his face. "Oh, I get it. This is the part where I'm supposed to place judgment on you, right?"

"I like sex, Leo, and I don't think you need to be in

love or married to enjoy it. I've never been pregnant, and I've never had a disease, but I know how to have a good time and I don't think that's a bad thing. I'm in control of my life, and my body, and there's no way in hell you're ever going to be okay with that, so don't . . . just . . . don't tell me . . ." I sputtered to a stop, unable to remember how I'd ended that speech in all my fantasies about the day Leo finally came back. Not that I thought it would ever actually happen; if I had, I would have done a better job preparing.

He was quiet for a moment, then he said, "So, you did all that so I'd never want you back? Is that it?"

"I did it because I like *sex,* you jerk!" I said, feeling the fury rise in my gut. "Jesus. Don't you listen?"

"Yes," he said, quietly. "I'm listening, and I heard it all, even the stuff you didn't want me to hear."

I threw my hands up in frustration. "What is that supposed to mean?"

"It means what I heard sounded practiced, like you've been saving this up to push me away if I ever came back. It also means that for someone who knows me better than anyone else, you don't know me as well as you think."

"How could I?" I said, my voice going shrill. "You were gone, Leo. *Gone.* And I had to find some way to protect myself from ever feeling the way I felt . . ." I swallowed against the lump in my throat and swiped at the tears on my cheeks, then took a deep breath before looking him in the eye again. "I'm never going to let anyone make me feel like that again, okay? Not even you. *Especially* not you."

"So . . . what do you want?" he asked, his voice soft. "You want me to judge you, to hate you? To go away and just forget about you?"

Unable to answer, I simply nodded.

"I'm sorry," he said. "I can't do that."

"You can go away," I said. "I know you can. I've seen you do it."

And then I got in my car on shaky legs, and I drove off.

Chapter 9

I made my way out to my shed on autopilot, almost running down the wooded path to get there. My mind darted all over the place like a frightened hamster trying to get out of an unfamiliar maze. It went from Leo and the way he'd looked at me on the side of the road today, to my glowing, delusional mother and the four messages she'd left on my phone bugging me to bring her more potion, to Ms. Troudt and her flying crown of bluebirds, to Desmond and the awkward aftermath of sex and how that was going to affect my magical supply. Then I'd cycle back to Leo, and the whole thing would start over again.

I needed to think about something else, and the only shot in hell I had of doing that was to work. Of course, I wouldn't be able to make potions for any of my waiting clients right now; they'd have to wait a little bit longer, at least until I figured out what was happening, and what I might have done to cause it. Today's work was going to be just for me.

I cranked the generator—this time it took four pulls, I was really going to have to get that thing replaced—and went inside, flicking on the twinkle lights. I swiped at my face, pushing away the stupid tears with shaking hands. I needed him out of my mind, out of my body, out of my life, and this was the only way I'd get respite. I shook my head violently, trying to use the velocity to shake him out of it, then went to my workbench and turned on my Mac-Book. It was still open to the recipe I'd tried last time, and I re-read my final note on the failed experiment.

What went wrong this time? Leo North.

I closed my eyes and breathed in and out, trying to find my inner calm. It took its own sweet time, but I found it eventually, and managed to shut down thoughts and feelings about Leo. I was at work now. This was where I needed to be.

I opened my eyes and went to work assembling the various ingredients, got an Edison vial ready, then went to grab a fresh Erlenmeyer flask and . . .

That spot on the shelf was empty. I glanced around, in case I'd misplaced it, but there weren't any. I thought there'd been at least one more on the shelf before, but I couldn't swear by it, and this kind of thing wasn't without precedent. When I was in that space, my focus on the work was complete, and sometimes the mundane details, like reordering supplies, would get past me.

"Shit," I said, and then glanced to the next space on the shelf, where the open-topped beakers with the pour spouts sat. Then I thought for a moment; that was one thing I hadn't varied from the original recipe. I'd always used the flask. And what the hell, right? It was probably going to fail anyway, but I needed to stay busy. I grabbed a beaker and set it on the counter, then went into my MacBook and started typing.

Sunday, June 24. Variation: All instructions as stated, with two exceptions. Replacing distilled with purified water. (Proven error.) Using 150ml Kimax beaker. (Unproven; first attempt.)

And then, I went to work. I moved through the steps on autopilot, I knew them so well, and the rest of the world faded away as I danced from instruction to instruction. Finally, after almost four hours of work that passed like minutes, I'd come to the pivotal stage. In the beaker, the liquid turned amber and the single bubble appeared, rising slowly from the bottom to the top, where it made an almost inaudible *pop* at the surface.

Here we go. I shut off the burner and used tongs to pull the beaker from its holder. I set it on the workbench to cool, right next to the Edison vial. I waited ninety seconds, then picked up the beaker.

Swirl. Swirl. The liquid inside went from amber to a cool, swirling blue. That had never happened before, but just because it was pretty and appeared pourable didn't mean success.

I didn't smile. I didn't whoop. I didn't rush to pour, either. There was still one more step before then.

Remain calm. Breathe 2x. I did as instructed, willing my calm to come to me. I opened my eyes and carefully poured the swirling blue liquid into the Edison vial, up to the first etch mark, measuring exactly one ounce.

No sludge. No turning black.

I poured more of the potion into another Edison vial. It had never occurred to me to do more than one at once, considering everything pretty much went to hell by this point. There was enough for three in total, and I filled the last one, too.

I put the top on the first vial, swirled it once clockwise as the instructions demanded, and did the same with the other two, then waited for another ninety seconds. The blue color deepened in all three, but kept swirling. It was working! I glanced at the instructions and stuck my tongue out at the nameless conjurer who had written them.

"It was the stupid flask," I said. "Jerk."

The timer dinged, and I turned my attention back to my beautiful Edison vials. The liquid was still swirling, as if on its own power. I picked one up, stood in the middle of my shed, and threw it to the ground, where it smashed, dissolving the glass and sending the liquid seeping into the packed dirt at my feet. For a moment, there was a hint of a stain, but then nothing to indicate that anything had happened at all, except for the metal cap that rolled on its side for a moment before falling flat on the dirt.

I waited, watching the space where the potion had sunk in, but still . . . nothing.

Huh. The recipe must still be wrong. The nameless conjurer had put *another* bad detail in? Sadistic bastard.

Disappointed, I sat down and pored over the recipe again. Maybe I'd added too much Persephone root. Maybe the Persephone root I had was too old, and had lost its efficacy. Maybe it wasn't even real Persephone root. When you worked rogue outside the mainstream magical world, those were chances you took, and I had gotten this stash from a traveling carnie before I found Desmond. Maybe I'd put in too much, maybe not enough, maybe it was old, maybe it was just dried lavender and I'd been had. Who the hell knew? There were a lot of charlatans in the magical world, just like the non-magical. I turned around and started typing notes into my MacBook.

And then I heard it, a subtle *thud* behind me. I turned to look, and there was still nothing. I thought maybe a bird had accidentally flown up against the Plexiglas windows I'd put in the shed—novice conjurers were known for blowing glass out of work spaces, it was a rite of passage, and I'd destroyed two sets of traditional windows before wising up—but then I saw dirt starting to displace at my feet, creating a small anthill, as though something were trying to burrow its way out.

Something *was*.

I knelt down by the space, watching in fascination as it grew, glowing green and yellow, the stalk pushing up first to about four inches above the ground, at which point the twinkling petals spread out as the blossom opened. I blinked a few times, to be sure I wasn't imagining things, then looked down at my denim-covered knees, which reflected the green-yellow glow. Then the petals started to turn as the tiny sunflower danced.

"Oh, my God!" I jumped up to my feet, looking around for someone to share this with, but of course, no one was there, so I spoke to the shed. "I did it! I did it! Physical magic! Holy shit!"

I hadn't brought my phone with me, and I didn't keep a camera in the shed. I glanced around me a little bit, in a panic to record the moment, but there was nothing. I had done this amazing thing; Stacy Easter, failed librarian, town slut, and mother's shame . . . *I* had created physical magic, on my own, without a mentor to guide me or years of training, and I hadn't thought to bring a stupid camera. It hadn't occurred to me that I would ever succeed. I had created a dancing, glowing sunflower, and no one would ever—

The MacBook! It had a webcam. I grabbed it off the workbench and sat down on the ground, keeping my eye on my sunflower as I tried to launch the right program. *Photo Booth? Argh!* The sunflower slowed down. In seconds, it would be nothing more than a puff of smoke. The fact that it had lasted this long was a damn miracle. The little beach ball spun on the screen, and finally, Photo Booth launched and the camera came on. I moved it out to the other side of the sunflower, leaned my face down so I'd be in the picture, too, grinned like a fool, and hit the button.

And it began to count down: *3, 2, 1* . . .

The screen flashed, and by the time my eyes adjusted, the sunflower was gone, leaving nothing behind but its tiny little anthill. I glanced at the screen, and there it was: the faintest outline of a glowing, miniature sunflower next to my soot-smudged, ebullient face.

What are you getting so full of yourself about? It's just a sunflower.

The voice in my head was cold and sharp, just like the bony limbs of the woman it emulated.

It's physical magic, I thought back. *It's a big friggin' deal. It means I'm good at what I do.*

It's stupid and pointless. You can't even tell anyone about it or you'll get in trouble for doing this unsupervised. What's the point if no one can even know?

I'll know.

Yes, just you. Alone. Like always. I wonder why that is?

I shook my arms out, trying to push the bad energy away. The voice was cruel, and it lied. I knew this. But when I heard it, cold and poisonous in my head, I couldn't help but believe it, at least a little, just as I'd believed my mother for all those years. Hell, part of me still did believe it. No matter where I was, no matter what I was doing, some part of me always knew I was ugly, unlovable, selfish, mean, and heartless, and that was just my nature.

That's why Leo left, and that's why he'll leave again.

I closed my eyes and released a breath through my nose as evidence of all my failures as a human being circled around me, like hunters coming in for the kill. My harshness, my coldness, my thoughtlessness, my cruelty. I remembered the night Leo had told me about sleeping with that girl at school, I had said horrible things to him, things that weren't even true. I'd just wanted to hurt him as much as he'd hurt me, and I'd succeeded. I remembered that night I'd slept with Tobias, years ago, when deep in my heart, part of me knew Liv liked him. I remembered that morning, how casual and curt I'd been with Desmond about our night together. And then there was the way I'd handled my mother after the rehearsal dinner, pushing her into the car, looming over her physically, bullying her.

If you think that pushing us to make a choice is going to end in your favor, lady, then you're gonna want to take a moment to think again.

"Oh, she deserved that," I said out loud to no one.

Maybe, the voice answered coldly, *but you enjoyed treating her that way, didn't you? What does that say about you?*

I didn't know. I looked at the picture of myself on my computer screen. Face flushed with happiness, a trace of soot from the bottom of the beaker streaked across my cheek, hair out of place, no makeup. But there was a glimmer in my eyes, something genuine and happy and proud, and I didn't see the meanness, the coldness, the anger. It was just me, the real me, right there for no one but me to ever see.

Classic Stacy Easter. Ugly, cocky, and dangerous. All that risk, all for ego, and damn the consequences.

I took a flash drive out of my back pocket and backed up the picture to it, just in case something happened when I shut my computer down. Carefully, so carefully, I put the two remaining Edison vials on the shelf. I had no idea how long the magic might last, if it was even still good now, but it didn't matter. I didn't intend to ever smash them. They were going to stay there, on that shelf, always reminding me that no matter what else I might be, I was also Stacy goddamned Easter, and I was good at what I did.

Surely that had to matter for something.

By the time I got back to the 'Bago, night had officially fallen. I still had a buzz on from my success with physical magic, but as soon as I returned to real life, the tension

started to creep in. Deidre Troudt still had power nearly
three days after taking her potion, and those bluebirds,
translucent and cartoony though they may have been,
didn't have the sputtering quality of waning magic. But
that didn't mean that my—or for that matter, my mother's—
powers were going to hang around. The three potions had
no ingredients in common aside from water. So if I was
going to figure out what was creating this magic, I was going to need more data.

Which meant I was going to have to pay a visit to my
mother. I took a quick shower, got in my car, and headed
into town.

My first thought when I saw the small crowd of maybe
fifteen people standing on her lawn holding candles was
that she had died or something, but if Lillith Easter ever
bit it, the town reaction would be closer to celebrating in
the streets, since she had a habit of working her unique
charm on pretty much everyone. I drove almost a full block
past my mother's house before I could find a parking space
on the normally quiet, dead-end street. I got out of the car
and rushed to her house, wedging myself through the
crowd, my heart in my throat.

Because there, on her darkened porch, stood my mother,
glowing like a stoner at a Phish concert. She wasn't giving
off quite enough light for her to illuminate the yard, but the
crowd held candles, and the atmosphere was creepily rem-
iniscent of a vigil.

"I don't have all the answers," she said, smiling as she
held out her hands to her followers in a beatific pose, "but
I do have one: Love one another, as you would love your-
selves."

Never heard that one before, I thought, and pushed
through another line of followers. I got to the front and
found Gladys Night—no connection to the singer, although
she did like to warble off-key during services whenever

possible—handing out candles from a wicker basket at the base of the porch.

"Here you go," Gladys said, holding a candle out to me then smiled as she looked at me. "Oh! It's Stacy!" She stood up straight and waved her arms. "It's her daughter! It's her daughter!"

The crowd, most of whom had either ignored or resented my pushing to the front, now all *oohed* at me. It was extremely creepy.

I walked up the steps and took my mother by the arm. "Tell them to go, Widow."

"Oh, my beautiful daughter!" She put glowing hands on each side of my face, little ropes of smoky green light dancing over them. I pulled back and jerked my head toward the door.

"Inside. Now."

The Widow hooked her bony arm through mine and turned to the crowd. "She doesn't want me to exhaust myself."

The crowd gave a low, disappointed moan, and I inspected the candlelit faces. Most of them were older, members of my mother's church, and as I far as I could recall, none of them had ever much liked the Widow. Even for Christians who tried to keep their hearts open to everyone, the Widow was hard to like, the kind of ranting hypocrite who gave normal, sane religious people a bad name. But still, here they were; a little glowing and a few creaking clichés and my mother had gone from a harridan to a saint.

My mother held out her hands to quiet the crowd. "Now, now. She's right. I should rest. But before I go, remember that one day, I will make the ultimate sacrifice to save you all, and when that day comes, don't be sad, but remember what an incredible blessing it is to witness a miracle firsthand."

The crowd broke into cheers and I muttered, "What the hell does that even mean?"

My mother smiled at me, as warmly as she had ever smiled at me. "It's okay, darling. I forgive you."

Slowly, she moved down the porch toward the front door, her glow reflecting on the windows as she passed. I stared after her until she disappeared inside, then looked back at all the people dripping wax on my mother's lawn.

"Go home," I said. "You got five minutes. If you're still here then, I'm calling the cops."

One by one, the candles were blown out, and the crowd began to disperse. I went inside and found my mother staring out the back window by the dining table. The glow was starting to fade, and her shoulders slumped a bit as she began to fall to the ground. I managed to get to her just in time, catching her and putting her in one of the tall-backed dining room chairs.

She smiled and let out a breath. "Thank you. It is exhausting, keeping that going."

I felt a twinge of nervousness at that. "You . . . you can control it?"

She put her hand to her throat. "Darling, would you get me a glass of ice water, please? I'm feeling a bit parched."

I was a little stunned by her easy use of both *darling* and *please*, but did as she asked. Once she'd taken a few sips of her water, she looked at me and smiled. "I've finally found it."

So far, even with as little as we'd said to each other in the last few minutes, this was the most tender moment I'd ever shared with my mother, and it put me off my guard. "Yeah? What's that?"

"My purpose," she said. "Why I'm here. What I'm supposed to do. I've seen the future, and I know what's supposed to happen, and now it all makes sense. Everything I've been through, all the ways in which I've been tested and suffered . . ." She smiled at me, her eyes brimming with tears. "Now I know why."

And it's still all about you, I thought, but said, "Yeah? So what happens?"

She shook her head. "I can't tell you that. Not yet. But when it all falls together as it has been planned, you will understand." And then she put her hand over mine and squeezed it. "You are such a beautiful girl."

I don't know why that got me, but it did. I pulled my hand away, remembering that whoever this woman was on magic, the Widow Lillith Easter was somewhere underneath, fangs primed and ready to strike.

"Look, Widow, you've gotta stop this. We need to keep this glowing thing under wraps until I figure out what's going on. You're not a prophet, and you're not a saint, and you're sure as hell not a martyr."

"And how do you know that?" Her voice was calm and happy, just innocently asking a question. She didn't appear angry in the least that I had contradicted her, and it was creeping me out.

"Go to bed," I said, speaking slow and in soft tones, as if I were talking to a child. "Stay behind doors for a few days, okay? Just until I get this all figured out. No more speeches, no more candlelight vigils. Can you do that for me?"

Before she could answer, the front door shut, and heavy footsteps thunked through the living room and into the dining room, where Gladys Night, round cheeks flush with pleasure under a helmet of steel-wool hair, set a plastic planter on the table that had sat empty on the porch since my mother's doomed attempt at porch gardening in the summer of 'ought-seven.

"Oh, my goodness, Lillith!" she squealed. "I haven't been able to count it all, but there are *thousands* of dollars in here!" She reached one hand into the planter and pulled out a handful of wadded cash, and then with the other, she pulled out a check. *"This one alone is for five hundred dollars!"*

"No." I stood up like a shot and took the check from Gladys. It was from Nat Payne, owner of Nat's Dry Cleaning and Spray Tan, and it was made out directly to my mother. *Crap.* "No. No, no, no. You can't do this. You can't take their money. You have to give it back and tell them all it's a terrible, terrible mistake."

The Widow stood up and walked over to peek into the planter.

"Oh, my," she said. "That is a lot."

I waited for it, heard her voice in my mind saying, *Enough to go to Switzerland and get all the plastic surgery my body can bear,* but then she said words I never thought I'd hear, words that took me a moment to fully comprehend.

"Stacy's right," she said.

"What?" Gladys said.

"Excuse me?" I said.

The Widow shook her head. "It must go back. I don't need their money. All I need is their faith. That's what sustains me." She looked at me and added simply, "That's what makes it possible for me to control it."

"But . . . but . . . ," Gladys blustered, looking down at the money. "Think of the *good* you can do . . ."

"Wait." I held up one hand, my mind racing. "What do you mean, that's what makes it possible for you to control it?"

Gladys shook her head, staring down into the only green that planter had ever seen. "We can return or rip up the checks, but the cash . . ."

"Mom," I said, and that got the Widow's attention.

"Yes, dear?" she said, doing her best June Cleaver.

"What makes it possible for you to control the magic?"

"Faith," she said, but I heard what she really meant, *Their faith in me,* and it all fell into place.

Of course. That made complete sense. What fuels a narcissist more than attention and adoration? It wasn't being beautiful that had made her glow; it was attention. That was her hook into the magic, the thing that was most important to her: *her.*

"I mean, people just threw the cash into the planter by the handful," Gladys was saying, still focused on the money. "I didn't have time to keep track of who gave us what . . ."

My mother stood still for a moment, her lightly drawn brows knitting together, and then she said, "Okay," and my heart dropped.

"I'm going to fix this, Widow," I said, "and when I do, your ass is going to get sued."

Returning to old form, my mother ignored me. "Gladys, I need to ask you a favor. Is that okay?"

Gladys, who had known my mother for a long time and had likely never heard my mother ask for rather than demand favors, nodded mutely.

"If you could write thank-you notes to the people who wrote checks and return the money to them, I would appreciate it." She motioned to the buffet behind her. "I have stationery and postage in the top drawer there. Then please give the cash to the church. Okay?"

With that, the Widow moved slowly out of the room, and in the distance I heard not her footsteps but just the light creak of the old stairs as she moved up them to her room.

I looked at Gladys, who stared back at me.

"I paid twenty dollars out of my own pocket for those candles," she said, her lower lip out in a bit of a pout.

I reached into my pocket, pulled out twenty bucks, and grabbed one of the candles out of the basket for myself.

"Give the money back," I said, and left. Then I stepped

outside, sat down on the porch steps, and put my two fingers together on the wick of the fresh candle. I closed my eyes and thought about my mother, letting the worry and fear over what she had done—and what she had yet to do—build up in my head. I thought about all the awful things she'd said to me when I was a kid, the way she'd let Nick go a week with a fractured rib before bothering to take him to a doctor, the way she had let us believe our father was dead for two days before I answered his phone call asking for money. Emotion roiled within me: fear, anger, hurt.

I opened my eyes; the candle wick was pure white, and there wasn't the slightest hint of red, smoky ropes around my hands. I hadn't even managed to soften the wax. I put the candle down next to me on the porch and sighed. It wasn't just any strong feeling that triggered the magic at this stage. It was about one emotion connected to the thing that was most important to you. For my mother, it was having her narcissism fed. For Deidre Troudt, it was Dr. Feelgood.

For me, it was Leo. Although whether it was specifically love or desire, anger or pain, I didn't know. All of my emotions involving Leo were tightly interwoven, and separating them to figure out which it was would probably prove impossible.

I got up, leaving the candle there, and walked down the street toward my car.

Chapter 10

There are times in a girl's life when she just needs waffles. The following morning was one of those times. I'd managed to sleep only in bits and snatches, dreaming in flashes of fire and the smell of singed satin, dancing sunflowers and glowing widows, the taste of Leo and flying purple potion vials. When I woke up, I pulled on my sneakers and went for a run.

When that didn't shake all the tension out, I showered, got in my Bug, and went to Crazy Cousin Betty's for waffles. It was early on Monday morning, and neither Liv nor Tobias was working, which was a relief. Much as I loved them both, I didn't want to see anyone I knew well at the moment. I just wanted peace and waffles, and to be left alone.

"Oh, my God, Stacy Easter! Just who I wanted to see!"

My butt had barely hit the vinyl in the booth seat before I heard my name called. I looked up to find the town's cutest baby boomer lesbians, Addie Hooper-Higgins and Grace Higgins-Hooper, moving toward me. Addie was physically striking: naturally pretty even without makeup, bright blue eyes shining under a fringe of wild silver hair.

She wasn't always the sharpest tack in the box, but she was so earnest that you eventually forgave anything she said or did, because no matter what, her intentions were always for the good. Grace was granite-faced, with bobbed gray hair the color of a summer storm. She was laconic and straight-forward, and you never had to forgive her anything because she never did or said anything without thinking it through thoroughly first. I had a lot of time for them both, but Grace was more my kind of woman.

"Morning, Stacy," Grace said simply as she slid into the seat across from me. Unlike Grace, Addie didn't slide; she bounced in.

"So, oh my *God,* the wedding!" Addie said in what was probably meant to be a confidential whisper, but her enthusiasm got the best of her. "What in the world *happened*? Was it Liv? Is someone trying to kill her again? Because you know, you really could have called us."

Being called in to help during the big fight with Davina last summer was one of Addie's fondest remembrances, and since she couldn't talk about it with anyone who hadn't been there—we'd made her swear on all that is holy to keep it secret, and to her credit, she had—she wedged it into every conversation she had with any of us who were there that night.

"It wasn't Liv," I said, "and no one's trying to kill her. It was . . . I don't know. A thing. A magical hiccup. I'm figuring it out, and it won't happen again."

I held up my menu between us. I knew it by heart and could recite it on command, but I was hoping they'd take the hint and leave me alone. Addie, who had never been big on taking hints, put one finger on top of my menu and pushed it down, leaning forward.

"It's already happened, honey."

The muscles in my shoulder and neck tensed. "What do you mean?"

"You know that mousy little girl . . . ," Addie began.

"She's not little, she's seventeen . . . ," Grace corrected.

". . . who works at the checkout at the grocery store? Well, she—"

"Her name is Clementine," Grace said, and I felt ice go down my back.

"—had an . . . *incident* in the middle of the grocery store yesterday afternoon. *Everyone* was talking about it."

I looked at Addie. "Clementine? You're sure? Red hair, thick glasses, eyes way too big for her face, looks kind of like a gawky Bambi?"

Addie nodded. "That's the one."

Crap.

"What happened?" I asked, and when Addie blinked, I prompted. "At the grocery store?"

Addie leaned forward; it was gossip time. This was her element. "Well, at first, it just seemed like another teenage drama thing. I mean, Bill hires all high school kids to be cashiers and stock boys, and there's always some kind of hormone-induced theater going on. But usually it's about that Barbie-doll blonde with the C-cup and the D-grades. Not Clementine. She's a sweet girl but . . . she hasn't exactly grown into her beauty yet."

I tried to relax my shoulder muscles. There was nothing to freak out over; I hadn't given Clementine anything, not even a fauxtion. Hell, I'd barely even given her five minutes of my time. Whatever had happened, it was just a coincidence. It had to be.

I shrugged. "Girls can do other things besides be pretty to make boys crazy, you know."

Addie gave me one of her world-weary, don't-tell-*me*-about-the-world, I'm-a-*lesbian* looks.

"I *know* what girls can do, but Clementine isn't one of *those* girls. She plays the cello, and not well. She got accepted to Cornell, early admissions. She'd probably scream if she saw a penis outside of an anatomy book."

"It's the smart, mousy ones that you have to watch out for the most," I said, thinking of Millie. But even as I said the words, I remembered Clementine's eyes when we'd talked, and I felt a niggle of doubt. Even in her mousiest moments, there'd always been an edge to Millie; Clementine was soft all over, no hint of an exoskeleton anywhere on that kid.

"Anyway," Addie said, "I wasn't there, but Eleanor Cotton was. She said that she was in the produce section, thumping melons, when one of the stock boys—the tall, skinny one—and one of the boys from the football team started beating each other to a pulp, apparently over Clementine. Well, mostly, it was the football player doing the beating and the stock boy being the pulp, but I heard he got one or two good swings in there—"

"They're teenage boys," I said. "She has breasts. There's nothing magical about that."

"Wait. Listen." Grace's eyes met mine with that serious look they got only when things were truly important. It was easy to dismiss Addie; she had a fanciful imagination and a love for gossip that verged on the pathological. She was a storyteller at heart, and the truth was no deterrent for her if exaggeration or outright lies meant a better story.

But if Grace said, "Wait. Listen," then you waited, and you listened.

Addie leaned forward.

"Eleanor doesn't know anything about the magic, and I swear when she told me this, I acted like it was weird and told her it must have been her imagination, but . . ." Addie glanced from side to side, then leaned in even closer and kept her voice super low. "She said that when she went out into the parking lot after buying her melons, she saw

Clementine just sitting in the front seat of her car, looking stunned. Eleanor went over to check on her, and Clementine waved her away, and when she did, that's when Eleanor noticed it."

Even as Addie paused to heighten the drama, I knew what was coming.

"Eleanor said Clementine had bright pink light flickering around her hands, like tiny streaks of lightning."

And with that, Addie sat back, looking proud and validated. She took Grace's hand, and the two of them looked at me.

"I don't think Eleanor would make something like that up," Grace said coolly.

"I *know* she wouldn't," Addie said. "Why would she? If you're going to make something up, you throw in a secret pregnancy, or a drug addiction, or a raunchy affair. Something at least a little interesting." Addie's eyes widened and she put one hand innocently to her chest. "Not that *I* would ever make anything like that up, but . . . if you're going to lie, you make it a lie that's worth the effort. Light around the girl's hands? There's no reason to make something like that up."

"No, right," I said absently, my mind in a whirl, trying to separate facts from assumptions. People were becoming magical; that was fact. I had assumed, because the first few instances happened around me, that it had been my potions, my fault somehow. But I had never made a love potion, and even if I had, I certainly wouldn't have given it to Clementine.

Something else was going on here, something that went beyond me and my potions.

I barely had time to start putting pieces together when Desmond Lamb walked through the front door to CCB's and took a seat at the counter. I watched his back as he picked up a menu and chatted with the eponymous Betty,

who was in her seventies and—up until Liv and Tobias—
had been the only magical in town.

Now we had at least seven.

Something is very, very wrong.

". . . has to be something magical, and if you need us
to help . . ." Addie prattled on in the background, but my
eyes were on Desmond.

Desmond, who was supposed to have left town yesterday.

". . . have my phone number, and you know I'm an in-
somniac, so even if it's the middle of the night . . ."

Desmond, who had been there when Clementine had
asked me for help.

". . . come over and have tea and we can talk about anything, and I won't say a word to anyone, Grace will tell
you how good I've been about . . ."

Desmond, who had been so careful to make sure the
potion he made for me was in a purple vial.

"That son of a bitch," I grumbled, and slid out of the
booth.

Addie stopped talking, although I'm sure she turned to
watch as I approached Desmond. Based on the look on
my face when I left the booth, she was probably expecting something juicy. But by the time I sat myself down
next to Des, I was all smiles.

"Hey, stranger. Fancy meeting you here." I gave a small
wave to Betty. "Hey, Betty. How's it going?"

"I'm old, and it's pissing me off," she said, "but other
than that, I'm still alive, so knock wood, right?" She winked
at me, then looked at Desmond. "One sunrise special to go.
You want coffee, too?"

"Black, please," Desmond said, then turned to smile at
me. "Well, Stacy Easter, this is quite the welcome surprise."

"What are you still doing here?" I asked, not wanting
to tip my hand, but not being overly pleasant, either. Even

if I didn't suspect him of screwing with my town, which was a castratable offense in itself, I wouldn't be too pleased to discover a lover I'd sent back to Canada had returned to my doorstep. *Act natural,* I thought, and narrowed my eyes at him a bit.

He gave me an appraising look, and for the first time, the expression in his eyes—which I'd always read as standard British aloofness—now appeared as something else: wariness.

The game was, apparently, afoot.

"I have a little vacation time coming," he said, "and I've decided to stay here for a while."

"Wow," I said. "How long?"

"Well, that's the beauty of being self-employed, now isn't it?"

His elusiveness was annoying me, but I kept my face impassive. "Huh. Where are you staying?"

"Oh, a charming little bed-and-breakfast owned by the woman who made the cake for the wedding," he said.

I took a moment to decide how to play that, and I went with the path of least bullshit.

"You're staying at Grace and Addie's? What a coincidence. I was just having breakfast with them."

Something lit in his eyes, respect maybe, and he gave a nod as though I'd just moved a chess piece to a smarter position than he'd expected me to. "I know. I saw you when I came in. I didn't want to interrupt your conversation, though."

"That was thoughtful." I stared at him in silence, waiting to see if he'd fill in the dead air, the way that 99 percent of people do. He said nothing, just stared back down at me. I wasn't ready to confront him directly, not until I knew more about what was going on, so for the moment, I was just going to throw a rock in the water and see what rippled up.

I leaned forward, speaking in low tones. "I know I'm really good in bed, okay? And sometimes that makes men think they're in love with me, but they're not. It was just good sex, and you'll have it again someday with someone else. Really. But I'm just not that kind of girl. So if you're in town to try to win me, you're wasting your time."

At that moment, Betty delivered his food. Desmond chuckled lightly, pulled out some bills and handed them to her, then took his coffee and to-go bag in hand and stood up.

"You have found me out, Stacy," he said, "although in one particular, you've misjudged the situation. While I enjoyed myself a great deal the other night, and while you are being modest when you state that you are merely 'good' in bed—I hope it doesn't embarrass you if I say that I have rarely had the pleasure of enjoying such enthusiasm and flexibility—let me assure you that I have no unwelcome designs on you." He raised his head as Betty gave him his change. "Thank you, Betty. I look forward to what I'm told is the best breakfast in town."

Betty gave me a quick look; she pretended to be old and doddering, but she'd just heard every word we'd said, and the only reason she wasn't repeating it to everyone else even as I sat there was because I mattered to Liv, and she loved Liv with a maternal fierceness that made you ache to watch it. Or at least, it made me ache; no one had ever loved me like that.

"This town has a lot of good things to offer," Betty said casually, then moved on down the counter, but I noted that she stayed within listening distance.

Desmond sorted out the bills, leaving most of his change for the tip. "Where was I? Oh, yes." He turned his focus to me, his smile simple and almost sweet, which made it even creepier. "Where you are correct is that I have fallen in love, but I am sorry to say, not with you. Nodaway Falls has charmed me, in a most unexpected way, and I couldn't bring myself to leave it. Not just yet, anyway."

He leaned over and kissed me on the cheek, then turned and walked out. I took a few minutes to indulge a feral growl, and then returned to my booth where Addie and Grace waited.

"So, you and Desmond . . . ?" Addie prompted. "You two made a very cute couple at the wedding."

"We're not a couple," I said, glaring out the window in the direction he'd gone, even though he was long gone. "He's just something I tracked into town on my shoes."

"Is everything okay, honey?" Grace asked. When Grace looks concerned, it's bad.

I forced a smile. "Everything's fine. I need you guys to do me a favor, though. Keep an eye on him. Tell me where he goes, who he sees, and what he does. Anything weird, call me. And try not to tip him off that we're watching. Okay?"

Addie's face lit up, and she clapped her hands in excitement. I honestly don't know if I'd ever seen anyone that happy, ever.

Grace gave a brief nod. "You got it, Stacy."

"Thanks." I got up and put money down on the table to pay for their coffees, then started to walk away before heading back to look at Addie.

"Addie?" I said, and she looked up at me, still smiling brightly.

"Yes, honey?"

"Put tons of flaxseed in his food, okay?"

She grinned, and I patted her on the shoulder on my way out. She was a good woman, that Addie.

Clementine Klosterman wasn't at Treacher's IGA that afternoon; Bill said she had the day off, and blew me off when I asked when she'd be back in. I was just about to leave when I saw a tall, lanky, freckled, and conspicuously banged-up stock boy working the soup aisle. His left eye was purple, and he had a cut over his right cheek that looked like it had been made with a ring of some kind—possibly a high school football state championship ring, NFHS had shocked everyone last year by actually winning—but his body was relaxed and he moved fluidly as he transferred the soup cans from the box to the shelf. His hands were strong and deft but still a little awkward, and I smiled, instantly liking him; he reminded me of Leo.

I figured I'd get more out of a casual encounter than an in-your-face interrogation, so I moved down the aisle casually, finally stopping next to him.

"Wow," I said, inspecting a can of alphabet soup. "What truck hit you?"

For a moment, he acted like I hadn't spoken, and then suddenly he looked up from where he was crouched by the lowest shelf. "Huh? Oh, Ms. Easter. I'm sorry. Did you have a question?"

I hesitated, a little surprised. I shopped in there whenever driving thirty minutes to the Wegmans in Erie was too much of a hassle, but that wasn't often. If Wegmans were a man, I'd have married him years ago. "You know me?"

The kid blushed a bit. "Yeah. I helped you find the salad dressing once." He jerked his head backward. "Aisle Three, next to the big crouton display. That display is gone now, but it was here when you came in. Remember?"

No.

"Of course." I put the soup back on the shelf and pointed to his face. "I was just wondering what happened to you . . ." I glanced down at his name tag. ". . . Henry."

"Oh." He started to smile, then said, "Ow," and touched his cheek. "I kinda got into a fight."

"Huh." I paused a moment, and then asked, "Over what?"

He hesitated, then said, "Nothing." He crouched back down next to his box and started filling the shelves again.

"A girl?" I prompted.

He stopped stocking and lowered his head. "I don't know what I was thinking."

I glanced around; no one else was there. It was still pretty early in the morning. I sat down on the floor, leaned back against the shelves facing him, and said, "It's okay. I do."

His eyes widened and he said, "No. I mean, it wasn't like that. It was just . . ." His face went taut. He shoved one of the cans in too hard and it knocked over some other cans. He shook his head, obviously frustrated. "Karl's such a jerk, you know? Always has been. In kindergarten, he stuffed another kid's head into the john on the first day."

"That's advanced," I said. "Most bullies don't get to toilet facials until the third or fourth grade."

"I don't understand what she sees in him," he said. "Clementine's smart and pretty. She can be really funny, when she relaxes around people." His face flushed a bit. He was obviously one of the people Clementine relaxed around, and I could see it meant a lot to him. "He's never even looked at her before. He's usually a jerk to the cheerleader type, you know? Then all of a sudden, he's at the checkout, calling Clementine Four-Eyes and Metal Mouth and just being stupid."

"Really?" I said, trying to put the pieces together. Was it possible Karl was advanced in bullying, but still in that pull-the-pigtails-of-the-girl-you-liked stage of flirtation? I thought back to the guys I knew when I was in high school and thought, *Yes*.

"He sounds like a jerk," I said.

"He is. Four-Eyes? Metal Mouth? Who says stuff like that anymore? Plus, she got her braces out last month. He didn't even notice. Idiot." Henry sighed and stopped with the soup, then turned to look at me. "Anyway, I got between him and Clem, and ended up with my head wedged in a watermelon."

I laughed. "Hey, at least you can joke about it."

He gave me a dull look. "I'm not joking. He threw it on the floor and it broke in half and he stuffed the bigger half on my head. Mr. Treacher's taking it out of my pay."

"Oh, man." I pulled my lips in between my teeth and bit down, trying like hell not to laugh, but I couldn't. As I've said, I'm a horrible person. "Oh, God, I'm so sorry. That's awful, really."

He laughed, too, and I felt a little less like a terrible human being. Poor kid.

"You think it's awful now," he said, "try getting watermelon pits out of your sinuses."

We laughed together for a bit, and then I patted him on the shoulder. "You're a good egg, Henry. Don't let the thing with Clementine get you down. Girls can be kinda blind at this age. They get all hot and bothered over the Karls of the world now, but when they get older and smarter, you'll be the one they go for."

Henry looked away. "I don't care about that."

"Yeah," I said. "I can tell."

He went back to stocking the soup cans, then stopped and stared down at the ground for a minute, his forearms resting on his knees and his hands hanging low. God, he had it bad for this girl. I wondered if she had any idea.

"She doesn't have to like me," he said, his voice low. "I just wish she liked someone better than Karl."

"That's setting a pretty low bar," I said. "If you really

like her, I'd think you'd want someone for her who was more than just 'better than Karl.' "

He nodded. "Yeah. It doesn't matter, anyway. She likes Karl."

He looked so sad and dejected, stocking the soup as though each can had CLEMENTINE LOVES KARL written in a little love heart on the label.

"Hey, Henry."

He looked at me. "Yeah?"

"I'm gonna let you in on something, and I want you to listen to me, because I know what I'm talking about, okay?"

He nodded.

"When I was your age, I had a Karl, and I had a Henry. I ended up picking the Henry, and it was the smartest thing I ever did. If Clementine is smart, she'll pick you, and if she's not, you don't want her. Just keep your grades up and get into a good school where there are smarter girls."

He stared at me. "You picked the Henry? Really?"

"Yeah, I really did." I remembered Leo at that age. So smart, so awkward, so sweet and vulnerable and goofy. I have never in my life loved anyone more, not even Nick.

Henry gave a little half smile and began stocking again, this time with a straighter posture. I didn't know if I was doing him any favors giving him hope about Clementine—if she really liked Karl, she had some serious problems—but it felt good that I'd made him feel better.

I patted him on the shoulder and stood up to walk away, then turned around, as if it were a last-minute thought. "Hey, did Clementine seem strange or different to you at all yesterday? You know, before this whole thing happened?"

He looked up at me, hesitating while he thought.

"Well . . . there was one thing." He shook his head. "I don't know. It might have been my imagination."

Bingo. "What was it?"

"She was moving really . . . well, fast. No one else seemed to notice, but when she was ringing Karl up the items were coming at me so fast I could barely keep up. Clementine is usually real careful about things. Not slow, just careful. But yesterday, she was flying. Then again, Karl was really being a jerk. And then . . ."

"And then you got your head stuck in a watermelon."

He smiled. "Yeah."

"Okay. Thanks, Henry." I turned to walk out for real then, and then turned back for real. "Hey, Henry?"

He looked up.

"You don't happen to know Clementine's home address, do you?"

As a woman who lives in a Winnebago, I don't place judgment on trailer parks. People do the best they can, and some of those homes can be kind of nice. I was surprised to find Clementine living in Findley Pines, though. Based on her preppy-on-steroids fashion sense, I expected her to be the kid of college professors, living in one of those planned neighborhoods where every house looks the same and no one drives a car that's more than four years old. I knocked on the rickety front door and a minute later, a tall red-headed woman in a diner waitress uniform with a name tag that read BECKY answered.

"Hi," I said. "I'm looking for . . . does Clementine Klosterman live here?" I was kind of hoping she'd say no, that Henry had somehow screwed up the address. Instead, she gave me a confused look.

"Who are you?" she asked. "One of her teachers or something? She didn't get in trouble, did she?"

I went blank for a moment, then said, "I'm a customer at the IGA."

In the empty space where I tried to think of a reasonable excuse why a customer at the IGA would stop by the home of one of its cashiers, Becky leaned her head back and hollered, "Clem! Someone's at the door for you!"

Becky riffled through her purse and pulled out a pack of cigarettes, holding it out to me. "You want?"

"No," I said. "Thanks."

She lit up, and then Clementine showed up behind her mother, dressed much the way she'd been dressed every time I'd seen her: a long-sleeved, buttondown shirt that had been ironed within an inch of its life and impeccably tucked into a pair of mom jeans with ironed creases in the knees. Holy crap, did this apple fall far from that tree.

"I have to get to work," Becky said to Clementine without looking at her. "You handle whatever this is about. As long as I don't have to deal with it, you're not in trouble."

And with that, Becky headed out, hopped into a rickety Dodge Dart, and backed up out of the one-car parking space in front of the trailer, driving over the corner of the anemic patch of grass that passed for their lawn.

I turned to look at Clementine, whose eyes were wide.

"You look mad," she said.

"Smart kid." I pushed my way into her trailer. It was small, but cozy. The walls were white, textured and thin, with join lines every four feet or so. The living room and kitchen were open, with a little island separating them, and the place was clean, if infused with cigarette stink. Clementine stood stiffly at the doorway, her hands clasped behind her back, watching me with a tense look on her face as I moved around inside.

"Um, can I get you something to drink? We have Diet

Coke and . . ." She hesitated a moment. "We have Diet Coke."

I leaned my butt against the kitchen counter and crossed my arms over my stomach, giving her the stink eye.

"I'd like a big tall glass of *What the hell were you thinking?* You got some of that?"

She lowered her head, her red hair hanging long around her face. "I know. I'm sorry."

"Oh, hell." I walked over to her, put my index finger under her chin, and raised her face until her eyes met mine. "It's really hard to yell at you if you just fold like that."

Clementine stared at me, eyes wide. "I'm not sure . . . I don't know . . . what do you want me to say?"

"I don't know. I'm new at this. I don't get the chance to yell at kids very often." I stood back and looked at her. "Let's try it again." I took a breath, released it, and said, "Do you have any idea how dangerous magic like that is?"

She lowered her head again. "I know. I'm sorry." Then, remembering, she raised her head and said, "I mean . . . I didn't . . . Um." Her brows knit. "Are you sure you don't want a Diet Coke?"

"Will you feel better if I have one?" I asked.

She nodded.

I shrugged. "Fine, then."

She rushed around to the fridge, got the Coke, filled a glass with ice, poured the Coke in, and handed it to me. I took it, set it on the counter, and said, "Clementine, seriously. What the hell were you thinking?"

"I . . . I . . . I . . ." She looked like a robot on one of those bad sci-fi shows from the sixties. *Does not compute. Does not compute.* "I don't know what you want me to say. Am I supposed to say I'm sorry, or defend myself, or . . . what?"

I leaned closer and lowered my voice. "You could say

that you came to me, and I wouldn't help you, so you went to someone else, and if I was so concerned about your safety, maybe I should have helped you when I had the chance." I waved a hand at her. "Go ahead."

She stared at me, wide-eyed. "I don't . . . I'm not . . . I mean . . . what?"

"Oh, hell." I ran my hand over my forehead. "This is exhausting."

"I'm sorry." She motioned toward the fridge. "Would you like some pie? Mom brought some home from work last night."

"No, thanks," I said. "How did you even get to Desmond so fast? He's only been here two days."

Her eyes went wide and she shook her head. "No, no, he came to *me,* I swear it. He told me you sent him, and I saw him with you yesterday, so, I thought, you know, that made sense. I thought you'd changed your mind."

My stomach turned. "The son of a bitch," I said under my breath. "I'm gonna kill him."

"He just . . . he seemed so nice, with that British accent . . . He reminded me of Sherlock Holmes."

"Have you read Sherlock Holmes?" I said. "Sherlock Holmes is not a nice man."

She blinked. "He's not?"

"No. He'd walk over your dead body in a heartbeat if it served his purposes, kid. You gotta grow some balls before you can mess with a Sherlock Holmes, or a Desmond Lamb." I let out a frustrated sigh. He must have gone to find Clementine right after leaving me yesterday. But how could he have gone back to his place in Canada, made the stuff, and gotten back in time to . . . ?

And then I remembered my missing Erlenmeyer flask. He must have waited for me to leave, then broken in and used *my* equipment and supplies.

Bastard.

"Never, *ever* sleep with Sherlock Holmes," I said pointing a finger at her. "No matter how much you want to forget the other guy."

"Um . . . o-okay?" she said.

I let out a breath. Back on track. "So, what was the potion for? Was it a love potion? Because you know that messes with free will, right? You know that's dangerous right?"

"He said it would be okay," she said.

"He *lied*," I said. "I told you it wouldn't be okay, and who's scarier? Me or him?"

"Right now?" she said, and swallowed visibly. "Definitely you."

"Okay." I let out a breath. "So he gave you a love potion. Was it the kind you take, or the kind you dump in someone else's drink?"

"Oh, the kind I take," she said quickly, then hesitated. "Um . . . is that better?"

"Marginally," I said. "But still bad, because you're still messing with free will."

"Right, right." She nodded so emphatically that her glasses shimmied down her nose, and she had to push them back up. I sighed; I just couldn't beat this kid up, no matter how much she needed a good beating. I leaned against the counter and shook my head.

"Here's what I don't get. Why Karl? You don't seem like a dumb girl to me, and Karl is a walking box of rocks. What's that about?"

She blinked. "Karl?"

"Yeah, Karl. I mean, I get he's on the football team and sometimes that's a draw for the dumb girls, but you're not a dumb girl, Clementine."

She smiled a bit. "Thank you."

"You're also not off the hook yet."

Her smile faded. "Okay." Then she shook her head, her face so earnest it was almost painful. "I didn't take the potion for Karl. I was supposed to take it right before seeing"—she flushed bright red—"the guy I was taking it for, so I snuck into the alley behind the store so I could go straight to the stockroom but then Karl was in the alley smoking a cigarette and he saw me first and . . ." She sighed. "It didn't work, anyway. Karl was super mean to me. Does that make it any better?"

I shook my head and stared at her, my heart softening to the point where yelling at her was going to be useless. "No, honey. It doesn't. First of all, your intention was in violation of free will, and intention matters."

She hung her head. "Oh. Right. Okay."

"And second of all, it *did* work."

Her brows knit. "But . . . Karl was really mean to me."

"Yes," I said, "because Karl's still eight years old inside."

She sighed. "Oh."

We stood in silence for a little while, Clementine nibbling her lip in anxiety, me wondering how the hell I was going to put Humpty Dumpty back together again. The effects of most potions were temporary, and she hadn't dosed Karl with anything, thank God. Aside from the magic she was displaying, most of this was going to go away. Still, I needed to know exactly what Desmond had given her if I was going to figure out what the hell he was doing, and how the hell I was going to reverse it all.

"Hey," I said. "Do you still have the potion vial Desmond gave you?"

"Oh," she said, "it won't work anymore. He said it would only last twenty-four hours."

I gave her a flat look. "What in the world makes you think I would want to use a love potion?"

Her eyes widened. "Oh, right. Yes. I have it." She went under the sink, pulled out a can of Comet, flipped off the top, and dumped the contents onto the counter. There was a big wad of cash, some old jewelry that looked like it had probably been in that can for a while, and a little purple vial.

I reached for the vial, whipped it open, and sniffed; it was empty, but the pungent scent of star anise was still strong enough to punch me in the face. Unfortunately, that was so strong that it masked the scent of anything else. I examined the inside and the underside of the cap, but I didn't see anything special about the vial. He had done something to the vials, I knew that, because the vial was the only common factor in the potions that had caused trouble, but what exactly he'd done . . . that was still a mystery.

I put the cap back on and tucked the vial in my front pocket, then watched as Clementine put everything back into the can and set it under the sink with the rest of the cleaning supplies.

"Aren't you afraid your mother is going to find all that stuff?"

"No," Clementine said, her voice sharp as she carefully closed the cabinet door. "She doesn't do a lot of cleaning."

"You know, your mom is probably doing the best she can," I said lamely, and for the first time, I saw a glint of anger in Clementine's eyes.

"Yes," she said. "She is." And in that moment, I could see that she knew full well that her mother's best wasn't good enough, and that she deserved better. At that moment, my heart cracked open and offered Clementine Klosterman a comfy place to curl up inside. I leaned back against the counter and crossed my arms over my chest, in a moot attempt to keep her out.

"Okay. First things first." I reached into my pocket and

pulled out a business card for her. "The effect on Karl shouldn't happen again, but if he keeps acting weird around you, you call me immediately. Understood?"

"Yes, absolutely," Clementine said.

"Good. Now, tell me about the pink light," I said. "Has it happened again?"

Her body stiffened, and she kept her eyes lowered as she spoke. "Um, I'm sorry, what?"

I put my finger under her chin and lifted until she had no choice but to look me in the eye. "The pink light, on your hands. It makes you super fast, right?"

She nodded. "That wasn't supposed to happen, was it?"

"I think it's exactly what Desmond meant to happen. I'm just not sure why, or what it is, or how long it's going to last. It happened during the day, though, right?"

"Yes."

"That means you have day magic. At night, it shouldn't happen. During the day, though, you're gonna want to steer clear of your trigger, which is usually some kind of strong emotion. Can you tell me what you were feeling when you started moving so fast?"

She blushed a bit, but to her credit, she met my eyes as she talked. "I was ringing Karl up, and he was being really mean to me, and then Henry told him to shut up and . . ." Her face broke out in a huge smile.

I shook my head. Me, Deidre, and Clementine, all brought down by men. I had to give my mother that, at least: She loved no one more than herself, but at least she wasn't a damn cliché.

"Okay, then. My guess is, Henry's your trigger. That means you need to quit your job at Treacher's. Plus, Bill Treacher is an ass. He docked Henry's pay for that watermelon."

She looked up at me in shock. "No! He docked *my* pay for it, too!"

"See? Ass. Quit the job."

She shook her head. "I can't. I need the money. I got accepted to Cornell. I've got scholarships for the tuition, but I have to pay for room and board and everything else myself. I've saved up all my babysitting money for three years, and everything I made at Treacher's this last year, but that's only going to get me through part of the first semester. I can get a job once I get there, but . . ."

I put my hand on her shoulder. "No, that's fine. You can work at CCB's. You know Olivia Kiskey? And Betty? And Tobias?"

She nodded. "Yeah. I mean, I know of them. Why?"

"All magic."

She stared at me, her face blank. "I think it might take me a little while to get used to all this."

"Join the club, kid. Anyway, they'll watch over you and cover for you if anything weird happens. I'll talk to Betty about it tomorrow and she'll let you know when you can start. You can get tips there, too, so it'll probably pay even better than Treacher's."

Her face brightened. "Oh, that'd be great."

"Don't get too excited," I said. "It's lots of hard work and people are jerks to waitresses, but that will teach you to stand up for yourself, so it sounds like a win to me."

She nodded emphatically. "Yes."

"All right, then," I said, and started for the door, but before I left, I turned around and looked at her. "You remember what I told you the other day? About not falling in love right now, and all that?"

Clementine nodded.

"Yeah, well . . ." I sighed, staring at her. Loving Leo had nearly torn me to pieces, but even with all the pain and torment, I still wouldn't trade a second of it. As much as I didn't want her to end up like me, I didn't want her to miss out, either. "Forget what I said. When all this is over, you should tell Henry how you feel about him."

Her face broke out in a mix of elation and nerves. "Really?"

"Yeah," I said, and opened the door. "What the hell, right?"

Chapter 11

I went home and immediately went out to my garden shed to look at the purple vials I had left from the stash that Desmond had given me. It was hard to see much through the purple glass, but even shining a flashlight into the vials, I couldn't see anything. I ran a Q-tip inside, but there wasn't anything I could see on it, and I didn't have the equipment to run any serious diagnostics on it.

"Damnit." I put everything away to head back to the 'Bago. I had half a mind to go over to Grace and Addie's B&B and rip Desmond a new one that minute, but I also had a strong feeling that I needed to know more before I took him on. He was smart, and he'd caught me by surprise. I wasn't going to let that happen again. I went into the 'Bago, sat at my dinette table, and stared at Nemo swimming back and forth in his little bowl.

What the hell was Desmond's game, anyway? Why would he want a small town to start spitting magic? Was it coincidence or design that he'd magicized only women? I had to figure out what was happening; of all the powers Desmond had unleashed, only mine was truly dangerous, and the sun was setting quickly. I'd managed to get through the night before without incident, but avoidance didn't solve this problem.

I needed to take action. What that action should be, however . . . well, that's what I needed more time to figure out.

The powers had first sparked in response to intense emotion, but I had no idea how they would evolve. *If* they would evolve. Maybe the powers would wear off after a couple of days, and that would be that. I could run Desmond out of town on a rail, and life would go back to normal. When Peach and I had our powers last summer, courtesy of Liv being dosed by a magic potion without her consent, that was what had happened. They'd just faded after a while.

But we'd been conduits, non-magicals temporarily given power through a magical source. This was different: Desmond wasn't magical, and we weren't conduits. This was a potion giving real magic to non-magical people, and I'd never even heard of that, let alone had any experience with it. The only thing I could look to as any sort of prediction of what might happen was my mother, whose powers *had* evolved. She'd found so much narcissistic supply that she'd been able to wield the power, rather than be wielded by it. The smart thing to do would be to go find her, make sure she wasn't getting into any more trouble, and talk to her about it. Feed her ego, and have her show me how she controlled it.

That would be the smart thing to do.

"But you know what, Nemo? I really don't wanna." I leaned on my counter and rested my chin on my folded arms as I watched the weird little magical fish scoot around in my glass water bowl. Unlike real fish, which usually had the good sense to up and die right away rather than go through the bother of waiting for me to forget to feed them, Nemo seemed to be doing all right. He didn't need care; he was plastic. He just zipped from side to side of the bowl, seemingly happy, showing me, Millie, Liv, and Peach grinning one way, and then suddenly our head angles would flip and we'd be grinning in the other direction. I stared at him, trying to wrap my mind around the fact of his existence, and it was disquietingly easy. It was weird how quickly you could get used to this kind of thing: the new normal. Even stuff that blows your mind at first becomes humdrum after a while.

Like having a glowing mother.

I wanted to just dive under the covers and hide from it all, but I couldn't. If the Widow had an intense dream, she might glow in a room by herself. No big deal. I was apt to set my bed on fire, and there was no way I was going to let myself char before I made Desmond Lamb pay a stiff fine for screwing with my life, my family, and my town. The only thing that outranked my stubbornness was my vengeance, and my sense of self-preservation.

It was time to make some concessions.

I zipped Nemo up into a plastic baggie filled with water, and got in my car. I chatted at Nemo as I drove, glancing at the smiling picture of the four of us whenever I started getting tense so I wouldn't accidentally melt the Bug's steering wheel while I drove through town, getting closer and closer to my own personal O'Leary's cow.

"This may be a stupid idea, Nemo," I said as I turned down Zipser Lane, "but it's the only idea I have, and I'm desperate."

I pulled over in front of Peach and Nick's house. The lights were off, and it was quiet and still, but Nick's truck was in the driveway. If Leo had gone to the airport, he would have left the truck there for Nick and Peach to grab when they came back from their honeymoon. He was either in the house and asleep at ten o'clock at night, or . . .

I let my eyes drift next door, to Liv's house. The lights

were on downstairs, but between the angle I was at on the street and the curtains in Liv's living room, I couldn't see if Leo was over there. If I knocked on the door to find out, Liv would insist I come in, and if Leo was there, I could end up burning down the whole place. Liv always hated how big her house was; she'd even put it on the market for a little while last year. But before too long, she and Tobias would be filling it up with little magical babies. Besides, it was all she had left of her mother. I wasn't going in there at night until this whole thing was over, and that was that.

I sat in the car for a little while longer, lost in my own thoughts until my body reacted to something I hadn't even processed consciously. *Leo.* I don't know how I knew he was near, but I felt him the way you feel a rumble in the ground when a plane is going overhead. It was always one of the things about our relationship that I'd found incredibly romantic when we were younger. Now it just seemed achingly sad.

I hopped out of my car and glanced down both sides of the street. A moment later, he came jogging around the corner, moving through the pool of light that came from the streetlamp. I took a deep breath to calm my heart rate; somehow, just the expectation that he would make me start a fire made it worse. I reached in through my open window, pulled out Nemo, and set his baggie on top of the Bug. I focused on him, on the four of us smiling as we zipped from side to side of the plastic baggie, and my heart rate calmed.

I could feel Leo moving closer, his jog slowing to a walk as he saw me, but I kept my eye on my magi-fish.

"Stacy?"

"I see you didn't go away."

He didn't say anything, just stood there looking at me.

"Good." I turned to face him. "I need your help."

"You got it," he said, without hesitation.

"I need to try something, and I need you to help me. That's all this is, okay? Just a test."

His brows knit. "What's going on?"

I stole one last look at Nemo. *Smiling faces. Happier times.* Then I took a deep breath and led Leo back behind the house where Nick kept the wood and kindling for the fireplace in a small shed in the corner of Peach's garden. I opened the door to the shed, grabbed two strips of kindling, then walked back toward Leo to stand over the slate patio. I held my arms out, each fist wrapped around some kindling.

"Kiss me," I said.

"What?"

"My mother's gaining control, and her trigger is attention. She got lots of it last night, and it fed the magic. Or it fed her, and it gave her control. . . . I'm not really sure how it works." I hesitated, fighting against myself to get the words out. "You're my trigger."

I couldn't see much more than the outline of his body in the moonlight, but I could tell by the set of his shoulders that he was unsure.

"Oh, come on, you big baby. You've kissed me a thousand times."

He let out a rough sigh. "Stacy . . ."

"You kissed me yesterday. I know you can do it."

"Yeah, I've been thinking about that all day," he said, his voice hesitant. "I'm sorry about that. I shouldn't have . . . It was a mistake."

I felt the stab of rejection, and glanced at my hands. No glowing smoke. I mentally checked *pain* off the list of possible sparking emotions, but it didn't make me feel much better about the fact that Leo's feelings about me had changed. Of course, the effect had been exactly what I told myself I'd been going for: He knew about the other men, he was disgusted, he didn't want me anymore. It was exactly what my plan had been. I just hadn't expected it to take such a chunk out of me. Why hadn't I seen that coming?

Because you're an idiot, I thought, but then shook the thought. This wasn't about love, or even us, really. He was just a catalyst, the chemical that activated the formula, and I needed that chemical in order to get myself out of trouble.

That was all this was.

"Leo, it doesn't have to mean anything. As a matter of fact, it's better if it doesn't. I just need your help. I can't control it if I can't test it, and I can't test it unless you kiss me. So just get over yourself and kiss me." I swallowed, almost unable to get the next word out. *"Please."*

He moved slowly, inching closer, and the anticipation and anxiety were torture. My body felt unhinged, like every part had its own individual opinion on the matter. My legs wanted to run, and my lower abdomen ached for him, wanting to take him inside with an unfamiliar desperation. My lips felt puffy and warm, and my arms were starting to get weak and trembly, claiming they were tired from holding out the kindling, but I knew better: They wanted to drop everything, pull him close, and never let him go again.

I stayed still, even as he moved closer, as his palms caressed my face. I closed my eyes and his breath fell warm on my face as he whispered, "Stacy."

His lips melded into mine softly, and chastely at first, but he kept the contact going. Slowly, he increased the pressure, his lips gently easing mine open. I dipped my tongue into his mouth, tasting him, and he groaned deep in his throat. I could feel his body grow hard against me, and as his arms wrapped tight around my waist I had to fight the instinct to run, to push him away, to protect myself. Instead, I let myself feel it, all of it. How deeply I loved him, how badly I wanted him, how achingly I missed him. I let the part of myself that he had taken with him find me again and settle back inside, comforting like hot cocoa on a cold night . . .

And that's when he let me go, so fast my head spun. My senses, which had all split, came to me in a quick succession, as though from unrelated sources. First, the pain of separation, then the smell of wood smoke. I felt a firm grip around my wrist as my fingers were pried open while Leo cursed. I opened my eyes to see one bundle of sticks in flames on the ground under my hand, which was covered with little glowing ropes of reddish smoke. It was almost pretty, the way it glowed, like the heart of a piece of charcoal on a dark night. Leo dashed to my other side, where I was still tightly clenching the other bit of kindling, ablaze in my hand. He tried to pry my fingers off it, and it took me another moment but finally I let go, and the burning wood fell to the ground. He stomped it out with his feet, then put his arm around me and led me through the back door, into the kitchen.

He flicked on the light, sat me down at the table, and went into the pantry, which was where Peach kept her first-aid kit. I watched him move, still a little stunned. He brought the kit over to the table and grabbed for my hands.

The smoke was gone, and there wasn't a mark on them. He raised his eyes to mine.

"What the hell is going on here, Stacy?" he said, his voice shaky and weak. That's when I noticed that while my hands were fine, his were charred and red.

"Jesus," I said, and snapped out of it. I stood up and pushed his shoulders down until he was sitting in the other chair, then went to work. I wet some gauze and cleaned his hands. His fingertips had taken the worst of it, probably from when he'd tried to pry my hands open, but the burns didn't seem too bad once the char had been cleared off. I put some burn cream on the worst of it and then reached for the gauze, but he said, "No, that's okay."

I stayed where I was, kneeling down in front of him, looking at his hands, still holding them in mine.

"I'm sorry," I said.

"I'm okay."

"I didn't think . . ."

"I know."

"I wasn't trying to hurt you."

He put one hand under my chin and tilted my face upward until I was looking at him. He looked worried and tired, but there was that eternal kindness and love that never left his eyes. At least, never when he was looking at me.

"I'm not hurt," he said again.

"Okay." I moved away from him and slumped down into my chair, then released a deep breath. "I need to think."

"Let me get you some water."

He got up, filled a glass with ice, and poured the water, then returned, setting it down in front of me with a decisive *thunk* on the old farmhouse table.

"You can't sleep alone," he said.

I let out a weak laugh. "Congratulations. You've hit on a line I haven't heard before."

He didn't so much as crack a smile. "Whatever's going on here, it happens at night. If you have a dream about . . ." He met my eyes and stopped; it was clear exactly what kind of dream he was talking about. "Just because your hands are protected doesn't mean the rest of you is."

"Yeah," I said. "I thought about that."

"Okay. So, what's your plan?"

I shrugged. "I don't know. Sleep during the day?"

He took a moment, then said, "Yeah, that could work."

"It's the simplicity that makes it genius."

He let out a soft laugh, then said, "Wait here for a minute. I'm gonna go grab some stuff."

"For what?"

He looked at me like I was an idiot. "I'm coming home with you."

I angled my head at him. "Boy, you really have been out of the game for a long time, haven't you? You're supposed to work it so I think it's my idea."

"You said that your mother got a lot of what she needed, and it gave her control."

"A *little* control," I said. "And that's just a theory. To be honest, I don't have the slightest clue how all this works."

"You said I'm your trigger, and I think we've got some evidence in support of that. So we'll go back to your place and I'll . . . I don't know. Set you off. Whatever. Maybe it'll give you some control, help you figure it out."

"Wow," I said. "Don't make it sound so romantic."

He made a very serious face. "This isn't about romance. It's for science."

I laughed, then shook my head. "Okay. For science."

He stood up. "I'm gonna go grab some stuff, and then I'll be down. Don't go anywhere without me, okay?"

I gave a weak half smile and for a moment he hesitated, then went upstairs to pack while I stared out the window and tried to remember what it had been like, all those eons ago, when I'd been in control of my life.

By the time we got back to my place, it was past one. I put Nemo back in his glass bowl and went about making us a pot of coffee.

"Really?" Leo said, leaning over the counter to stare at Nemo. "Liv did this? She had magic powers all along?"

"They were latent, apparently," I said. "Even she didn't know about it until last year."

He shook his head and straightened. "Wild, huh? I mean . . . *life*."

"I don't know if I'd call it *life,* exactly," I said over the coffee grinder. "She's got a bunny made out of a red ceramic mug. One of those Japanese-folded cranes that flies blind into walls. Betty has a bird made out of a square of sparkly linoleum in her apartment. And of course, there's Nemo, but . . ." I dumped the grinds into the filter basket. "I don't know if they think or feel or anything. Liv treats them like pets, but I don't know. I'd put it somewhere between a pet rock and a cat. Probably closer to a pet rock."

Leo watched Nemo swim back and forth for a bit then said, "Whatever it is, it's a miracle."

"Yeah. Okay." I slid into the seat in my kitchenette, and he sat opposite me. We sat in silence for a while as the coffeemaker gurgled.

"So . . . ," I said.

"So . . . ," he said.

Gurgle gurgle gurgle.

"Tell me what it is," he said finally. "You know, that makes you spark the magic."

I sighed, relieved to have some kind of conversational ground to stand on. "I'm not sure, exactly. It's an emotion, of some kind, but they're all bundled together with you."

"All right," he said and leaned forward. "What do you feel when you're with me?"

I closed my eyes, trying to sort it all out. "Pain. Anger. Hurt." I swallowed. "Desire." I opened my eyes. "Love."

There was a tense silence for a few moments, and when he opened his mouth to speak, I held up one hand.

"Don't take that the wrong way," I said quickly. "You and me, we are off the table. But if this is going to work, I'm going to need to be honest, so I'm being honest."

"Okay," he said.

"Loving you doesn't mean that all this . . ." I motioned awkwardly between us. ". . . is going to be a thing again."

He nodded. "You got it."

"As soon as I don't need you anymore, the second I have control over this thing, you're going back to South Dakota."

He watched me for a moment, then shook his head. "No."

I stared at him. "What?"

"Look, if you don't want"—he mocked my awkward hand gesture—"*this,* then okay, I accept that. You get to dictate whether or not I'm part of your life, but you don't get to dictate where I live."

My body stiffened. "What? Why would you stay? What could there possibly be for you here?"

He kept his eyes on mine. "Home."

"Yeah, *my* home. You left. I got it in the divorce."

"I have a house here, I have friends here. You always wanted to get out, go somewhere new." He made a shooing motion with his fingers. "So, you go."

I stared at him, incensed. "Exactly where the hell do you get off, telling me where I can and can't live?"

"Apparently, the same place you get off, telling me where I can and can't live. If I want to come home, I'll come home, and you don't get to say a goddamn word about it."

I started to sputter, I was so mad, and then the chime dinged on the coffee and Leo's expression transitioned easily from angry to perfectly calm.

"Cream, two sugars?" he said, and pushed himself up from the table. Before I could answer, he said, "Oh, and I think you can scratch *anger* off your list. I didn't see so much as a wisp of smoke."

I blinked twice, trying to make my way back from wanting to strangle him to understanding what he'd just done. I glanced down at my hands, and he was right: There wasn't a trace of any red, glowy smoke. I took a deep breath and tried to relax as he set the coffee down in front of me, and I stared down into my cup.

"I take it black now," was all I could think to say. Without a word, he swapped my mug with his.

"No, you don't have to do that." I reached to switch the cups back. He pulled his mug away.

"You like it black, take the black," he said, then took a sip of the one with cream and sugar and cringed. "Fuck, that's awful." He dumped it out in the sink, rinsed the mug, and poured himself another cup.

"So, you can say 'fuck' now, huh?"

"Hmmm?" He turned to face me, leaning against the counter as he sipped his coffee. "Oh. Yeah. I can curse, I can get drunk, I can fornicate—"

"Fornicate?" I laughed, and he allowed a small smile.

"It's a church word. Some things get kind of drilled in." He sat down opposite me, all business. "So, anger's off the list. We have to try to isolate pain, hurt, love, and desire now." He sipped from his mug. "Not sure how to do those, exactly."

"Pain and hurt are very close," I said carefully. "So are love and desire."

He met my eyes, then said, "Well, let's start with pain and hurt, then."

I felt a twinge of nervousness creep down my back, making me antsy. "Okay, but . . ." I glanced around. "I don't want to burn this place down. It's all I have. That and a garden shed out in the clearing. I can't afford to lose either of those."

I got up, pulled open one of the countless little latched cabinets that the 'Bago had for storage, and pulled out a sleeping bag. I went to the front door and stepped off my cement stoop, then knelt and reached under the 'Bago to where I'd tucked the exterior light switch. I hit it, and the string of lights I'd lined the side of the 'Bago with lit up. They were just simple lights, each covered with a tiny tomato paste can that I'd painted and punched with holes myself, but I liked the patterns they set on the side of the 'Bago, and the soft way they lit the front.

"Come on," I said to Leo as he stared at the lights, smiling. "This way."

The night air was warm on my skin, and it had a calming effect, which probably worked against where we were planning to go, but still: I liked it. I led Leo to the small clearing of lawn I kept maintained just off the front of the 'Bago. I unrolled the sleeping bag and spread it out over the space, then sat down. Leo waited until I had seated myself, then handed me my coffee mug and sat down opposite me. This was better. There was enough light that we could see each other, but still enough darkness to hide in, at least a little.

"Okay," he said. "Pain and hurt, then?"

I held the coffee mug in my hands. "This thing is microwave-safe, so . . . it should be okay if I start to burn it, right?"

"Don't worry," he said. "It's all going to be okay."

"Don't comfort me," I said. "Comfort isn't on the list."

"Right." There was a long moment of silence, and just as I was about to give him a nudge, he said, "I don't think I can do this."

"It's gotta be done," I said, my voice cracking a little.

"I just . . . I want to tell you that I'm sorry, not make you feel worse."

I took a breath, and thought of it like the dentist. No one likes it, but you suck it up and push through because it needs to be done. I cupped my hands around the mug and spoke.

"You have nothing to be sorry for."

I could see enough to know that Leo raised his head to look at me, but not so much that I could decipher his expression. I didn't need to; I heard the tension in his voice.

"What are you talking about?"

"I was awful to you." I lowered my head, staring at the mug. There was definite pain, but so far, no smoke. Of course, we'd barely gotten started. I took a deep breath and pushed at my own soft spot. "I was . . . mean. I screamed at you. I threw things at you."

"I deserved it." His voice was quiet, and while he might have been working the moment to bring me back to all that pain and hurt, I didn't think that was the case. If I had money to bet, I would have put it on the fact that he was right there with me. "Stacy, I swear, there is nothing in my life I regret more than leaving you like that."

"You should have left," I said, verbalizing the thought for the first time. "You saw me for what I really was."

His head tilted a bit to the side, but his voice came out steely, not confused. "You said that the other day, that I saw you. What does that mean?"

I swallowed against the lump forming in my throat. I hated this, hated every moment, mostly because it was all stuff that wasn't going to get better for talking about it. Shit is shit, and no matter how much you talk about it, you're not going to make it into anything but shit. Still, I had to woman up and keep going.

There was science to be done.

"It's . . . me," I said carefully, working hard to keep my voice even. "I'm ugly."

"Stacy, what the . . . ?"

"Not physically, okay. I know I'm pretty physically. But *inside*, where it matters. I'm an ugly person."

He huffed in the darkness. "That's the stupidest thing I've ever heard."

"Oh, come on. You saw me. When I was screaming,

when I was throwing things at you . . . I saw the look on your face." My voice caught, and I took a breath to keep things steady. I knew I was supposed to give in to the emotion, that was the whole point, but you had to ease into these things.

"I was upset," he said, "but not at you. At me."

"But a little at me, too, right?" I said, meeting his eye. "I scared you."

He went silent, and I could see from his expression that I was right, so I kept talking to keep him from trying to make me feel better. The point of this was specifically *not* to make me feel better.

"When I get angry, I get ugly. I know that. And once someone has seen that . . . I mean, how can I expect them to want to be around me?" I blinked hard, squeezing the tears out silently but not swiping at them. Leo would have seen me swipe. It was possible that in the darkness, I could get away with the tears alone if I just didn't let them seep into my voice.

"You're wrong." Leo's voice was soft, but with steely undertones. "I didn't leave because I saw you for what you really are. I know exactly what you are. I've always known."

"Stop it," I said. "Don't try to make me feel better. You're ruining the science."

"I'm not trying to make you feel better," he said. "I'm trying to make you hear the damn truth."

I looked up at him, surprised by the harshness in his tone.

"I did a terrible thing to you," he said. "I was confused and drunk and I slept with her and it was awful. I wanted to talk to my dad about it, so he could tell me what to do, but I couldn't. So I talked to you. And yeah, there was something honorable about confessing and living with the consequences of what I'd done, but there was also something incredibly selfish about it, too. It made me feel better, and it made you . . ."

"A monster," I said.

"No," he said firmly. "Listen to me, please. You didn't do anything wrong."

I swallowed again, took a deep breath. All I had to do was keep my voice even, under control. "I saw your face, Leo. I remember it, every day, the way you looked at me . . ."

My voice squeaked. *Goddamnit.* I swiped at my eyes.

"Stacy." Leo moved across the space between us to sit by my side. "Look, your hands are fine. There's no smoke. Let's pull up from this a little, okay?"

"I don't blame you," I said, leaning my head on his shoulder. "You were right to leave me. You should have left me. *I* would have left me."

"No." He put his arms around me. "That's not how it was."

"It's okay, really." I pushed back from him so I could face him. "It's like what you said when you first came back. I'm hard to reach when I'm mad." I took in a stuttering breath, remembering how calmly I had taken that when he'd said it, and how many times it had repeated in my head since.

"That's not what I meant."

"It's just who I am," I said, the words coming in bursts over hard sobs. "It's . . . really . . . okay. I've . . . accepted . . . it . . ."

"Stop it."

I felt a shock when his hands clamped down on either side of my face, turning me to look at him, even though it was too dark and my eyes too full of tears for me to really see him. I could feel his breath coming in hot puffs on my face, though, and I could feel the heat coming from his hands.

"You're spinning, and it's all bullshit, and you need to stop," he said. "There's no smoke on your hands. This isn't helping you control the magic. It's not doing you any good, and you won't listen to me telling you you're wrong, so stop. Please, stop."

I felt the whine escape from deep inside, coming out like the whistle of a teakettle, releasing the steam that had built up there for so long, and I collapsed against Leo's chest, sobbing. He pulled me into his lap and held me to him, and I wrapped my arms around his neck and cried all over him.

"It's not true," he said. "None of it's true. Please tell me that somewhere inside, you know that."

I didn't say anything. I couldn't. I just held on to him while he smoothed my hair and rubbed my back, until I finally fell into darkness, cradled and safe in his arms.

Chapter 12

I woke up the next morning to the sound of birds, and the feel of a soft breeze on my skin. I was on my side, my back shielded by Leo, who spooned me from behind, one arm draped around my waist in sleep. I felt the heat of his hand on my lower stomach, the pressure of his morning erection against my backside, and tiny ripples of desire coursed within me.

I opened my eyes, saw the daylight, and sighed. Best to save the science for later. Besides, a morning erection was just biology. It didn't mean anything other than that Leo was a normal guy waking up next to a girl. Or, you know, just a normal guy waking up.

I shifted under his arm and put a little space between us, watching his face as he drifted from sleep into consciousness. He opened his eyes a little, smiled, and pulled me closer to him, nuzzling his nose into my neck.

"Good morning," he said.

I lay stiffly on my back, staring up at the morning sky as the ripples in my stomach became crashing waves. I considered for a moment the luscious possibility of rolling over on top of him and taking full advantage of his morning condition, but at the same time that the idea warmed me in all the right places, it also scared me, and I wasn't ready to face that fear.

"It's time to get up," I said. "I have to check on my mother."

Leo groaned and flipped onto his back as well. "Why'd you have to bring her into it?"

I sat up. "I also have to flip Desmond over and see what's crawling underneath."

He opened one eye. "Your mother *and* Desmond?" He reached down and adjusted the crotch of his jeans. "Yeah, that pretty much takes care of that."

"Should I mention that Nick is probably on a nude beach in Spain right now?"

Leo laughed. "Now you're just being mean." He caught my eye and his smile faded. "I'm sorry. I didn't mean . . . you're not . . ."

"Oh, dear God, are you going to tiptoe around my tender feelings now? Because if you start with that shit, seriously, I'm gonna hit you in the head with a shovel and bury you out back where no one will ever find you."

Something in his eyes cooled, and he looked almost disappointed. "Nope. Not gonna start with that shit."

"Good." I stood up, yanking my jeans up on my waist and pulling my shirt down. "I'm gonna go take a shower and wash off the gross. If you want, you can do the same and then I figure, we'll leave about . . ." I glanced at my watch. "Ten-ish?"

He sat up and rested his arms on his knees. "You're inviting me to go with you?"

I shrugged. "Yeah. Unless you've got something better to do."

"No," he said, smiling. "I don't have anything better to do."

I crossed my arms over my middle, feeling a rush of comfortable antagonism. "What are you smiling about?"

He gave a snort of laughter, then got up and shook out the sleeping bag. "Nothing."

I picked the coffee mugs up off the ground as he folded the sleeping bag and started to roll it up. "What?"

"Nothing. I just thought you were going to argue with me."

"About what?"

"About me going with you today."

"I don't care if you go with me today," I said. "You don't have to."

"I want to."

"Then, fine. What's the problem?"

"There is no problem." He huffed in frustration. "I was just a little surprised that the morning was starting without a fight, and now somehow, it's a fight. You're like a Jedi Master."

I laughed in mock offense, enjoying the feel of being on familiar ground again. "I see we're done tiptoeing around my tender feelings."

"Yeah, we're done." He shook his head, laughed again, and tucked the rolled sleeping bag under his arm. With his other arm, he motioned toward the 'Bago. "Ladies first."

"You're such a baby," I said, starting toward the front door of the 'Bago. "That wasn't even a fight."

"Mmm-hmmm," he said, noncommittally.

"I'm serious. If that was a fight, I would have bounced this coffee mug off your cranium."

"Okay."

I stepped up on the cement stoop, then turned to face him. "I'm a dangerous woman, you know. You shouldn't push me."

He stepped up onto the cement block below where I

was standing, his body close enough for me to feel the heat coming from him, and the warm ripples inside me began to work their way ever downward.

"Maybe *you* shouldn't push *me*," he said, his voice quiet. "I may have been a man of God once, Stacy, but I'm still a man."

One side of his face quirked in a smile, but the heat in his eyes was serious. I swallowed, gripping the coffee mugs tight to keep my hands from doing what they desperately wanted to do.

"Save it for after dark, Science Boy." I dumped the coffee mugs into my tiny sink, pulled the curtain that separated my bed from the rest of the place, and fell backward onto it. I closed my eyes and thought of my big, bald brother running around naked on a beach full of fat, old Spanish nudists. Five minutes later, I hopped in the shower, turned the water on cold, and turned my focus to the tasks at hand.

It helped, but not a lot.

It wasn't like the last time I was at my mother's house. There weren't as many parking spaces on the street as usual, but I didn't have to park three blocks away, either. Things seemed to be calming down, at least a little. When Leo and I stepped out of my car, I noticed that one of the parked cars had Pennsylvania plates, and for some reason, it made me tense. It really shouldn't have. The Pennsylvania border was twenty minutes from Nodaway; you saw those plates all the time, but they were always in town, dropping by for waffles or antiques on their way to somewhere else. Not typically in my mother's residential neighborhood.

"You all right?" Leo asked, taking my elbow naturally as we headed across the street to my mother's house.

"Yeah, I've just got a really bad feeling, and I'm not sure why."

"You're going to visit Lillith Easter. That would make anyone tense."

"You've got a point there." We hit the sidewalk in front of my mother's house and I stopped and turned to Leo. "She's been really weird since all this started. Prepare yourself."

He smiled. "I've known your mother since I was five years old. I don't think there's much she can do that will surprise me."

"Leo North!"

The Widow stood on the porch steps, wearing a flowing floral dress, hair falling freely around her shoulders, her arms spread out wide to embrace Leo.

Leo gave me a wide-eyed, slightly freaked look.

"Hey, I warned you," I said, and we started toward the house. The Widow met us halfway up the walk and pulled Leo in for a tight, and what appeared to be warm-ish, hug.

"Leo North!" She pulled back, kissed him on the cheek, and laughed. "I thought you'd gone home! So wonderful to see you!"

"Hi, Mrs. Easter," Leo said awkwardly.

Then, she turned on me.

"Stacy, darling!" Another hug. I'd been prepared for how sweet she acted when she was under the influence of narcissistic supply, but still. This was starting to get creepy.

She pulled back from me, her face beaming. "It's so good to see you again, sweetheart. Come in, come in, there's iced tea in the fridge!"

We followed her up the walkway, and that was when I noticed the woman sitting in the rocker on the porch. She looked to be in her mid-forties, hair graying and cut into a wavy bob, wearing a blue floral dress that looked like she'd made it herself. As we started up the steps, she pushed up from her chair. I was about to hold my hand out and introduce myself when she knelt and lowered her head.

"It's so wonderful to see you both," the Widow said, not looking at the woman even as she held her hand out to her. "We have so much to catch up on!"

The woman kissed my mother's knuckles and remained on her knees, head lowered, as we walked past. I stared, rude but unable to stop myself, almost stumbling as my mother grabbed my hand and pulled me inside after her.

"What the hell was that?" I whispered as the Widow shut the front door behind us.

"What, darling?" my mother said, her face blank.

"The crazy person on the porch who kissed your hand." I looked at Leo. "Just me?"

He shook his head slowly, eyes wide. "Nope. Not just you."

"Oh, that!" The Widow waved a dismissive hand in the air. "It's just the adoration."

I almost choked. "The *what*?"

"You know, like at church, how we all sign up when the Eucharist is out so someone is there adoring it every hour of the day? They're doing that for me."

"Eugh," I said. My mother gave me a stark look, and I held up my hands. "Sorry, Widow, but isn't that sacrilegious or something?"

"Of course not," she said. "I'm a miracle, and this is Tinsey's hour to witness the miracle."

"She knelt and kissed your hand," I said. "That's just . . . wrong." I nudged Leo. "Tell her, Leo. You were almost a priest."

"Yeah, I'm gonna stay out of this one," he said under his breath.

"See? I told you it was fine." The Widow made a dismissive gesture at me and then smiled at Leo. "Tinsey came all the way in from Erie just to see me! Can you believe it?"

"Erie," I said to Leo.

"Eerie," he said back.

The Widow glanced at her watch. "Although I thought she was being replaced at ten. Maybe she's pulling a double." She shrugged. "It is a bit of a distance for her. Oh, well. Iced tea?"

"I can't believe you think a twenty-four-hour adoration is okay," I said as we followed the Widow to the kitchen. The table was covered with baskets and tins and unlit candles. I grabbed Leo's hand and he squeezed mine back, and we sat down in unison.

"Well, it was hardly *my* idea," she said, but the huge grin on her face said it was absolutely her idea. She turned to face me with the pitcher. "Lemon? Sugar?"

"Bitter and bland is fine," I said.

She began to pour. "Leo?"

Leo kept his eyes on her, his brow crinkling as he watched her, looking like a geologist watching a rock suddenly defy the law of gravity: fascinated, but even more disturbed. "Yeah . . . that's fine. Thank you."

She poured the drinks and sat down at the table, sliding her chair to our side so she could see us over the pile of offerings. There was a long silence during which she looked at us expectantly, and I'll be damned if she didn't have her kissing hand ready and in position, just in case.

"It is just so good to see you again, Leo," she said finally, turning her focus on him. "I heard you left the priesthood, and I want you to put your mind at ease; you are forgiven."

Leo stared at her blankly for a moment. "Thank . . . you?"

"Well, you were practically my son. Your mother

abandoned you to your father when you were so young, and from the day Nicky brought you home from kindergarten, you were here more than you were home."

"Oh," Leo said, seeming to understand.

"What?" I looked from the Widow to Leo, then back to the Widow. "What?"

Leo leaned closer to me, not taking his eyes off the Widow. "When a child becomes a nun or a priest, there is a belief that it gets the parents into Heaven, no matter what."

"Not a belief," the Widow said earnestly. "It *does* get them into Heaven. No matter what. I could rob a drugstore if I wanted to."

"Yeah, except he's not your son, Widow," I said.

She ignored me, focusing on Leo. "And when you left the church, you took that away from me." And there it was, that tiny, familiar glitter of meanness in her eyes.

"Ohhhh, there she is, " Leo said, seeing it.

I patted his arm. "She never left, she was just in hiding."

"I get it." He smiled at the Widow. "Good to see you again, Lillith."

She raised her brow and said, "Are you two quite done with your comedy routine?"

"I think so." I gave my mother a gracious wave of permission. "Continue."

She gave me a disapproving look, then turned her attention to Leo and smiled with magnanimity. "As I was saying, I forgive you. God saw that you had stolen that precious gift away from me, but He gave me another way in."

"Yeah, what way is that?" I asked, but again, she ignored me, keeping her focus on Leo.

"I was sorry to hear about your defection—" she began.

"Well, I never actually became a—"

The Widow spoke louder over him. "—but if God has other plans for you, then sometimes you just have to follow your heart to find them. That's where God lives." She tapped her chest twice, then cut a quick look at me before returning her gaze to Leo. "It was your . . . *heart* . . . you were following, right?"

I nudged Leo. "She's like those Whack-A-Moles. Just when you think she's gone, *poof!* She's back."

Leo shot me a look, then returned his focus to my mother. "Yes, I was following my heart," he said with more kindness and patience than she deserved. "But let's talk about you. How are you, Lillith?"

The Widow's face lit up. "You know, thank you so much for asking. I'm doing *amazing,* I have to tell you." She reached out and grabbed my hand, squeezing it in her cold, bony fingers. "My beautiful daughter has changed my life, and now I've seen God's plan for me, and everything suddenly makes sense."

"Yeah, about that." I pulled my hand out of her grasp, losing my patience for the game. I waved my hand in front of her face, and she switched her weird, smiley focus from Leo to me. "It's not God's plan, Widow. You're being magically influenced by something weird and decidedly unholy. You need to send these people home and draw as little attention to yourself as possible until we get this figured out. Okay?"

The Widow blinked at me as though I'd just started speaking Russian. "I'm sorry. I don't understand."

"All this? It isn't God, Widow. It's your narcissism and their delusion, all feeding each other into huge monsters that, left unchecked, will most definitely crush Tokyo. Once I figure this out and get rid of the magic, it's going to be hard to come back from this, so—"

"Get rid of it?" Her smile faded and her expression

hardened and for the first time since we'd arrived, she looked like my mother again. "You will *not* get rid of it. What God has done, no man can undo."

"Oh, for—" I nudged Leo. "Tell her it's not God, Leo." I looked at the Widow. "He used to be a priest. He knows these things."

"Almost-priest," Leo corrected.

"Fine, whatever. An *almost*-priest. Tell her, Leo."

Leo was quiet for a moment, then said, "I can't do that."

I blinked in shock and stared at him. "What?"

"I don't know God's will. No one does. That's why He's God."

"Oh, dear sweet Leo." My mother reached across the table and patted his cheek. "Such a good boy." She pulled one of the tins from the big pile on the kitchen table, opened it, and shoved it at him. "Have a cookie."

I clenched my teeth and spoke through them to Leo. "You're not helping."

"I'm not going to lie," he said, his voice low.

An uneasiness settled in the pit of my stomach. "I thought you didn't believe in God anymore."

"I never said that."

"You said you lost your faith."

"In me," he said. "In whether I really belonged in the church. Maybe even in the church itself, a bit. Not in God."

I felt a mix of disappointment and anger, although I couldn't quite figure out why. "Oh."

He held my eyes for a moment, and I could sense a disappointment of his own in there, and then he turned to my mother.

"Lillith." His voice was soft and kind as he reached his hand out to my mother, who beamed and placed her hand in his. "I think the question of whether or not this is God's will is not what's at issue here. If it is God's will, it will be, no matter what. You don't need to have adoration and vigils and sermons to fulfill God's plan for you."

She pulled her hand out of his, and the beam in her face dimmed significantly. "I should have known you'd be on *her* side."

"I'm on your side," Leo said. "I'm not sure all of this is good for you."

Her little beady eyes went dead and cold, glittering like black glass. "*Good* for me? It's *amazing* for me. My entire life, I knew I was special. I knew I had a purpose. A *destiny*. But over and over again, I was disappointed. An unworthy husband, a tramp for a daughter. Now a Babylonian Whore of a daughter-in-law, here to ruin the only pure thing in my life, my good boy. And right at the moment when everything seemed darkest, when I began to question how I could be this special and yet so unappreciated—"

"Here we go," I muttered.

My mother ignored me. "—at that very moment, I got my answer. And every day, that answer is clearer and clearer." She slammed the flat of her hand down on the table. "Look! I'll show you!"

With that, she pushed up and headed out at a clip. By the time we got to the front door, she was already on the lawn, and Tinsey the Insane Adorer was on her knees on the porch, her hands out to receive my mother's knuckles for a kiss, but the Widow swooshed past her without a thought, and Tinsey just lowered her head and made the sign of the cross.

The Widow trudged to the middle of the lawn and held out her arms, then gave a meaningful glance back at Tinsey, who gasped and whipped her cell phone out. She didn't talk into the phone, just hit a few buttons, and within a few moments, doors up and down the street began to open, and people were coming up the street.

Leo moved a little closer to me where we stood at the base of the porch stairs. "What is she doing?" he whispered.

"I have no idea," I said. "It's still daytime. She doesn't have any power now. Maybe she just wants to show us how many people she can call in on a moment's notice?"

Leo shrugged. People began to gather, all silent, watching, their faces rapt. I moved closer to Leo, and he took my hand. My mother held her arms out even farther, and lifted her face to the sky.

"Father, creator of all that is good in this world, I ask you to act through me, to show the unbelievers and the cynics what your power can do. In your name, I humbly give myself to thee."

"Amen," someone said from behind me as the crowd gathered closer to her, circling her on the lawn.

At first, I thought it was just a ray of sun coming through the clouds—which, granted, would have been freaky enough. But as the crowd gasped and I stepped closer to get a better look, I saw that it wasn't the sun.

It was the Widow.

"I thought her power was night power," Leo said.

"It was."

"I thought you said people with night power couldn't use their power during the day."

"Yeah, that's what I thought, too."

"Okay."

I moved closer and wedged my way through the crowd until I got to my mother's side. Light emanated from her, a multihued halo that shimmered around her entire body. The green ropes of smoky light that had come from her hands the first few times were now electric-charged, like day magic, and they ran all over her body, only just visible under the glow of the other rainbow colors undulating around her body.

It took me a moment to see past the light to the extreme strain on her face. Veins were popping out on her forehead, and a trickle of sweat slid down her cheek.

This wasn't an act.

"Mom!" I rushed to her, catching her just as she fell. The light went out in a few flickers, and her chest heaved with shallow breath. She was cold to the touch, which wasn't unusual for someone with no body fat, but still. It was easily eighty degrees outside; even a snake got warm in the heat.

"Back off!" I yelled over the mumbling prayers as people huddled in to touch her. "Tinsey, call nine-one-one! Someone get her a blanket!"

I laid her down on the lawn, rubbing my hands up and down her arms as her body started to shake.

"Hang in there, Widow," I said. "You're going to be okay."

"Of course I am," she croaked, her voice weak. "I haven't made my sacrifice yet." And then she shut her eyes and passed out.

The crowd dispersed, and I glanced back to see Leo coming with the old quilt from the back of the couch. He wrapped her up in it and lifted her easily, like a child, carrying her up the steps and inside, where we could close the door against the insanity behind us. I tried to follow him, but I had to fight my way through the throng of people trying to touch my mother's limp, unconscious body.

"Back the fuck off!" I hollered, and they split like the Red Sea, glaring at me as I passed through them. I glared back and slammed the door shut behind us.

When she wouldn't wake up, the EMTs sent her to the hospital in Buffalo, where she was immediately admitted. Leo was at my side pretty much the whole time, but somehow managed to get in a call to Liv and Tobias, who were there by noon. Liv got ahold of Peach, and told me that Peach and Nick were going to be on the next plane stateside, but that was going to take at least a day.

Meanwhile, the Widow slept. Tests were run on her blood, on her brain. An unreasonably tall doctor told me that they weren't sure what had caused all of this, but they'd work hard to figure it out. Deliveries of flowers started pouring in almost the minute we got her admitted, and strange people began holding vigil outside her room. I processed everything from a place far away from the rumble and activity. I talked to doctors and nurses, I signed papers, I functioned, but I and my thoughts were elsewhere.

With Desmond, mostly. He'd done this, to *my* people. Me, my checkout girl, my English teacher, my mother. The rules of what he was doing didn't work the way that natural magic worked; this was a whole new ball game. It may have started out as day and night magic, but apparently, whatever this was, it was evolving past that. Was that Desmond's intention? Or was it the consequence of messing with free will? Maybe he was skating by on a free-will loophole; after all, we had all taken the potions willingly, even if we didn't realize the full effect of what we were taking.

And hell, some of those consequences would be mine, wouldn't they? Or was I going to skate by on my own loophole, since I didn't know that my purple vials had been contaminated at the time I made the potions?

Whatever was going on, it was time to get all cards on the table. He wanted something, and it was past time I knew what that was.

"Knock knock."

I glanced up from the cold, untouched vending machine coffee in my hands to see Liv standing in the open doorway of my mother's room. The bed was empty; my mother was out getting an MRI so they could look inside her brain.

"Hey," I said.

She sat in the visitor's chair next to mine. "It's past one. You need to eat. Leo and Tobias went down to the cafeteria for food."

"Not hungry." I went to the bathroom, dumped the coffee into the sink, and tossed the cup in the garbage. "Actually, I need to head out for a bit. Can you keep an eye on things here?"

Liv blinked in surprise. "They'll be bringing your mom back soon . . ."

"Maybe, but they're going to have no idea what's wrong. Desmond is the only one who knows what's going on. I need to go see him."

I started toward the door, but Liv got up and stood in my way.

"Desmond did all this? You're sure?"

I nodded. "Pretty sure. He gave a potion to Clementine Klosterman, and now she's Speedy Gonzales with pink light around her hands."

Liv's brows knit. "Who's Clementine Klosterman?"

"She used to work at Treacher's IGA. I sent her to Betty to get a job at CCB's, where you and Tobias can keep an eye on her. And, oh yeah, would you and Tobias mind keeping an eye on Clementine Klosterman for me?" I gave a weak smile. "I know. I'm sorry. I should have called you. It's just that a lot has been happening."

Liv nodded. "Yeah, it has. Okay, so, what's your plan? You're just going to, what . . . go ask Desmond what he's up to? What if he's dangerous? What if he does something to you?"

"He's already done it," I said. "What's he going to do? Make me *more* of a firestarter?"

She sighed. "Fine. I'll go with you."

"No."

"Then wait until after dark, when your power is in. You can set him on fire."

I shook my head. "I can't control it." *Not yet, not without Leo,* I thought, but I couldn't think about that now.

"Then wait and take Tobias. He can stop Desmond . . ."

Our eyes met, and Liv's flickered away. Tobias's power, the ability to stop any movement—a pumping heart, for example—was rare and incredibly dangerous. It had gotten him taken away from his family at the age of thirteen after he accidentally killed a school bully, and he hadn't used it since. Most of the time, we didn't even talk about it. We pretended he was just another magical, like Liv or Betty, making ceramics into squirrels or creating blueberry muffins out of thin air, but he wasn't. And there were people watching who knew it.

Which made what I was about to ask for even harder.

"Hey, I've got a favor to ask, but—"

"Done. What?"

"Wait until I've asked," I said, meeting her eyes. "It's a big one."

She crossed her arms and gave me an expectant raise of her eyebrow. "What is it?"

I pulled a folded piece of paper out of my pocket and handed it to her. "This is everything I know about Desmond, which isn't much. His last name, his address in Niagara Falls. I did some basic GoogleFu, but nothing came up, which makes me think that maybe he changed his name or something. . . . I don't know. But there's something there, something in his past, and I think if I know what it is, it might help."

Liv's brow creased as she glanced over the sparse notes I'd hastily scribbled on the back of a Wegmans receipt. She looked up at me, worry in her eyes. "Christ, Stace. You're usually the one I go to when I can't find something on the Internet. I don't know what I can do that—"

"Actually, I was . . ." I hesitated, barely able to get the words out. "I don't think we're going to get anything through public channels. I know Tobias had some contacts in the magical agencies."

I couldn't look at her. I knew what I was asking. Tobias was floating nicely under the radar of the magical agency that had taken him away from his family when he was just a kid. Asking him to get in touch was risking them taking notice of him again, and if they did that . . . who the hell knew? Magicals like Tobias disappeared into thin air all the time, and no one ever saw them again.

"You can say no," I said, "but he's causing some real damage here, and I have to ask."

She raised her head to look at me, determination in her eyes. "Done."

Part of me wished she'd said no. "Liv . . ."

"Stop it." She tucked the paper into her pocket. "He'll be careful."

I released a breath. I'd gotten the asking out of the way, and had expected it to be the hardest part, but it wasn't. Letting her take this risk for me was even harder.

"You know, maybe don't do anything for a little while," I said. "There are private detectives in Erie, they might be able to—"

"Shut up," Liv said, and that ended the conversation. I wanted to hug her, to say thank you, but I couldn't. How did you thank your best friend for risking everything that mattered to her because you screwed up? I just stared at the foot of my mother's empty bed.

"I gotta get going," I said after a long silence.

"Be careful."

I looked up and our eyes met, and once again, it was me and Liv, in the center of a crazy magical shit storm. We'd come through last summer, but the cost had been way too high. And here we were again: another summer, another magical catastrophe threatening to take another chunk out of us all.

The only difference was, last summer hadn't been Liv's fault. She hadn't asked for any of it. Me, I'd been practically begging for it.

"I'm sorry," I said, and looked away.

We were quiet together for a while, and then she said, "Start amassing your canned goods now. Next summer, we're holing up in an underground bunker."

I called Grace and Addie on my way to their B&B, and by the time I got there, Addie was looking fierce outside of Desmond's room, a thick broom handle in her hand.

"He's inside," she said when I got there.

I smiled and squeezed her hand. "Good work, soldier."

She nodded, pulled on a thin chain around her neck, and produced a key from inside her shirt. She slid the chain over her head and unlocked the door.

"This doesn't unlock from the inside?" I asked.

"Oh, yes. It does. That's what the broom handle was for." She opened the door. I stepped in and almost felt like laughing. Everything was flowers and ruffles and a four-poster bed with the frilliest canopy allowed by New York State law.

Desmond was sitting on the floral Queen Anne chair by the window, an open book in his hand. When I entered, he smiled.

"Well, if it isn't the indomitable Stacy Easter," he said, putting the book down as he stood to greet me. "It appears I've been made out as the villain of this piece. Kept under lock and key in the tower, awaiting judgment." He nodded toward Addie, who glared at him as she shut the door behind me. The lock clicked over and Desmond smiled. "It's actually quite adorable."

I crossed my arms over my chest, digging my fingers into my own arms to keep myself from going for his throat. I needed him talking now, and punching my thumbs into his larynx, as gratifying as that might be, wasn't conducive to my goal.

"You got me, my mother, Diedre Troudt, and Clementine," I said. "Anyone else?"

"I can't say for sure," he said.

"I haven't used any other purple vials," I said, making my guess as to how he did it; the slight rise of his eyebrows confirmed I was right.

"Well, then . . . no," he said. "No one else should have been affected."

I moved forward. "Addie? Grace? If you've done anything to them, I swear to God—"

He laughed, and the sound of it grated on my spine. "You talk as if I'm some sort of monster."

"No, I talk as if you're the entitled asshole who put my mother in the hospital. What the hell did you do to her, anyway? For that matter, what did you do to all of us?"

His eyes lit with what I can only describe as the glittering illumination of pure crazy, and with a voice almost too quiet to hear, he said, "I *proved* it."

"Proved what?"

"I believe you call it magic," he said simply.

"I believe I call it *fuck you*," I said, just as simply. "My *mother* is in the *hospital*."

He waved a hand in the air. "Don't fret. Her brain is just overworking itself, trying to re-create the chemical it needs to make the 'magic.'" He put air quotes around the word, and the gesture made me want to slap him. "Just mix some liquid in one of the purple vials I gave you and administer it to her."

"I checked the purple vials," I said. "There's nothing in them."

He smiled, face beaming with pride. "Nothing you can detect. But trust me, the vials are coated inside with a very fine water-soluble powder. It dries, invisible, undetectable, and then dissolves into any liquid to which it is introduced. Fill a purple vial with water, and have her drink it. In a few hours, she'll be fine."

"She's not going to be fine," I said. "She *glows*. I'm setting things on fire. Deidre Troudt is manifesting bluebirds. The cashier is moving like the Flash. I don't need a temporary fix. I need a *cure*."

He watched me in silence for a moment. "Are you sure that's what you want?"

I sputtered for a moment. "What the hell are you talking about? *Yes,* that's what I want. And once that's done, I want you out of my town."

Desmond stood, looking even taller and thinner than usual, and more foreboding. It was then that I noticed his eyes; it wasn't so much a coldness there as an emptiness. How had I not seen something missing in him earlier? I had chalked everything up to cool British reserve, but this—this was something else. This was an absence of any feeling whatsoever, and it was creepy as hell.

"Stacy, think about it. You have *power*." He moved closer to me. "You have passion. Spark. Heat." He took a lock of my hair in his hand, twirling it around his finger, and I could smell the faint whiff of celebratory whiskey on his breath. "People would kill for what you have."

I clenched my fist and thrust it as hard as I could up under his solar plexus. He let out a *whoof* of air and fell back onto the most feminine bed in the world, chuckling. "Oh, I do so enjoy you, Stacy Easter."

I advanced on him. "Give me the cure or so help me God, I'll remove your manhood with dull scissors right here in this room."

"Darling, this room has your work half done already." He leaned back on one elbow and winced a bit, which I found slightly gratifying. "Besides which, I haven't got a cure."

I felt ice trickle down my spine. "You're lying."

"Well, yes, but it's just so rude to refuse to give it to you outright. I am British, you know." He pushed up from the bed, holding his hand on his gut as he advanced toward me. "You've got quite a hook there."

I held up my fist. "Take one more step and you'll feel it again."

Before I knew what was happening, he'd grabbed my wrist and pushed me against the door, his body lean and strong against mine. I struggled, but his grip on my wrist tightened, and I cursed as the pain shot up my arm.

"I'll allow you to strike me exactly once," he said in low tones, his eyes cold on mine, "and you've used up your grace. Now, are we going to handle this as civilized people, or is this going to devolve into bloodied fists? Because you do know the win goes to the person willing to get bloodiest. Are you certain that person is you?"

There was a knock on the door, and Addie's voice came through, muffled. "Stacy? Stacy? Are you all right?"

Desmond released me, the threat still present in his eyes. I shifted my head, keeping my eyes locked on his, and said, "Everything's fine, Addie."

"Are you sure?" she called. "I have a broom. I'll stick it right up his back end."

Desmond chuckled. I took a breath and said, "It's fine."

There was some shuffling outside the door, but then

Addie quieted down. I pushed myself away from the door and crossed the room, sitting casually in the Queen Anne chair. Desmond sat again on the bed and faced me.

"So what now?" I asked.

He smiled. "Now we negotiate. I give a little, you give a little."

"Fine." I rubbed my wrist, which was still throbbing, and beginning to bruise. "Give a little."

He sighed. "The purple vials are coated with a mix of chemicals that activate the limbic system in the brain."

"And what does that mean?"

He gave me a condescending look, as if to say, *You poor stupid girl.* I ground my teeth and let it go. I had bigger fish to fry.

"The limbic system is the emotional center of the brain, but it's also the magical center of the brain, in people for whom that genetic code is switched on. Your friends Liv and Tobias. That sweet old lady from the waffle house. Betty, was it?"

His eyes glittered; he knew exactly who she was, although it was sure as hell I hadn't told him she was magical. He was playing his cards slowly, one by one, to let me know that he had a much better hand than I'd thought. He wanted me to be intimidated, but hell if he was going to get that from me.

"Yeah? So, what about those people who don't have the magic genetic code switched on?"

He smiled, although his eyes still held that hollow emptiness that I was just now realizing they'd always had. "I switched it on. You are looking at the most powerful man in the world, darling."

I wanted to shrink down into my chair, but I would be damned if I was going to give him the satisfaction of seeing me sweat. "Not so fast, Optimus Prime. It doesn't work like natural magic. It's traveling, from day or night to all the time, and it's making my mother sick."

He shrugged. "Well, this is still in the trial stage, so there are quirks to be worked out, but I must say, I'm quite pleased with the results we're having."

My heart pounded in my chest, fear sending a cold prickle over my skin. "Let's revisit those quirks." I swallowed. "Exactly what is going to happen to us?"

He held my eye for a moment. "I can't be entirely sure. Everyone is different, and this is the first time I've worked with this exact mix of chemicals. Some people can go on for quite some time without manifesting serious symptoms. There does seem to be a connection to how hard they push the magic. Those who resisted the power and used the vials regularly lasted for as long as three, sometimes four months."

"Lasted?" I said, my throat choking on the word. "What do you mean?"

He held my look, his own deadened and emotionless.

My breath stopped in my chest, and I had to force it out. "Are you telling me that I'm going to die? Because I have to say, that really changes my motivation not to kill you right now."

"But you forget," he said, "I have the cure."

"Or maybe you're just saying you do so that I won't kill you," I said.

He shrugged. "That does sound like something I would do. I think for the moment, you're just going to have to take it on faith, until we've finished our negotiations."

I ran my hand over my face, took a breath, and said, "Okay. Tell me what drinking from the vials will do for us."

"Readministering the original cocktail has a stabilizing effect. The non-magical brain isn't working so hard to

re-create the chemicals it doesn't have the natural capacity
to create, and so it relaxes, and doesn't abandon the rest
of its duties, which seems to be what happened before."

"Abandon its duties?" I said. "What do you mean?"

"The brain is a beautiful thing," he said, a glint of
fascination in his eyes. "It keeps us breathing, keeps our
hearts beating. Makes us want, makes us feel. Everything you see around you . . . buildings, vehicles, books,
wallpaper . . . so much beauty, so much imagination, so
much magic . . . all because of the human brain." He
looked at me, and got back to the point. "When the brain
neglects its duties, when it can only focus on one area
of its function, the body naturally suffers. Breathing
stops, or maybe the desire to eat. Some find it unbearable and bring things to an end at their own hands." That
emptiness took over his eyes again, and he seemed to be
gazing at something only he could see. "It's sad, very sad,
but knowledge is the key to the advancement of man, and
it must be pursued. At all costs."

I took in a deep, shaky breath. *Jesus.* "So, that's what
happened to the women you've done this to before? They're
all dead now?"

He seemed to pull out of his memories, and focused
again on me. "Not all of them," he said coolly. "Every
trial has been different. There are some from the early
trials who simply sneeze whenever they see the color blue.
As I tinkered with the formula and dosages . . . well." He
shrugged, not a hint of guilt or regret in his expression.
"It is because of them that I now have the cure, which re-
verses it all. They are heroes; they sacrificed all for the
greater good."

"No, they *were* sacrificed," I said. "Different thing."

He met my eye. "You say potato . . ."

"Why women?" I said. "Why not men?"

"The effect on men is . . . different. My theory is it's

because men tend to have a less developed limbic system." He waved a hand in the air. "At any rate, I'm finding my best results coming from women at the moment. And your mother has been my most successful subject by far."

My stomach turned sour at the tone in his voice, but I tried to keep my expression flat. "Leave my mother out of this."

"Oh, your mother is what this is all about. She's spanned the gap from day to night. She controls the power. No one has ever done that before." He let out a greedy chuckle. "Your mother is the reason I'm still here. She is . . . exquisite."

I asked the next question with as light a tone as I could muster. "Why do you think she's been able to do that? What is it about her that makes her so special?"

He smiled. "You can't expect me to give all my secrets away. It'll kill the mystery in our relationship." But even as he spoke, I could see a hint of doubt in his eyes: He didn't know. That gave me what was probably my only advantage in this fight, so I changed the subject.

"So, let me get this straight. You're going to keep us dependent upon you to provide this stuff for a few months while you use us as lab rats until we all go crazy and die? Have I got that right?"

"Not at all," he said. "I will willingly give you the cure, in time."

I relaxed a bit at that, but I knew we were far from done here. "But not until you get what you want."

He gave me a small smile. "Yes."

I crossed my arms over my chest. "And what do you want?" He leaned forward and smiled lecherously at me, and I said, "Yeah, you'll have to kill me before you get that again."

He laughed. "As much fun as our time together was, that's not what I want from you."

"Yeah? What do you want, Desmond?" I said, my nerves zinging with tension.

His eyes flickered up to meet mine.

"All I want," he said, simply, "is one."

Chapter 13

My mouth went dry, and I swallowed, hard.

"One *what*?"

"One of you," he said, "to go with me."

"Go with you? Go where?"

"Back to Niagara Falls, to my lab. I'm so very close to gaining the data I need to publish, to prove what I have done, what I can do. I just need one subject with me who can control her magic and show it to the world."

"No," I said, pushing myself out of the chair and backing up until my ass hit the radiator under the window. "You can't *have* one of us. What are you, crazy? You dosed us all without our consent, and now you want one of us to be your lab monkey for the rest of her life? God, didn't they teach you anything about free will? You do know those consequences come back to hurt the conjurer, right? That would be *you,* idiot."

"Rubbish," he said, waving his hand as he stood up. "There are no magical consequences. What, do you actually believe there are little consequence elves who trace your actions back to you and take their pound of flesh?

Really, Stacy. I expected more from you than silly superstition."

"I believe in right and wrong," I said. "There are some
things you just don't do."

"Yes, well I believe in *reality*," he said in a low growl,
moving closer. "Those women sacrificed for a reason, and
I won't have that sacrifice rendered meaningless because
some upstart bitch is having a crisis of conscience."

I flinched back a bit, and the dark aggression slowly
left his face, as if by force of will. When he smiled again,
his eyes were completely blank.

"It's not my intention to hurt you," he said, his voice
softer. "But this is my work, and I've given over everything that ever meant anything to me for this. I can't stop
now, no matter what. I will let you, your friends, and
everything you love die if you thwart me on this. All I
have to do is leave, disappear into the world, and you'll
never have your cure. And how many vials do you have
left? Six? Seven?"

I had seven. I'd counted them the last time I was in my
shed. Apparently, so had Desmond.

"Divided among four people . . . that won't last long.
At the rate your mother is going, she'll use them all up
before the more restrained of you needs her first dose.
Or . . ." His eyes lit up, the emptiness gone as excitement
and greed took over. Apparently, he was only sociopathic
with regard to specific emotions. Sadness? Guilt? I tried
to remember the specific times I'd seen his eyes deaden
that way, and it was then that I realized he was still talking and I hadn't been listening, so I snapped back to attention.

". . . in the long run, it will be worth the sacrifice," he
said. "The world will be forever changed."

"Right," I said. "You'll out magic, and scientists will
descend on my friends wanting to cut their brains out.

You know there's a reason why magical people stay in the closet, right?"

"It's not like that anymore. We can study the human brain without making a single incision, without harming anyone. You needn't worry. I will be kind to her. I will treat her like a queen. I will protect her. I will honor her. You have my word."

"Oh, good. The word of the man who raped her brain that he will honor the woman he abducts. All my worries are put to rest now."

He shrugged the comparison off. "I did what I did. It's done. Now we simply need to move forward, working with what we have. One of you will go with me, or all of you will wither and die."

I let the radiator hold me up, unable to hear anything but the rapid beating of my heart as the bile rose in my throat. There were no choices here, and no way out. I was the one who'd started this whole mess in the first place by trusting Desmond, and even though the thought of subjecting myself to whatever he had in mind made me sick, this was my mess. I had to clean it up.

"Fine," I said, moving toward the door. "I'll go pack my things. We leave in the morning."

"I'm touched," he said, "but you're not my first choice."

A sick feeling came over me, probably because I knew the answer even as I formed the question. "Who do you want?"

"Why, the merry Widow, of course," he said. "You give me your mother, and I give you the cure. Then we go on our happy way, and you save the world. Considering your feelings about your mother, it sounds like a win–win to me. If you play your cards right, you might never see her again."

I was surprised at how *not* mixed my feelings were on that. She was narcissistic and often cruel, and there were times when I wished she'd move away to Florida like Peach's parents, but she was my mother. More than that, she was Nick's mother, and no way in hell was I putting Nick through that.

"The Widow isn't mine to give away," I said, "and she's not yours to take."

He rolled his eyes. "Are we on the free-will thing again? What makes you think she wouldn't *want* to go with me? She and I got on quite famously at the wedding." His mouth curled up at one end in a cold smile. "She might jump at the chance to run off with a younger man."

"To be your lab rat? I don't think so."

"If there's resistance, that's where you come in," he said. "You know her better than anyone else. You convince her to go with me. I can see where it might be difficult for someone of your *high moral fiber*"—he said this with more than a hint of sarcasm—"to make this choice, but I do believe it's an easy one. Everyone lives versus everyone dies."

"You son of a bitch," I spat.

He gave me a cool nod. "Based on the number of purple vials you have left, and the rate at which your mother will need them, I'd say you have about a week or so. Once your mother is in my custody and we have safely disappeared into the ether, I will provide you with cures for the remaining three. That is the deal. Take it or . . . well." He met my eyes, and again, I saw nothing but blackness in his. "You have a few days to think about it. No action need be taken today, if that's any comfort."

I stood there with my hand gripping the doorknob, my body shaking with fury and panic. "Before I go," I said, releasing a breath, "I want you to know one thing."

He looked almost bored, the bastard. "And what is that?"

I met his eyes, holding his gaze for a moment so he

would see how serious I was. "You've made me very angry, and I think you should be warned. I can be really ugly when I'm angry."

He stood up and walked toward me, his eyes locked on mine. He was close, too close, by the time he stopped, raising one hand up to gently graze my cheek.

"Ugly?" He chuckled. "How can someone as beautiful as you ever be ugly?"

"Trust me."

His eyes grew heavy-lidded and his breath escaped in a slow vent of steam. The bastard was getting off on my fury.

"Stacy Easter, how I do enjoy you," he said, and knocked on the door, his eyes still on mine. "Guard! My visitor is ready to go."

There was a click in the lock. I pulled on the knob and stepped out of the room, my legs wobbly beneath me, but I didn't let them visibly buckle until Addie shut and ceremoniously locked the door behind me.

"Honey?" Addie said, looking at me warily. "What did he do to you? You're white as a ghost!"

I took her by the elbow and walked her down the hallway. "Do you have any other guests here?"

She shook her head. "They all cleared out after the wedding."

"You guys still have that apartment above the antique store, right?"

Addie nodded, her face concerned. "Yes. Why?"

"Pack some things. Plan on staying there for a while. I'll pay for the empty rooms here, just until he's gone. It'll be . . ." I took a breath. "Six or seven days, at the most."

"Nonsense," she said. "I can just kick him out—"

"No," I said. "At least here, I know where he is. I just don't want you or Grace or anyone else near him."

Addie lowered her voice and leaned in. "You don't

need to worry about us. We're tough old lesbians." She moved down the hall and took a letter opener off the half-moon hall table. She tucked the tip of the blade under the top and wiggled it a bit, and then a hidden drawer popped open.

"Oh, my God," I said.

"I know," she whispered proudly, showing me the edge of the letter opener, which had some uneven serrations at the tip. "It's a key." She pointed to the stash inside the drawer and lowered her whisper even more. "I have pepper spray, Mace, throwing stars, and a tranq gun. He gets out of line, he's gonna regret it."

I stared at her, unable to speak for a moment. "Wow."

"I look sweet, but seriously, you don't wanna fuck with me."

"No," I said. "I don't think I do."

"I can stay here, keep an eye on him. It'll be fun."

I glanced back at the room, then shook my head as I carefully shut the drawer. "Thanks anyway, but . . . think of it like termites. Just close up the place and go. Please. Promise me."

Addie nodded, eyes wide, then looked back at Desmond's closed door. "He's really *that* bad?" she whispered.

"No," I said. "He's worse."

An hour later, I walked into my mother's hospital room, a purple vial filled with tea in my hand. Leo hopped up from the visitor's chair when I walked in.

"Where the hell have you been?"

I ignored him, just moved toward my mother's bed. He grabbed my wrist lightly, but I still winced as the pain shot up my arm. He released me immediately and looked at my wrist, which was blotched with purple.

"Stacy . . . ," he said, his voice softer. "What happened?"

"I went to see Desmond," I said, and uncapped the vial. "Help me raise her up?"

Leo did as I asked, his expression concerned, but to his credit, he remained quiet, allowing me to pay attention to what I was doing. He lifted her up and I tilted her head back and emptied the vial into her mouth. Absently, automatically, she swallowed. I capped the vial and nodded to Leo, who laid her back down on the bed.

"She'll be fine." I put the empty vial back into my purse. "We just have to wait."

I started for the chairs, but Leo put his hands on my shoulders and turned me to face him. "You're shaking."

"Still?" I let out a small laugh. "You'd think an hour in the car would take that down a notch."

"He hurt you." Leo's face was grave, and there was a dangerous light in his eyes. "What happened?"

"I've got it under control," I said, although I wasn't at all sure that was true. I'd had some time to think, to come up with a plan, sort of. I needed more time, but I didn't think I was going to get it.

Leo led me to the chairs and we sat down. He turned his chair to face me and leaned forward to lightly take my hands in his.

"What do you need?"

I blinked in surprise. "What, no third degree about what happened? You're not going to insist that I tell you everything so you can take action while I wait safely at home?"

He met my eyes. "I don't know what's going on here. I'm so far out of my depth, I can't even begin to see the surface of the water. All I can do is offer you . . . well, me. If I can help, just tell me what to do and it's done."

I touched his face. "You are the best man I've ever known."

He let out a small laugh. "You obviously need to get out more."

"Shut up." I leaned forward and kissed him lightly on the mouth. "I love you. Whatever happens, I want you to know that."

A worried expression washed over his face, but before he could say anything, there was movement from the bed, and a moment later, the Widow spoke.

"Where am I and what in God's name am I *wearing*?"

They decided to keep the Widow overnight for observation, but by the time we left the hospital, she was in typical Widow form, enjoying the attention of the doctors and nurses and the many, many flowers and gifts that came flooding in, while also being horrified at the hospital gown she was being forced to endure. I hoped that indignity would be enough to keep her from glowing while she was still in the hospital, but there wasn't much I could do about it, so I decided not to worry about it. Liv and Tobias returned to check on her again, and by the time visiting hours were over at eight, the Widow was happy. I didn't tell Liv or Tobias or the Widow about anything that had happened with Desmond, and I kept the sleeve of my shirt pulled over my injured wrist. There was nothing anyone else could do, anyway.

This one was on me.

"We'll be back to get you tomorrow," I told the Widow as Leo and I were leaving. "But no funny stuff, okay? If you glow, they're gonna keep you here longer. Possibly forever."

She crossed her finger over her heart just as a nurse came in with another floral arrangement. I was going to need to get the 'Bago driving again in order to transport all that crap from Buffalo to Nodaway, but that was tomorrow's problem. I turned to wave once more before we left, but the Widow was so enthralled with her gifts, she didn't notice.

The ride home was long, and quiet. Leo tried to start a few conversations of idle chitchat, but I couldn't keep up with it. I tried, but my mind would wander back to work on the problem with Desmond and I'd trail off mid-sentence. Eventually, Leo just allowed the silence and drove us back to the 'Bago while I stared off into the horizon, watching the sun set.

It was dark when we got home. I took Leo by the hand and led him into the 'Bago. I made some coffee and told him every detail of what had happened with Desmond, leaving nothing out. Leo's face grew stony over the course of my narration, and by the time I hit the end, there was nothing to give me any clue what he was thinking aside from the tiny light of fury in his eyes.

"Okay," he said after a while, staring down into the mug of coffee he'd let grow cold. "What's the plan, then?"

"I don't know," I said. "I haven't quite gotten that figured out yet. But I do know the backup plan."

He raised his eyes to mine. "What's the backup plan?"

I hesitated a moment, knowing this wasn't going to go over well. "Me."

Leo didn't seem to react much. "What does that mean?"

"It means . . . the one thing we have over Desmond is that we know how the magic evolves. It's the emotional supply—"

"No," he said, his voice firm.

"—and if I can develop my power—"

"Out of the question. That's what put your mother in the hospital, pushing that magic. And you only have enough vials to keep her going for a week. If both of you are pushing it—"

"What else am I going to do?" I said. "I can't give him my mother. I'm certainly not going to give him Clementine, or Ms. Troudt. I made this mess. It's my job to clean it up."

"You think I'm going to let him just take you? Do you think there's a universe in which that would ever, *ever* happen?"

"I don't think it's your call," I said, keeping my voice as even as I could.

"Yeah, it is," he said, slamming one hand on the table and pointing the other toward the door. "I'm your source. If I walk out that door—"

"If you walk out that door, that monster takes my mother," I said quietly.

He opened his mouth to speak, and then closed it again. He ran his hands through his hair and said, "I hate this."

"Me, too," I said. "But right now, he's how the four of us are going to stay alive, so let's focus on that."

"Okay," Leo said. "You've got some vials. You think there's any way you could reverse-engineer that formula? Maybe buy us some more time?"

I shook my head. "I'm nowhere near that level. There's a friend of Liv's, though, a guy named Cain. He's a conjurer, the one who got me started. He's smart, and he knows way more about this stuff than I do. He might be able to do that. Maybe."

Leo stared at me for a long time, then said, "You've thought this through, then."

"Yeah. But . . . that's only a temporary solution. What we need is that cure." I sighed and ran my hands through my hair. "Right now, I've got six vials left. I'll have to give one to Cain to try to figure out what it is. If I push my magic, I'm going to end up needing to take some, too, and assuming we can keep Clementine and Ms. Troudt away from their sources, then we've got about three, maybe four days to figure out what we're going to do before the Widow and I need more. And once we're that desperate, the game is over. We've lost."

Leo was frozen so still, for a moment I wondered if he was even breathing. "We can't lose."

I touched his arm. "We won't."

"Yeah? You can guarantee that?"

"No, Leo. Of course I can't. We don't know anything, and what we think we know could be wrong. But . . . fuck it. The world could get hit by an asteroid tomorrow. The super volcano could blow and make one big Pompeii out of North America. Aliens could land and destroy the White House."

He shook his head, a warning look in his eyes. "Don't make light of this. Please." He picked up our coffee mugs, stood up, and dumped them in the sink.

I got up and leaned against the table, staring at his back. "I'm not making light of any of this. I'm just saying . . . this is what we have. We can bury our heads, or we can try something and see what happens."

He was quiet for a long time, then said, "You can't go with him."

"I don't want to go with him, but I need to work every angle to make sure that doesn't happen, and I need your help to do that." I moved forward and put my hand on his chest. "Besides, it could be fun."

He gave me a pained look. "Stop."

I trailed my hand up his chest, over his neck, sliding my fingers into his hair. "Desire's the only thing left on the list, Leo."

He took my hand in his and pulled it down, holding it away from him. "You want me to fuck you until you burst into flames? That it?"

"No," I said, keeping my eyes on his. "I want you to make love to me because I love you."

Our eyes met and I could see the conflict in his, the love and the caring and the connection we always had. I moved closer, twining our fingers together.

"I have loved you every day of my life, Leo North, and I will love you until the day I die. If that day is coming sooner than I originally thought it would, then I don't have time to waste with this bullshit dance anymore." I pressed my body against his, kissed his neck, and whispered in his ear. "I want you because I have always wanted you, only you."

"Shit!" Leo dropped my hand and shook his own out. I looked at my hand; the ropes of red smoke were starting to form.

"Oh, God, I'm sorry," I said.

Leo laughed. "Well, I guess we figured out what it is that gets you fired up."

"Are you okay? Your hands . . ."

He shook his head. "Don't worry about it." He put his hands on either side of my face and pulled me to him for a kiss, then looked me in the eye. "I love you."

Happiness mixed with fear and I started to shake. "I know."

"I need you to know that," he said. "This isn't just about sex for me. It's you, and you are everything to me. You have to know that."

"I know."

"Good." And then his hands were on the buttons of my jeans. "Someone has to keep his head here," he said quietly, tucking his thumbs inside my jeans and underwear. "I'm running this show, okay?" He slid my jeans off and lifted me, bare-assed, onto the table.

"Okay," I said, breathless, holding my hands out and watching them as the ropes of smoke started to intensify and move faster. Leo put his leg between my knees, nudging them apart.

"What about you?" I asked, motioning toward him. "You're still dressed."

"Don't worry about me," he said, then took my face in his hands and kissed me, hard, his tongue demanding my mouth with power and certainty. He grabbed my ass and pressed me against him, allowing me to feel him hard under his jeans. I groaned into his mouth as the core of me melted into him.

"Oh, God," I said when he pulled away. My eyes fluttered open, and I could see waves of heat distorting the air around my hands.

He touched my chin and turned me to face him. "If it becomes too much, you tell me to stop. If you start to feel weak or dizzy—"

"Stop talking," I said, and kissed him. I could feel my heartbeat, warm and throbbing where we touched, and then he moved down my body, laying kisses on my collarbone, on my breasts through my T-shirt, and finally—

"Oh, my *God*," I said as he shifted me under him, laying me on my back and pulling my thighs up to rest on his shoulders. I held my hands out in the air, careful to keep my eyes open, watching the heat radiating from me as his tongue gently opened me up. I swallowed and watched the ropes of smoke as they danced over my hands, starting down my arms.

"Leo," I said, and he looked up. The cool air from his absence made my stomach tighten with desire, and the ropes moved up my forearm, toward my elbow.

"Control it," he said, his breath warm on my stomach as he spoke. "Focus."

I met his eyes and nodded. "Okay." I looked at my hands, wrapped my mind around the power, and the ropes of smoke pulled back toward my wrist.

He kept his eyes on mine as he went down again, and I held the contact, watching him as he adored me with his mouth, and then I slowly pulled my eyes away, looking at my hands.

Focus. The waves of heat intensified at my palms, and the air around my lower arms began to look normal again.

He slid one finger inside me and I groaned and closed my eyes. *Oh, God, yes.* I writhed under his touch, pushing myself against his tongue, and he withdrew.

"Stacy," he said, his voice quiet but tense, and I opened my eyes again. The ropes of smoke were moving down my wrists again.

"I can't," I said, arching my back to slide closer to him. "I need you . . . I can't . . ."

"You can," he said, and slid one finger back inside. "Focus."

He moved his finger lightly, curling it toward my stomach, and a bolt of heat shot through me, making me quiver.

"I want you," I said, breathless. "I want all of you."

"You'll have me," he said, letting the breath from his words dance over my wetness. "Control it."

I let out a breath and looked at my hands. *Focus. Control.* He slid a second finger inside at the same time as he moved his tongue and a flame shot out from my left palm, just the palm. Leo raised his head, but I said, "Keep going," and he did, moving faster with the rhythm of my hips. I held out my right hand and he used his teeth and I hollered and shot flame out of my right palm, dissipating into the air. The ropes were gone; this was just me, my power, under my control.

Mine.

Leo looked up at me. "Good girl. How are you feeling?"

"Like I'm going to kill you if you don't take off your pants," I said.

He grinned at me. "I thought I told you I was in charge here." He moved his fingers inside me, making me tighten around his fingers as I fell farther, closer . . .

"Oh, fuck," I said, and released a breath on the verge of climax, holding back, controlling. "I need you. Now."

I heard the rip of a condom wrapper, and when I looked up, his pants were off.

"About damn time." I let my head fall back, waiting, but there was nothing but cold air on me, and I lifted my head to see him stroking himself, watching me.

"How long is that going to take?"

"I'm ready," he said, his face flushed. "But I need something from you first."

"What?"

He put his hand on the flat of my stomach, and I could feel the hardness of him moving against me, not entering, just poised, making me insane with the need of him. He reached for my face, and with one finger gently angled my head to look at my right hand.

"You're not ugly," he said, and entered me, just a little. "Say the words."

"Leo," I said in breathless complaint as he teased me.

"Say it," he said, his voice firm, "and mean it . . ."

"I'm not . . . ," I began, but the voice in my head said, *Yes, you are.*

"Mean it," Leo said, pushing a little farther into me, but still not near enough.

"I . . . I can't . . . I'm . . . oh, God, this is cruel."

He leaned his body over mine, still holding back, making me insane with need for him. He put his cheek against mine, angling both of our faces toward the flame coming from my hand, and then he turned his head and nibbled at my collarbone. I arched against him, dying for him, but he pulled back.

"I know you better than anyone in this world," he said. "I've loved you, all of you, every day of my life. I'm inside you. I have looked at you more than anyone on this earth and I know. Trust me. You are not ugly."

I looked at him, and our eyes met, and I saw all the

love, the need, the honesty in him. He was telling the truth. All I had to do was trust him more than I trusted anyone else, even myself.

It was easy.

"I'm not ugly," I whispered, and within a second Leo pushed fully inside me and I screamed with the pleasure of it as the flame in my open hand burst out. I angled it away from Leo, sending the flame into the air, where it dissipated harmlessly.

He pushed in again, a sound of pleasure coming deep from his throat, and I clenched around him.

"Oh, please," I whispered, and he kissed me on my cheek, then turned his head to watch the flame with me as he slowly, so slowly, moved within me.

"Control it," he whispered, and began to move faster.

I took in a deep breath, and closed my right hand, finger by finger, into a fist, pulling the heat in, making it mine. The fire curled into my hand and disappeared as my hand closed.

"What are you?" he asked, kissing my neck and pushing himself into me.

"Beautiful," I said, and laughed. I could feel the power in my hand, but I had it locked down, locked within, ready to burst free only when I told it to.

He took one finger and angled my chin until my eyes locked on his. "True, but not the answer I was looking for." He withdrew, almost to the point of leaving me, and I whined.

"No, finish me," I begged, and he moved my chin until I was looking at my left hand.

"Tell me you're not vicious," he whispered, moving back into me so slowly, too slowly. I arched my back against him and he reached between us, where we connected, and moved his fingers against me as he pushed inside.

"Tell me," he said.

"I'm not vicious," I breathed, looking at my left hand. Leo pushed into me, working up the rhythm again, and I watched as flame began to shoot from my hand. I concentrated on the power, commanded it to be mine, as I slowly closed my left hand into a fist. I held the wave off, slowly closing my left hand, pulling the power into me, making it mine.

I dropped my head back against the table and laughed. "Ha! I did it!"

He cupped his hand under my head and lifted me until I looked at him. Between us, he pressed his other hand against me as he pushed the full length of himself inside and I gasped, allowing myself to feel it all, to hold nothing back.

"Now," I whispered. "Finish me."

He went still. "Tell me what you are."

"Frustrated," I said, and laughed a little as I writhed beneath him.

He smiled and used both hands to shift my hips beneath him, pushing into me. I cried out, and he leaned down, putting his lips next to my ear.

"You're powerful," he whispered. "Say it."

"I'm powerful," I said, feeling the words rush into me even as his rhythm picked up, as though each thrust sent the message home, into my core, where it could never be touched by anything anyone said to me, ever again.

"Say it again," he said, his voice breathless as he moved inside me.

"I'm powerful," I said.

"And mine," he said through clenched teeth as he pushed harder and faster. "God, Stacy, please. Say you're mine."

"I'm yours," I said. "I have always been yours."

"Mine," he said, moving faster, pushing harder, reaching places within me I hadn't known were there.

"*Yes!*" I screamed as colored light exploded behind my eyelids. My orgasm hit in waves and he held me tight and released himself into me, the slow bursts from him keeping my climax afloat in the air longer, making me cry out again and again until I fell back on the table, grateful for the cold linoleum against my steaming skin. He fell over me, using his elbows to hold himself up even as his head dropped between my breasts. I opened my hands; there was no red smoke, no distorted air. The heat was gone, controlled, and I wrapped my arms around him, holding him to me.

"I am yours," I said. "Always and forever."

In what seemed like a split second, I was in darkness, and Leo was calling my name, with some urgency, but from far away. I felt the pull of him as I looked back and forth, unable to find him, unable to tell where I was, and then in a sudden *whoosh* I was back in my body, lying in my bed, with Leo hovering over me, frantic.

"Stacy! Stacy!"

I opened my eyes and took a moment to focus on him. Then I reached up with my arm and tried to touch his face, but my arm felt like rubber.

"I'm here," I croaked, my throat suddenly dry. "I'm here."

"What do I do? Do I just mix water in it? You didn't tell me. I don't know what to do."

I blinked a few times, then managed to focus on the purple vial in his hand. I clumsily pushed it away. "I'm okay."

"You're not," he said. "What do I do?"

"Water," I said. "No vial. Just water."

He gave me a look, as though he was preparing to argue, and then got up and poured me some water. A moment later, he was at my side, holding me up while I drank it. I finished it and lay back on the bed, staring up at the ceiling as he put the glass away. He sat down on the edge of the bed, and I reached out, able to control my fingers again, and touched his back. It was tense, hard as rock. I sat up and put my arms around his neck.

"I'm okay," I said. "A little exhausted and dehydrated. It's been a hell of a day, and I shot fire into a room that was already hot while every bit of moisture I had was directed at a very specific place. Plus, I don't think I've had anything to eat or drink today but coffee." I thought for a moment. "Yeah. That's it. Pretty stupid."

He got up and refilled my glass of water, then held it out to me and watched as I drank it. When I handed it back to him, I smiled.

"I feel a lot better now," I said, and it was true. "I really think it was just dehydration."

He nodded, not looking convinced, and took the empty glass. He got up, set it on the counter, and stood there, leaning his hands against the counter as he hung his head.

"Are you okay?" I asked.

"No," he said simply. "But I will be."

"Come here." I patted the bed next to me. He came to me, angling my body facing away from him so we could spoon together. He wrapped me tight in his arms and kissed my cheek.

"I will always love you," he said. "I need you to know that."

I pulled his hand up to my lips and kissed it.

"I know," I said, and then snuggled against his strong body, gave in to the warmth of his touch, and fell into a deep, satisfied sleep.

ment later, he was at my side, holding out the water while I drank

was already hot while hovering bit of moisture. I had was all

moment. "Yeah. That's pretty much it."

out to me and waited until I drank it. When I handed it
back to him, I smiled.

"Come here." I patted the bed next to me. He turned to
me, stalking my body, coming away from him so we could

kissed my cheek.

that."

deep satisfied sleep.

Chapter 14

I woke up just before dawn, my eyes flying open suddenly as whatever I'd been dreaming about poked me into consciousness. Leo had rolled over, his back to me, and I carefully crawled out of bed, slid into my jeans, snaked my phone out of my bag, and went outside. I leaned against the hood of the Bug, scanned through my contact list until I found the number I was looking for, and dialed. It rang twice before he answered.

"What is it?" His voice was clear and fully conscious, as if I hadn't woken him up.

"Hey, Cain. It's Stacy."

"Yeah, I know. Liv okay?" The southern sandpaper in his voice was just as I remembered it, and I smiled. I'd kind of missed the guy.

"She's fine. It's me who's in trouble."

He chuckled. "Why am I not surprised?"

"Because you've met me. Hey, what do you know about Anwei Xing?"

There was a long pause. "Tell me you're not messing with Anwei Xing."

"What I've stepped in is way worse than Anwei Xing,"

I said. "Can you tell me what happens if you take it for an extended period of time?"

"Huh." He was thoughtful for a moment. "Well, depends on how you mix it. Brewed straight up, like a tea, it'll dull your emotions for a while. There's some other things you can do—distillation, fermentation, hell I heard of one guy who even shot it up in a needle. Mess with it at that level, and you can target some specific feelings, but you've got to be a damn master to pull that off. Not many people can do that."

"This guy can. He made me a potion that cut off my emotions surrounding one specific person."

"Huh," he said.

"Yeah." I nibbled my lip and tried to figure out how best to phrase the thought that had woken me up. "The thing is, that's a rare herb. People don't just have that sitting around in their stores unless they're actively using it, right?"

"Depends on the person," Cain said,

"Do you think someone that good might be able to shut off his own conscience? Maybe accidentally? Like, maybe, if he was upset about something else, and it just spread to block out his entire moral center?"

He was quiet for a moment. "That's a lot of maybes there."

"Yeah, I know, but . . . let's just say I'm grasping at straws. Because I am. Would he have to keep taking it to keep up the effects?"

"Depends. Anwei Xing is pretty powerful. If you brew with the leaves, it's a temporary effect. Use the root and you can do something lasts longer, but it's dangerous."

"But possible?"

"Easter, anything's possible. Doesn't mean that's what's happening. It's possible your guy here is just an asshole."

"Well, he's that, too, but let's just play with this idea

for a moment. Is there something that might counter the effects of Anwei Xing? Even if it's permanent?"

"What? You wanna give him his conscience back?"

When I'd woken up, the idea had seemed like genius, but saying it out loud to Cain made it sound kind of stupid and amateurish. Whatever; anything was better than leaving Leo to go off and be Desmond's lab rat. I was desperate. "Yeah. Might there be a way to do that?"

"Off the top of my head . . ." He let out a long sigh. "Maybe, if he's using just the leaves. If he distilled something with the root . . . damn, Easter. Hell if I know."

"Well, I'm up to my ass in alligators here. Any chance you could check into it for me?"

He let out a heavy sigh. "Yeah. I guess. You need me to get on a plane?"

"Can you?" I asked.

"They've got planes here," he said cryptically.

I sighed. "Get on one, then. At the very least, it'll be nice for you to come and visit Liv. You're the closest thing she's got to family."

The only reason I knew Cain was still on the phone was because of the background noise. Liv had never known her sister Holly, and Holly had died before she and Cain could get married, but still. Cain was family to Liv, and I knew she missed him. If she wasn't going to tell him that, I would. Cain wasn't a guy who expressed his emotions a whole lot, but he'd loved Holly, and he cared about Liv, and it wouldn't kill him to drop in every now and again.

"You still there?" I asked, even though I knew he was.

"Yeah," he said. "I'm here."

I hesitated a moment, about to let him go, then I said, "Hey, what would you say if I told you I made a sunflower? Physical magic? All on my own, with no formal training?"

There was no hint of laughter in his voice when he

spoke next. "Christ, Easter. What the hell are you getting yourself into out there?"

I cringed. He was right, and I knew he was right but I couldn't help myself. "I'm getting into some extraordinary shit out here, that's what I'm getting into."

"You coulda blown the damn windows out your house!"

"That's why I did it in my garden shed. Plexiglass stands up a lot better, by the way."

"You could have killed yourself. Physical magic is nothing to mess with, you hear me?"

"But you're impressed, right?" I said. "No training. All by myself. I mean, if you were Desmond, you wouldn't want to mess with me, right?"

He grumbled something that sounded like it could have been agreement and I said, "Get your plane ticket. Liv misses you."

"Yeah, okay," he muttered, but there was a pleased note in his tone. I didn't know much about Cain's history, but my guess was that when it came to family, Liv was pretty much it for him, too.

I heard a noise and looked to see Leo stepping out the front door, barefoot, one eye open, hair all mussed on one side, arms crossed over his bare chest, boxers hanging off his hip bones. He was an early-morning wreck, and the most beautiful damn thing I'd ever laid eyes on.

"Just get on a plane," I said to Cain, and cut off the call. I slid the phone into my back pocket and smiled at Leo. "Hey, sailor."

He padded down the cement steps and walked over to me, leaning against the Bug's hood next to me.

"Morning," he said.

"Morning," I said, and rested my head against his shoulder. He put one arm around me, kissed the top of my head, and said, "Who was that on the phone?"

"Cain," I said. "He's the conjurer guy I told you about. I had a thought."

"Was it a good thought?" he asked.

"It was a desperate thought," I said. "Probably nothing, but beggars can't be choosers."

He tightened his grip around my waist. "You'll figure it out."

"Yeah, I will," I said.

He looked at me, his eyes dark and worried. "How are you feeling? I mean . . . with the magic and everything. Are you . . . dizzy? Headache? Is there something we're supposed to look for, to know when to worry?"

I glanced around; although we were sitting in the midst of what looked like gray predawn, the sky above was blue. The sun had come up; it just hadn't made its presence entirely felt through the thick growth of trees on my property. I held out one hand, closed my eyes, and tried to find it, that source of power I had touched last night. I remembered the spark that had come from Leo, the place in my soul his touch had brought back to life, showing me where the power hid in my mind. I approached it, and once I got close, I opened my eyes.

Focus. Control. I felt the heat move through me, and the air in my cupped hand began to distort a little, like the space over black asphalt on a hot day. An awkward flame burst and shot from my palm, and then sputtered out, and I felt a wave of exhaustion run through me, as though I'd just put all my life force into that one paltry, sad display. I was breathing as though I'd just run a mile, and I leaned against Leo's chest.

"I did it," I said, my voice weak to my own ears. "In the daytime. That means I was right. Yaaaaaaaay." I put up a weak fist of victory in the air and laughed, then noticed that Leo wasn't laughing with me.

"Hey," I said, looking up at him. "Please. Don't."

He forced a smile, but it didn't reach his eyes. "Don't what?"

I slid off the hood, stood in front of him on wobbly legs, and took his hands into my own.

"This sucks," I said. "It's awful and if I was in your position, I would feel exactly the way you're feeling now. But there's no way out of this but through. I need you to believe in me right now, because if you believe in me, then I'll believe in me."

"It's not about believing in you." He watched me for a while, then said, "I just got you back."

"I know. I've gotta power through this thing first, though, and I can't do it if I'm constantly worrying about you worrying."

"Then I won't worry." He pushed off the Bug and pulled me into his arms. It was strange how comforting that felt, how just the physical touch from this one man could make my world so much better. I closed my eyes and let myself fall into him, let him hold me up for a few moments until I got my strength back, at which point I tilted my head back to look up at him.

"We need to make breakfast and get ready."

He smiled and kissed my nose. "Already?"

"Already," I said. "I've fallen into a big pile of shit and I have to start shoveling my way out."

"Aw," he said, smiling. "That's my classy girl."

I sat Deidre Troudt and Clementine Klosterman down on the stolen stools that furnished my little garden shed, and explained everything as best I could, considering there was no small amount of it that was currently baffling me.

"You have to stay away from your triggers," I said at

the end of my speech, and handed a vial to Deidre Troudt. "That'll keep you safest for longest, giving me time to figure out something better. If you find your magic getting out of control, if it's happening at night, if you feel exhausted or you pass out, put some liquid in the vial and drink it down." I glanced behind me at the case of purple vials. After the one each I was giving these two, that left four for me and the Widow. *Tick tock, tick tock.* "Let me know as soon as you use the one you've got, but if you stay away from your triggers, you shouldn't need it at all before I get you the cure."

Ms. Troudt looked at me. "And when will that be?"

"Soon," I said, and hoped I looked confident. I needed these two happy and out of my hair for the moment. I turned to Clementine. "How have you been doing?"

Clementine pulled her wide eyes away from the vial in her hand, then pushed her glasses up on her nose and said, "Good, good. I got the job at CCB's. Thanks for that. It's so much better than the IGA."

"Any more incidents?" I asked, but before Clementine could answer, Ms. Troudt stomped back into the conversation.

"So, you're telling me all I have to do is stay away from Dr. Feelgood, and all this goes away?"

"Um, excuse me, Ms. Troudt?" Clementine said, her voice low.

"No," I said, keeping my focus on Ms. Troudt. "I'm saying that if you stay away from Dr. Feelgood, it'll get bad less quickly."

"Ms. Troudt?" Clementine said, her voice a little louder.

"How am I supposed to do that?" she said. "I finally find the love of my life, and you want me to just stay away from him? I need to talk to him, I need—"

"*Hey!*"

Both Ms. Troudt and I stopped and looked at Clementine, whose face was flushed and whose posture was straight. I smiled.

"Yes, Clementine?" I said.

"I was about to answer you when Ms. Troudt interrupted me," Clementine said, and she raised her eyes to meet Ms. Troudt's, pushing her glasses up on her nose. "That was rude."

Ms. Troudt stared at her, her eyes wide. "Who the hell are you?"

"Cl-Clementine Klosterman," Clementine said, glancing at me for reassurance as her confidence started to fail her. I gave her a nod, and she looked back at Ms. Troudt. "You don't remember me?"

"You were in my class?" Ms. Troudt asked.

"Mm-hmm," Clementine said, nodding cautiously. "A couple of years ago, in the tenth grade."

Ms. Troudt gave her an appraising look. "Yeah, I recognize the top of your head. You always had it lowered. It's good to see your face, and you're right. I was rude. I apologize." She motioned permission for Clementine to speak. "Go ahead."

Clementine took a deep breath and shifted her eyes from Ms. Troudt to me. "I, um . . . it did happen again, but only during the day."

"What happened?" I asked. "Did Henry come into CCB's? You gotta tell that kid to keep his distance, Clementine."

"No, no . . . it was at home." She swallowed hard. "My mother and I had a fight, and then I was doing the dishes, and I moved really fast, and I broke three plates, and that only made things worse . . ."

I paused. "Your mother? But she wasn't at the IGA that day when everything first started, was she?"

"N-no," Clementine stammered, and lowered her head.

"But Karl called me stupid, and that's what my mother says . . . sometimes . . . and I thought of her and that's when I started moving really fast and . . ."

She trailed off. Deidre Troudt and I exchanged horrified looks.

"Your mother calls you stupid?" I asked.

Clementine kept her eyes lowered, and meekly shrugged one shoulder. "Sometimes. But only when I do stupid things. Sometimes . . . I do stupid things. She's just trying to make me better." Clementine's eyes darted to meet mine quickly, then lowered. "She just wants me to have a boyfriend, you know. Be normal."

"Your mother says that stuff to you?" Ms. Troudt said, her voice softer than usual.

Clementine raised her head and nodded.

"And that's why you took the love potion?" I asked. "To get a boyfriend and get your mother off your back?"

Clementine sighed. "I really do like Henry, but . . . yeah." And then her posture sagged and she hung her head again.

"Oh for fuck's sake," Deidre Troudt said. She reached over and poked Clementine in the side. "Sit up straight."

Clementine did as commanded.

"Hold your head up."

Clementine did that, too.

"Look at me."

Clementine met my eyes first, and when I nodded encouragement, she timidly shifted her gaze to meet Ms. Troudt's.

"Your mother's a bitch," Ms. Troudt said. "You're not stupid, and you're perfectly normal. You were in my class, and I'm telling you, you're not stupid."

Clementine sort of half rolled her eyes. "You don't even remember me."

"Right," she said. "I remember all the stupid ones."

"Okay," I said, "all this is great, but if your mother's your trigger, we've got a problem. We've got to get you out of your house and away from her for a while. How the hell are we going to do that?"

Deidre Troudt waved a hand in the air. "I've got it." She hopped off the stool she'd been sitting on and turned to Clementine. "You're staying with me. I'll drive you home to get your things. I'll tell your mother we're doing some kind of English summer camp thing. Think she'll buy that?"

Clementine nodded. "She won't care. She'll be glad I'm out of the house. But . . . are you sure it won't be too much trouble? I can clean up, and I can cook . . ."

"It's no trouble," Ms. Troudt said, although her voice was more annoyed than comforting.

Clementine nibbled her lip and Ms. Troudt swatted at the air in front of her face. "Stop that. Every time you nibble your lip, you're ruining your looks because your mother's a bitch. Don't let her have that."

Annoyance flashed over Clementine's face, and her posture straightened. "My mother's a bitch. I'm gonna nibble my lip for a while. Back off."

Ms. Troudt's eyebrows raised in an expression of respect. "Okay, then."

Clementine smiled, a real, proud smile. I smiled, too, and entertained the idea of setting up a secret camera in the Klosterman household for when Ms. Troudt returned Clementine to her mother. I kind of wanted to see that.

"This is good," I said to Ms. Troudt as I walked them out of the garden shed. "She can keep you away from Dr. Feelgood, and you can keep her away from her mother."

Ms. Troudt pulled her car keys out of her purse and gave them to Clementine. "You go start the car and put the AC on extreme. I hate getting into a hot car."

"Okay," Clementine said, then smiled wider than I'd

ever seen her smile and disappeared down the path. Deidre Troudt touched my arm, keeping me from following. Once a moment or two had passed, she spoke.

"I don't know what's going on here, but I know it's not good," she said, her voice low. "I'll take care of the kid. You take care of this."

I nodded. "I will, Ms. Troudt."

She rolled her eyes. "You made me a magical Disney princess foster mother. You still can't call me Deidre?"

I hesitated for a moment, and then said, "Look. You know the whole story with my family, right?"

Ms. Troudt gave me a wry look. "I'm forty-eight years old, and you were in my class ten years ago. No, I don't remember the details of your family."

"Oh," I said. "Yeah, well. My dad deserted us when I was six, which was just as well. I don't think he much liked being a father anyway. My mother has been pretending he's dead for twenty-three years, because she's afraid of how it'll make her look if she publicly acknowledges that her husband ran off to be a drag queen. Nick played football, he made her look good in town, so she liked him. I didn't do anything that made her look good, so I got ignored."

Ms. Troudt's expression softened, and I had to look away in order to keep talking. "No one aside from Nick gave enough of a crap about me to correct me, on anything. I remember at least three times when you kept me after class to give me a hard time about how I dressed, or what I ate. That mattered to me. A lot. And calling you Deidre, it just . . . I feel like it makes you into someone else, and that feels like a loss to me. I don't deal well with loss."

"Oh, honey," she said, and pulled me in for a hug. It was warm, and soft, the way a mother's hug is supposed to be, and I had to fight to blink away tears. "When someone your age calls me Ms. Troudt," she said into my ear

as she held me tight, "it makes me feel like the oldest fucking person in the universe. I will gladly give you a hard
time about anything you want. We can start with your hair,
which desperately needs cutting." She pulled back and
smiled, and I could see there was some moisture in her
eyes, too. "But, please. For me. Call me Deidre."

I laughed and wiped at the space under my eyes. "Okay.
Deidre."

"Excellent," she said. "Now go fix this colossal clus-
terfuck and then we'll have lunch and I'll tell you you're
too skinny."

And with that, she disappeared down the path behind
Clementine.

We brought the Widow back to Peach and Nick's house
that afternoon. At first, she wasn't thrilled with the idea
of needing babysitting, but once she realized she'd be able
to torture her new daughter-in-law 24-7 seven, she perked
up a bit. Leo and Nick got her settled in the guest room
upstairs while I sat in the living room with Liv and Peach
and talked about the honeymoon.

"Oh, it was beautiful!" Peach said, flipping through the
pictures of white beaches set against implausibly blue water.
"We went to this little town called Mijas, and it's kind of off
the beaten tourist track so no one there speaks English, and
they were so sweet about Nick's terrible Spanish . . ."

I kept one eye over my shoulder, waiting for Nick to
come back down, and by the time I looked back, both Liv
and Peach were watching me.

"Everything okay?" Liv asked.

"No," I said. "But it will be." I reached out and touched
Peach's hand. "I'm sorry I ruined your honeymoon."

Peach lowered her eyes. "No. It's fine. Two weeks is
too long for a honeymoon, anyway."

"Four days is too short," I said. "And now you've got the Widow upstairs. This sucks and I'm sorry."

Peach shrugged. "Nick was already getting twitchy about getting back to work."

I heard footsteps on the stairs and I stood up. I kissed Peach on the top of the head and said, "I'll make it up to you. I promise."

I left the living room to meet Nick and Leo at the base of the stairs. Nick didn't even look at me, which was what he did when he was pissed. It wasn't punishment; he just hated being mad, especially at me, so he tended to avoid me until he wasn't mad anymore. Ordinarily, I'd give him a few days to cool off, but I didn't have that kind of time now.

Leo shook Nick's hand, kissed me on the forehead, and went outside to wait in the Bug. Nick took one quick look at me then headed to the kitchen. I followed him out to the backyard, where I caught up with him.

"Nick, I need to talk to you."

"Now's not a good time, Stace."

He walked all the way to Peach's garden before realizing that there was no door in the back fence, no way out, and he had no choice but to turn to face me. His eyes were a solid wall of blue ice, and my stomach sank.

"Please," I said. "Just yell at me and get it over with. I don't have time for you to be mad at me."

He narrowed his eyes. "Why not?"

I sighed. "This whole thing is really complicated and there's a chance . . . there's a chance I might be going away in a few days . . ."

"Going where?"

"I don't know."

"With who?"

I hesitated, then said, "Desmond."

His eyes went wide. "Desmond? What about Leo?"

"I wouldn't be going *with* Desmond . . . not romantically. It's just something I might have to do and I might not have much time for good-byes before I go and if that's the case, I don't want to go away with you being mad at me."

He shook his head. "You're something else, you know that?"

"I know," I said. "So yell at me and get it out of your system now because if I go . . ." I drifted off and Nick filled in the empty space.

"You might not be back? Is that what you're saying?"

I didn't answer. He turned away from me, slammed his open hand against the fence, and then turned back, eyes glittering with anger.

"You want me to yell at you? Fine. I've been protecting you and taking care of you my whole life, and I took *one* thing for me, and look what happens. You blow it up. What, Millie dying last year wasn't enough for you? You had to go poking around in magic some more, see what else it could fuck up for us?"

My breath caught; I wanted to defend myself, but I couldn't. He was right. Last summer Nick had been unwittingly central in everything, and I knew that even now, it all frightened him more than he cared to admit. Millie, who had loved Nick since we were kids and had never told him, didn't take it well when Peach and Nick got engaged. She turned to magic to get her vengeance, hurting Peach and almost ruining Nick's life. Still, Nick had been close to Millie, she'd been his secretary for ten years, and when she died, it hit him pretty hard. I think that was also partially because he understood the least out of all of us what had happened and why. And now he stared down at his shoes, fuming and furious with me for bringing this all back into his world, and I couldn't blame him.

"Last summer," he said slowly, his voice sharp as steel, "Peach got hurt. Millie got killed. Liv . . ." He huffed and shrugged. "Okay, fine, Liv made out all right, but still. We survived that whole mess last year by the skin of our teeth, and you gotta go overturn that rock, see what's crawling under it? And now you got Mom involved . . ."

"None of that was my intention," I said, my voice shaky. "I didn't do it on purpose."

"Yeah," he said, his words hard and cold. "But you didn't take a lot of time to think before you just rushed in, did you? Magic, it spreads, like cancer. It touches everything around you, like it did with Liv last summer. Did you even think about that before you started this mess?"

"I'm trying to fix it," I said, working to keep my voice level. "I'm telling you I'm sorry. What else can I do?"

He let out a hard breath, then shook his head. "You can be done."

I blinked. "What do you mean?"

"I mean, *done*." He sliced his hand through the air like an ax. "No more magic. After this, it's over."

My mind went blank. I hadn't even considered that as an option. "Nick," I said finally. "It's what I do."

"You're a librarian!" he shouted.

"I got *fired*!" I shouted back.

"*Laid off.* Not the same thing. You could get a job at another library. Commute to Buffalo, go to Erie, whatever. They're looking for a librarian at the high school. You could do that. You could get a job. Instead, you do this. You're doing it to Mom, to me, you don't care. Like always, you just do whatever you want and who gives a fuck about anyone else?"

"Wow," I said, and tried to catch my breath. "That's what you really think of me?"

Nick went silent, his eyes on the ground, unable to meet mine. I took that as a yes.

"Okay," I said, and started toward the fence gate next to the house.

"Wait," Nick said, and I stopped where I was. I listened as his footsteps came up behind me, until he was standing at my side, neither one of us looking at the other.

"If you go with him," he said, "if you leave without saying good-bye to Peach and break her heart, don't expect me to do a jig if you ever bother to come back."

And with that, he went through the gate. I stood outside, listening as his steps stomped up the porch, as the front door slammed behind him. I stood in the dark for a while, trying not to fall apart, and once I thought I had a handle on myself, I went out to the street where I found Leo, leaning against the Bug, waiting for me.

"Everything okay?" he asked when I reached him.

"Yeah, sure," I said on a jagged breath, forcing a smile.

Leo didn't smile back. He'd seen Nick storm out from the backyard, and they had been friends long enough for him to know how bad it had to get for Nick to get mad. "You sure?"

"No," I said, and when I didn't say any more, we got in the car in silence and drove home.

Chapter 15

I spent the rest of the afternoon futilely searching the Internet for anything I could use against Desmond until I got so tense that Leo sat me back on the bed and . . . well. Relaxed me.

"For science," he'd said, with a glint in his eye.

I controlled my magic perfectly. I was now at the point where I didn't need sex to do it, but I wasn't about to tell Leo that. I needed the sex to block out everything else: the sadness, the fear, the guilt. In his arms, with him inside me, everything seemed right, even when it was horribly, horribly wrong.

Afterward, while he napped, I stared up at my ceiling, watching it spin above me, first one way, then another, like a ball twirling back and forth on the end of a string. There was a moment when things started going dark, and I realized I had stopped breathing. I took in deep breaths, consciously willing the air in and out of my lungs, until the world stabilized enough for me to sneak out to the shed. I retrieved a vial from my dwindling supply. After the vial I gave to Peach to take care of the Widow, that left only two remaining. Something had to work out, fast, or this

was going to end really, really badly, really, really fast.
With shaky hands, I filled it with water and drank it down.
I settled on my stolen bar stool and waited until the world
started to look normal again, then went back to the 'Bago,
crawled into bed next to Leo, and slept, taking it on blind
faith that I would wake up again.

I did.

Liv and Tobias stopped by at eight that night. We made
coffee and sat around my little kitchenette table. It was
crazy how intimate and casual it felt, like we were just
two couples getting together to drink some coffee and play
some cards.

"Turns out, Desmond has been on the radar with the
magical agencies for a while now," Tobias said, sliding a
manila folder across the table to me. "And with good reason."

I flipped the folder open and scanned over the print-
outs inside.

"Desmond Benedict?" I pointed to the name on the
top of the first page, which was full of sparse, simple
sentences typed in a stark Courier font. Some of the information was blacked out with marker; it looked like
one of those leaked governmental reports you find on
conspiracy websites.

"He changed it to Lamb when he emigrated to Canada," Tobias said.

I flipped a page; it was a photocopy of a page from the
Haslemere Herald. In the middle of the page was a gray
smudge that indicated a highlighted name and there it was:
Desmond Benedict, one name in a list of graduates from
the local high school. I flipped another page, and found
another photocopy with another gray smudge highlight,
this time a mention in the alumni newsletter that Desmond
Benedict had graduated at the top of his class at Oxford
and gotten a full scholarship to medical school.

Liv leaned forward. "Most of this is just background stuff. It gets interesting about . . ." She flipped through a few pages, then stuffed her index finger on one. "Here."

I glanced at Leo, then read out loud. *"Dr. Desmond Benedict, a neurologist originally of Haslemere, Surrey, had his medical license revoked for the unauthorized use of the brains of human cadavers for personal research . . ."* I pulled back, trying to gain distance between me and the page. "Eww."

"Yeah," Liv said, and reached over to flip a few more pages for me. "This is also interesting."

It was a blog post from a woman named Alysia Creek, a journalism student from London, talking about the day she spent shopping with her boyfriend. There was nothing particularly interesting about it, just your standard navel-gazing, but at the bottom of the page, there was a picture of her with the boyfriend. She was stunning. Dark eyes; long, curly brown hair; a creamy complexion most women would kill for. She was laughing and turning her head to look at a tall man, who held her from behind and smiled at the camera, awkward but delighted. It took me a moment to recognize him.

"Oh, my God," I said, and leaned in to get a closer look.

"Hey, is that . . . ?" Leo said, coming to the same delayed recognition.

"Yep," Liv said. "Took me a minute, too."

The post was some eight years old, but still . . . even in the photocopied printout, I could recognize Desmond. The high cheekbones, the wide-set eyes, the curly brown hair a little longer than he kept it now. But at the same time that it was Desmond, it wasn't. This guy's eyes were warm, and he had the distinct look of a dork in love: happy, surprised by his own good fortune, and vulnerable to the point where it almost hurt to look at him.

"Maybe . . . is this his twin or something?" I asked. "Because that's him, but that's not him."

Liv pointed her finger to a spot on the page. "Not unless both twins were named Desmond."

And there it was. Alysia had written, *Desmond was a darling about all the shoes I bought.*

A darling? Huh.

"Notice anything else?" Liv asked.

I stared down at the picture, scanned the text of the post quickly, and raised my head to look at her. "No. What?"

"She looks like you," Leo said, his voice stiff.

I looked at the picture again, trying to see the resemblance. Aside from the long, dark hair, I didn't see it. "No, she doesn't. She looks sweet."

"You're sweet," Liv said in that automatic way best friends use to when they're lying to your face.

I gave her a look. "Please."

"Deep, deep . . . you know, *deep* down," she said.

Leo pulled the picture closer to take a longer look, and I focused on Tobias.

"Anything else of note?"

"Yeah," he said darkly. "A few weeks before he left England, she went into a mental institution, and a month after being admitted to the institution, she hanged herself with a bedsheet."

I heard Desmond's voice in my head. *Those women sacrificed for a reason, and I won't have that sacrifice rendered meaningless because some upstart bitch is having a crisis of conscience.*

"Doesn't say much about why she went into the hospital in the first place," Tobias went on, "but something went south in her brain about six months after Desmond got his license revoked for messing with brains. It's a hell of a coincidence."

Leo shut the manila folder and set it back in front of

me. I could feel the tension coming off him in waves. I reached out and took his hand, then looked straight at Tobias.

"Thank you," I said. "I hope this doesn't cause you any problems. I know it was a big thing to ask."

Tobias shrugged. "I have some friends I trust on the inside. I'm not worried." He seemed to be genuinely unconcerned when he said it, but when I looked at Liv, there was strain in her smile.

"If it helps you fix all of this, it's worth it," she said.

"Well, that sucked," I said to Leo later as we were getting ready for bed.

"We got some good information," he said.

"Yeah, and I risked Tobias's safety and Liv's happiness to do it. And I don't even know if it's anything I can work with." I sat on the edge of the bed and threw myself backward. "Maybe Nick's right."

Leo got on the bed and pulled me into his arms. "What did Nick say?"

"He said that I do whatever I want, and to hell with everyone else."

Leo kissed me on the forehead. "Do you think he's right?"

I sighed. "Yes."

"Okay."

I looked up at him. "Do you think he's right?"

Leo smiled. "Yeah."

"Gee. Thanks."

"Stacy . . . it's not a bad thing," he said. "You always look at yourself in the most negative possible light. You have to stop that. It's not good for you."

I rolled over on my side. "Fine. You tell me how being selfish and not caring about how what I do affects other people is a positive thing."

He reached out and moved my hair away from my face. "That's not what I said. Look, when things are important, you do what needs doing. You're a person who gets things done, who makes things happen."

"I'm Stacy goddamned Easter," I said, and closed my eyes.

"Yes, you are," he said softly, "and don't ever forget what an amazing thing that is."

I put my hand over my face. "I've run out of time, Leo."

He moved closer to me on the bed. "Don't say that."

I lifted my head. "There are two vials left, that's it. Best-case scenario, I talk Desmond into taking me with him as his lab rat—"

Leo's eyes flashed. "You're not going anywhere with him."

"—and the worst-case scenario is that he runs off and leaves us with no cure, no more of the vials to keep us going, and we all die."

"That's not going to happen," Leo said.

"You don't know that. You can't know that."

He raised his eyes to look at me. "I know."

"How?" I said, lowering my hand, fully frustrated. "How in hell can you know that?"

He smiled at me, the most simple, beautiful smile. "Because I have faith." He pulled me into his arms. "Because you're Stacy goddamned Easter, and I know you. I know what you're capable of, and I know that Desmond Lamb or Benedict or whoever the hell he is has no idea what he's dealing with."

"Oh, you sweet, sweet man," I said, putting my hand to his face. "Get out now. Save yourself."

Leo's eyes darkened. "I hate when you do that, you know."

"What?"

"I'm not perfect, Stacy. I've made mistakes. I was the one who cheated, I was the one who left. You act like you're so broken and I'm so good—"

"Because it's the truth!" I pushed up to sitting, slamming my hand on the bed, unable to contain my frustration. "And I mean it, Leo. You should get out while you still can, before my damage breaks your heart. Before . . . before I do something to make you look at me with disappointment, and that breaks mine."

Leo sat up as well, pulling his legs up and resting his forearms on them as he looked at me. "Do you really want me to leave?"

"No," I whined, "but you should. Any idiot can see that. I'm trouble. Nick can see it, my mother can see it . . ."

"You gotta stop letting your mother into your head," Leo said.

"Even if she's right?"

"She's not."

I turned my face to the wall and swiped at my eyes. I was too tired, beyond exhausted, scared to death, and this was too much for me to handle. There was a reason why I'd never had a serious relationship since Leo left: It was too much damn *work*.

"Do you want me to leave?" he asked quietly.

"No," I said, then followed that up immediately with, "Yes."

"Okay, let me put it another way. Do you love me?"

"Oh, God, not this," I said.

"Do you love me?"

"It doesn't matter, Leo."

"It matters more than anything else," he said, his voice calm and quiet. "Do you love me?"

I didn't say anything. I couldn't. He spooned me against him, his body warm and comforting behind me, making me feel safe for the first time since he'd last held me like that in high school. That last of my strength to fight left me, and I snuggled next to him and let the comfort in.

"I love you," he said softly in my ear, "and you love me. Why can't we just do that?"

I tightened my grip on his arms around my middle. "I won't survive it."

"Won't survive what?"

"Losing you," I said.

"Then don't," he whispered, and held on to me tighter.

"It's not that simple."

"Close your eyes."

I did, and Leo smoothed my hair back and gently kissed my neck.

"It's possible this could all go horribly wrong," he said. "You could die. I could die. Bad things can happen. There are no guarantees."

"Wow," I said, glancing over my shoulder at him. "Did you fail Comforting 101 in priest school or what?"

He smiled. "Close your eyes."

He waited until I did as told, and then he tightened his hold on me.

"It's also possible that things could work out. We could figure these problems out. We could be happy every day for the rest of our lives. We could grow old together. We could have children, grandchildren. Adventures. It is possible that we could love each other freely and without restraint for the rest of our lives."

My eyes whipped open. "Wow."

"What?"

I turned over onto my back and looked up at him. "I just . . . I never thought . . . ."

"You never thought for a moment that the Universe wouldn't punish you for just being you?"

I lowered my head and rested it against his arm. "No. Never."

He gave a small, sad laugh. His eyes trailed over my face until they met mine again.

"You're not broken," he said. "You weren't born Wrong, and the world hasn't been punishing you. You're an amazing, strong, beautiful woman and you deserve good things." He kissed me behind my ear. "Tell me something?"

"Something," I mumbled, snuggling up next to him.

"What does your perfect world look like?"

"I don't know," I said sleepily.

"Imagine it," he said.

I took a moment, and did just that. I imagined Leo and me, happy together. Sex on a blanket under the stars. Dancing to Frank Sinatra at our wedding. Sunshine and hot days and a grubby, grinning kid with chocolate ice cream smudged on his chin. Leo teaching him how to ride a bike, then looking back at me with excitement when he takes off, zooming down the street on his own power. I saw us having Thanksgiving dinner with Peach and Nick and Liv and Tobias. I saw us decorating Christmas trees, taking a horde of kids out for Halloween.

Up until that moment, when I thought about my future, I never saw . . . anything. Just a flat expanse of pretty much the same life: alone, predictable, under my control. Never loving anyone, and never allowing anyone to love me. I had always been okay with that. It had always seemed like the only way life could work, and I'd always felt kind of sorry for the people who tried to make it work any other way. Too much pain, not enough benefit.

But watching Leo teach that imaginary kid to ride that bike changed me, in an instant. I *wanted* that life. I wanted it so bad that it felt like my insides were reaching out for it, pushing me into a place I didn't think existed. I fell asleep dreaming about that world, and believing for the first time in my life that it might actually be possible.

Even now, I don't entirely know what I was thinking. I woke up at two in the morning. Leo was fast asleep, and I slid easily out of bed without waking him up. All I meant to do was sit at the table, look over the information, see if maybe I'd catch a useful detail in there somewhere. When I picked up my car keys and slid outside, even then, I wasn't really intending to confront Desmond. I was just jumpy, and I thought a drive might soothe my nerves. It wasn't until I pulled into the little parking lot at the back of Grace and Addie's B&B that I realized I was doing exactly what I'd intended all along.

"I see we have something else in common," Desmond said as he stepped aside to let me into the foyer. "We are both night owls."

I didn't say anything, but he didn't seem concerned about my lack of response.

"My hostesses have abandoned the place to my care," he said, leading me through the foyer to the living room, "and they were kind enough to leave a fully stocked bar behind."

I followed him to the living room, sat down on the pink antique chaise longue, and set Tobias's folder beside me while Desmond dipped behind the bar.

"Thanks. I'll pass."

Desmond shrugged as he poured himself two fingers of whiskey. "Surely you don't think I'd dose you with something now?"

"Surely I do, jackass," I said.

Desmond snorted out a laugh. He bent down, pulled a bottled water out of the mini fridge, and walked over to me.

"It's perfectly safe," he said. "As you can see, it's got one of those little pull-tabs at the top. No tampering."

He held it out to me. I kept my hands in my lap.

"As you wish, m'lady." He set the water on the coffee table and downed a sip of his whiskey before settling in the Queen Anne chair opposite me. "I see you've brought some reading material with you. Anything interesting?"

"Yes," I said, "Mr. Benedict."

He hesitated mid-sip to meet my eyes. "I'm sorry. Is that supposed to have me shaking in my Wellies? I expected all that to come up when you ran the background check on me before you started buying my product."

I lowered my eyes, and he chuckled. "No background check? Tsk, tsk. For a woman of the world, Ms. Easter, you can sometimes be horribly naive. Although I must admit I'm pleased to have inspired such trust in you."

"I don't care about your name, and I don't care about your revoked medical license." I opened the folder and pulled out the page with the picture of him and Alysia. "I care about her."

His head angled a bit to look at the picture, and whatever light was in his eyes deadened. "Yes. I see."

"You loved her," I said quietly.

His eyes flicked up to meet mine. They were cold and hard, almost inhuman. "I did, yes."

"And you're the reason she killed herself," I said.

He blinked slowly, almost as if something inside were fighting the effects of the potion. "Yes."

"You know what I find interesting?" I said. "In that picture, you're a man in love. I've seen them before, I know the look. But now, you look at the picture and there's nothing. No expression at all, as if you have no feelings about essentially killing the woman you love. How'd that happen, Des?"

He reached out and flicked the paper over, then took a deep breath. "You know exactly how that happened. You've felt it."

"I remember," I said. "When I saw Leo at the wedding, it felt like I was trying to move through mud. When I was with him, right up until it wore off, I felt kind of dead inside. It took energy and effort to feel connected to anything when he was around. Is that how it is for you?"

He narrowed his eyes at me. "What is this about?"

I picked up the picture of the two of them and studied it. "I almost didn't recognize you when I saw it. There's something missing now, like you've hacked out a piece of your soul. Is that how Anwei Xing works when you use the root?"

"Am I supposed to be impressed by your cleverness?" he said, a small curl of a smile on his face even as his eyes remained unamused. "I will gladly applaud if it's what you're searching for. You'll forgive me; my ability to read social cues has suffered a bit under the influence."

He lifted his glass, and I could see the tiniest shake in his pinkie as he drank. The Anwei Xing was working, but there was an edge zone to it, a small area where he could touch the feelings about Alysia that he was trying to bury. I couldn't stop myself; I poked.

"How do you think Alysia would feel," I said carefully, "if she knew that even her death didn't stop you from killing other women?"

The slap came so fast, it wasn't until I hit the floor that I even realized I'd been hit. I blinked to get my bearings, and at first all I was able to process was how clean the hardwood on Addie's living room floor was. No dust bunnies under the couch. Amazing.

Desmond sat in his seat, patiently waiting for me to push myself up. I got up on shaky legs and stood before him. He raised his eyes to me.

"When I was young, I accidentally hit a girl in the

mouth with my elbow during a football game." He glanced at me. "Our football, not yours. Anyway, I suffered over that for days. Fifteen years old, and I cried myself to sleep that night because I'd hit a girl by accident. And now . . . here I am." He looked at his hand, the back of which was red from the force with which he'd just hit me, and his eyes were lit with amazement. I touched my lip and winced, then drew my hand back; there was blood on my fingertips.

"It's sort of a miracle, isn't it?" he went on. "To be free from all that debilitating guilt, all that horrible self-loathing? You also lose something, to be certain. The kind of simple joy other people have when watching children at play, or littering their Facebook pages with captioned pictures of cats. The joy associated with those first moments when love blooms." He smiled at me, as though we were friends. "Well, I guess you don't have that, either. Love is nothing but pain for you, isn't it?"

The shock from being hit was beginning to wear off, and I was able to catch my breath and speak again. "No. It's not just pain."

"No? It certainly seemed that way that night in my apartment, when you came to me, crying, begging me for the smallest taste of what I have every day." He raised his brow at me. "And if I recall correctly, love was pain for you the night you took me to your bed, just on the chance that it would help you forget him for a few moments."

"Don't bring him into this," I said, and Desmond's eyes lit with fury as he slammed his fist down on the table.

"You brought *her into it*!" he shouted, and bolted up from his chair. Instinctively, I cringed away from him, and he stopped.

"Good," he said. "I see I've gotten my message across.

I mean business, and I guarantee you, I'm the party willing to get the bloodiest here."

"Only one of us is bloody right now," I said, "and I'm still standing here, aren't I?"

He held my eyes for a moment, then his face broke out in a cold, dead smile. "Yes, you are." He glanced back at the papers on the table. "I'm not sure what it was you wanted out of this meeting, but I do hope you got it."

"Not yet." I moved forward and put my hand on his arm. "I'm here to give you a message."

There was a quizzical look in his eyes, and his nose twitched a bit before he realized that the burning smell in the room was, in fact, his shirtsleeve. He jerked his arm away and batted at the flames on his arm.

"Let me make myself clear here," I said. "I have power, as much power as my mother, and it's all under my control."

He batted away the last of the fire and looked at me. "That's your message, is it?"

"No," I said. "The message is subtext, but I see you're a little preoccupied, so let me state it outright: If you ever raise a hand to me again, I'll kill you where you stand."

"I see," he said. "And who will keep your friends alive when I'm gone?"

"I've got a bit of a temper, Desmond. You don't want to bet your life on the hope that I'll have time to think about that before it gets the best of me."

I leaned over to grab the folder off the chaise when he moved closer and put one hand on my arm. I straightened slowly, my entire body tense, waiting for the attack, but it didn't come.

"For someone with so much concern for consequences," he said, his voice cold in my ear, "you certainly seem to disregard them with vigor."

"Screw you, Desmond," I said and walked out, shutting the front door quietly behind me before going out to my car and driving in dazed circles around town until the sun rose.

Chapter 16

Leo was sitting at the kitchenette table dialing a number into his cell phone when I walked in. He hung up and stood, smiling. Based on the pillow crinkles on his face and the way his hair was still mussed on the left side, I guessed he'd woken up pretty recently.

"Hey, you," he said, his voice still creaky. "I was just calling you to—"

His expression went dark as he looked at me, and his voice was strong and serious when he spoke again.

"What happened?"

I dumped my keys on the counter. "I went to see Desmond."

"Why didn't you wake me?"

I turned to the cabinet and pulled out the ceramic canister I kept my coffee in. "Because I didn't want to see him with you."

"Because I would have stopped you," he said. "Because it was *stupid*."

He moved close and touched my chin, and I swatted his hand away. I pulled the top of the canister off. "Crap. I'm out of coffee."

"Hey." He took my shoulders in his hands and turned me to face him. I could see the anger in his eyes and I could feel my face crumple as the tears filled my own. Leo's expression went from anger to concern in a split second, and he pulled me into his arms. "Hey, it's okay. You're safe. I've got you."

I held on to him. "It was that stupid little boy," I said, sniffling into his shoulder.

"All right," he said patiently, then added, "What little boy?"

"You were teaching him how to ride a bike, and you were so happy."

Leo pulled back a bit and looked at me, his hands feeling my head through my hair. "I have no idea what you're talking about. Did you hit your head?"

"No," I said, and gave a little laugh-sob. "I saw him. In our future. Last night, you asked me to imagine . . ."

I trailed off, and Leo's expression softened as he smiled at me. "Oh."

"And I woke up at two in the morning and I couldn't sleep because I kept thinking about that little boy and I want that boy. I want that life, with you, and I couldn't stand the thought of just waiting here for Desmond to take that away, so I went over there and I pissed him off and he hit me, which was predictable because . . . you know . . . crazy." I sniffled, glanced down at the empty coffee canister, and started crying again. "And now I'm out of coffee."

"It's all right." He pulled me into his arms again and kissed the unbruised side of my face. "I will make sure you have coffee, every day, for the rest of your life, okay?"

He held me tight and I wrapped my arms around his neck. Deep in the back of my head, I heard the old me saying, *It's too good to be true, don't count on this, it won't work,* but I shushed her. She was stupid. She was the *reason* things never worked, and I wasn't going to let her ruin my life. Not anymore.

I pulled back and looked up at him. "I'm really sorry. I would want to kill you if you did what I did."

"I don't get to tell you what you can and can't do," he said, his voice resigned. "I just ask that you remember that if you get hurt, I get hurt. Okay?"

I nodded. "I'll remember. I swear. No more stupid stuff. I promise."

He laughed. "I can't expect that. I just . . ." He let out a huff, and I noticed that his eyes were a little reddened around the edges, and my heart cracked.

"God, I'm so sorry, Leo," I said. "I'm so—"

"Marry me?" he said, his voice so rough and cracked with emotion that I almost didn't hear him.

"What?" I asked.

"Marry me," he said again, his voice stronger, and there was no question in his tone this time.

"Leo," I said, a little too stunned to say more than that, and he swiped at his eyes.

"I know I'm supposed to do this better," he said. "I know I should plan it, and there should be a nice dinner and a ring and getting down on one knee and enough wine to make you just stupid enough to say yes, but—"

"Yes," I said.

"Wait, I need to say something to you first—"

"Yes," I said again.

He took my hands firmly in his. "Let me finish? Please?"

"Yes," I said, and grinned, and he gave me a why-I-oughta look, but then took a breath and went on.

"You don't have to say yes now," he said, enunciating carefully to get his point through my thick head. "There are a lot of things going on, and everything would be hellishly confusing even without all that, but I don't want anything to happen without you knowing that I love you

and I want to marry you and someday, I'm going to do this right. I need you to know that."

I waited a moment, then said, "Are you done?"

He sighed. "Yes."

"Yes," I said.

His face broke out in the widest grin I'd ever seen. "Really?"

"*Yes!* God, what does a girl have to do to accept a marriage proposal from you? You want it in skywriting? Then I gotta make a few calls."

He pulled me into his arms and lifted me up and kissed the side of my face. I held on to him tight, loving him more than I ever thought possible, and feeling happier than I ever had in my life. He set me down and kissed me gently on my bruised mouth, then pulled back and smiled at me.

"God, you're beautiful," he said.

"I know," I said. "I'm also going to drop on the floor if I don't get some coffee."

"All right," he said. "CCB's?"

"Awesome."

I reached for my keys on the counter, but he swiped them into his hand before I got to them. "I'm driving. Tired driving is just as dangerous as drunk driving, and you've been taking enough chances lately."

"All right," I said, my voice sweet and accommodating. "See how I'm learning to compromise? It's like I was born to be married."

He gave me a wry smile, and then my back pocket buzzed. I pulled out my cell phone and swiped to answer the call.

"Hello, Mrs. North speaking," I said, and giggled.

There was dead silence on the other line, then a sandpapery southern voice said, "Yeah, I think I got the wrong number."

"No!" I said quickly. "Cain! Are you here? Are you in town?"

"Easter? That you?"

"Yeah, it's me. Where are you?"

"I'm just turning off the highway. You okay?"

"Yeah," I said and smiled at Leo, who grinned back at me. "I'm just happy."

"Happy?" he said, as if he didn't understand the meaning of the word.

"And in dire need of coffee," I said. "Meet me at CCB's, ten minutes."

I hung up and took Leo's hand. "This is your day, babe. You're about to meet a bona fide southern conjurer."

Neither Clementine nor Liv was working at CCB's that morning. Betty was running the crowded front counter and the day waitress, Brenda, was flying through the dining room, so I just nabbed a booth in the back where we could keep an eye out for both Cain and, just in case, Desmond. Leo and I sat together on one side of the booth, facing the empty seat.

"God, I swore I would never sit like this," I said, rolling my eyes at us both. "It's so dorky."

Leo smiled. "You want me to sit over there?" He motioned to the other side with his chin.

"Shut up," I said, grinning, and took his hand in mine.

We had just gotten our coffee when the bells on the door jingled and a tall, scraggly, dirty-blond southern boy in dire need of a haircut walked in.

"There he is," I said, and waved. Cain noticed me and ambled over, as much as a guy could amble in a crowded waffle house at breakfast time.

"I can never get used to this town," he grumbled as he

slid in across from us. "There's a lady up at the counter wearing a damned fedora."

"Her name is Filly Jones," I said. "She was my pre-school teacher."

Cain gave me a dead look. "Filly Jones. You shitting me?"

"It's small-town charm," I said. "Shut up."

Cain gave me a one-sided smirk—his way of saying it was good to see me—and then he held out his hand to Leo.

"Cain Taggert," he said.

"Leo North." They shook and Leo added, "I'm Stacy's . . . um . . ." He looked at me and we exchanged an entire conversation in a glance, in which we both agreed that we wouldn't tell anyone we were getting married before we told Liv.

"He's just mine," I said, and Cain's eyebrow went up a bit. Then he reached into his pocket and pulled out a small black metal box, which, for all its tiny size, looked like serious business. It even had a metal latch.

"Oh, cute." I grinned at him. "You brought me a hamster's Samsonite. How thoughtful."

He stared at me, looking uneasy. "What'd he do to you?"

"Who?" I motioned to Leo. "Him?"

"No. The bad guy." Cain watched me, on alert, eyes darting suspiciously around CCB's. "You're beaten up, and acting weird."

I fiddled with the catch on the box. "What do you mean, weird?"

"I don't know." He paused for a moment, thinking. "Happy, I guess."

"Well, the bruise is because of the bad guy. The happy is because of Leo." I flipped the top on the box and en-cased in black foam was the smallest little brown vial I'd ever seen. I held it up to the light; inside was maybe five drops of solution.

"Wow," I said, tucking it back in the case. "What is it?"

"The best shot you've got," he said. "You need to get that into his system fast, and undiluted. Every drop. That means no mixing it with a drink."

I stared at him. "Huh? How am I supposed to get it in his system?"

"You can try skin contact but you've got to get all of it on his skin, and he's got to leave it there long enough for it to seep through, without washing it off. I'd say hypodermic is your best way to go. Inject him wherever you can, but the neck's the best place. Right into the jugular."

"Ew," I said, and Leo put his arm around my shoulder.

"Man up, Easter," Cain went on, his eyes sharp on mine. "This is how it works. You got one dose, one shot, and it's good for another forty-eight hours to get it into his system, max. It was hard enough getting my hands on that one, so you gotta get it right the first try."

"You didn't make it yourself?" Leo asked.

Cain looked at him. "No, I had to go out of house on that one. The guy wouldn't give me the formula, and he got on a plane back to Kenya last night, if he was even telling me the truth about where he was going."

I put my hands over the small case. "So, it's just one dose? And this will make him feel again?"

"Maybe," Cain said, his voice grim.

"Maybe?"

"Got a lot of cloudy variables here, Easter," he said. "I don't know how your guy mixed his Anwei Xing. I don't know how long ago he took it. Permanent magic like that is a big deal."

"Magic, or science?" I said, mostly to myself, but Cain said, "Huh?" and I looked at him.

"This guy," I said. "Desmond. He's a neurologist. Or he was, anyway. He says it's not magic, it's science. Chemicals. He says there are no magical consequences for violating free will, that it's all just superstitious rubbish."

Cain shrugged, and I felt a twinge of uneasiness.

"Hey," I said. "You were the one who told me about the consequences. There are consequences, right? I mean, magic is going to come back and find you if you break the rules, right?"

"There are consequences," Cain said. "I don't know if I'd call 'em magic. You reap what you sow. You violate free will, it's my belief that someday, you're gonna pay for that. You just have to decide whether it's worth it or not."

I carefully tucked the small case in my pocket. "It'll be worth it. I'm pretty sure."

"Yeah, well, don't forget. You're looking at maybe a fifty–fifty chance this will even work. I hope you've got a backup plan."

"I always have a backup plan."

"Yeah?" Cain huffed. "What is it?"

I smiled. "I'll tell you when I think of it."

Next to me, I could feel Leo tense. I had just turned around to look at him when he bolted out of the seat and pushed his way to the door. Through the open venetian blinds at the front of CCB's, I saw the faintest glimpse of brown tweed moving away at a pace.

"Oh, shit," I said, and ran out after him. I shouted, "Put the coffee on my tab!" at Brenda and nearly knocked Filly Jones off her counter stool as I ran out.

I looked first left, then right, and there was no sign of either Leo or Desmond, but I heard a shout from the alley to the right, and ran that way. When I got there, Leo had Desmond up against the brick wall, his forearm pressing against Desmond's throat.

"Leo!" I shouted, but he was focused entirely on Des.

"I swear to God, I should kill you now," he said.

Desmond moved his neck against the pressure of Leo's arm, and when he spoke, his voice was strained. "If you do, she dies. That's worse than a split lip, isn't it?"

Leo's eyes narrowed and he cursed, then gave Desmond one last slam against the wall before releasing him.

"This the guy?" I heard Cain say behind me, but I put my arm out to stop him from getting into the fray, and he stayed where he was.

"You touch her again," Leo said, "and I will kill you."

Desmond smirked. "I doubt much you'll care."

He tipped his imaginary hat at me then turned to walk down the alley and disappeared into the shadows. I watched after him, my panicked heart thrumming in my ears to the point where I didn't hear Leo talking to me until he touched my arm.

"Hey, Stacy," he said, his eyes shrouded with concern. "You okay?"

He couldn't have, I thought. *How would he . . . ?*

I blinked twice and looked at him. Leo, my Leo . . .

"Oh, God," I said, and reached out to touch a spot on his neck, a tiny red dot that I might never have noticed if I wasn't looking for signs of a hypodermic injection. "Did you fight? Did he touch you?"

Leo stared at me, confused. "A little. I got the better of him, though."

He let you get the better of him, I thought, and I pulled Cain's arm and tilted Leo's head to the side for Cain to see the tiny dot.

"Um . . . Stace?" Leo said.

I didn't respond, just looked at Cain, whose expression was grim.

"Wait here," he said, and disappeared out to the street.

"Stacy?" Leo blinked and looked at me, his eyes growing hazy. "What's going on?"

And then he pitched forward. I caught him just in time before he cracked his head on the brick wall, and I eased him to the ground.

"It's gonna be okay," I said. "I promise."

He looked at me, our eyes locked . . . and there was nothing there. Just a dead expression.

Like Desmond's.

"Move back."

I jumped at the sound of Cain's voice; I hadn't even heard his footsteps behind me.

"Leo." Cain knelt next to Leo and handed him a small vial of clear liquid. "Drink this. It's gonna taste bad, so do it fast. Got it?"

"Yeah." Leo took the vial from Cain and stared at it as if trying to focus. "What is it?"

"Just drink."

Leo took the cap off and shot the liquid down, then made a face and gagged. "Ugh, Christ!"

Cain took the vial back, then looked at me. "It'll just be a minute."

We all went still. I could hear the sounds of traffic moving down the street behind us, normal life continuing on as though it had any right. Then Leo leaned away from us and vomited onto the asphalt.

"That's a positive," Cain said.

"A positive what?"

"That reaction means he's got something magic in him," Cain said.

"Okay," I said, the panic throttling my voice into shrillness. "Okay. He's throwing it all up. It's okay."

"It's not in his stomach," Cain said darkly. "It's in his blood. All this does is confirm that Desmond shot him up with something powerful. It doesn't . . ."

Cain trailed off, and I closed my eyes, but all I could

see was Leo staring at me with that dead look, and all I could hear was Desmond's voice.

I doubt much you'll care.

"Desmond gave me something," I said. "He used the Anwei Xing to cut out my feelings for Leo."

"You sure that's what's what's going on here?"

I nodded. "Yes. He lured Leo out here. He's using Leo to get to me."

Leo retched again, but there was nothing left to come out. He leaned back against the brick wall, breathing heavy, his head hung low.

"It only lasted twelve hours when he gave it to me," I said, rubbing the gooseflesh that was prickling all over my arms. When I looked up, Cain was staring down at me under dark brows, an unusually concerned look in his eye.

"What?" I said.

"He administered this hypodermically," he said. "You only do that if you mean business."

On instinct, I stood up and reached for the small case in my pocket.

"Easter, wait," Cain said, grabbing my arm to stop me. "Getting you one of those was a damned miracle in itself. I don't know if I can get you another one."

I looked down at Leo. His head was still low, as if he didn't have the strength to hold it up on his own.

"I can't lose him," I said weakly. "Not now. I can't. You don't understand . . ."

"All right." Cain's voice came from behind me, but I didn't look at him. "You got a workshop?"

A sharp stab of hope sliced through my heart. "Do you think you can make another dose of that stuff?"

Cain's expression was grim. "No. But maybe we can put together that backup plan. Show me your workshop. Tell me everything you know. We'll figure something out."

I hesitated, staring at Leo.

"It's better than doing nothing," Cain said. "Sitting here in an alley isn't helping anyone."

"Okay," I said. "My workshop is at home."

"All right," Cain said, and got to the business of helping Leo to his feet.

Work was comforting, at least. Three hours later, Cain and I were no closer to having a real plan in place, but we'd made a handful of potions and even though they'd be all but useless in this fight—I could use a Lie Detector potion, but Desmond was a sociopath, not a liar—it felt good to be doing something. And the longer I was away from Leo, the more I could imagine him waking up from his sleep back in the 'Bago, loving me again.

"I'm sorry," Cain said as we were cleaning up, his voice uncharacteristically gentle. "It was a lot of work, tracking that magic down for you. I haven't slept and I'm tired. Once I get some sleep, maybe I'll think of something. You got a little time."

"Right." I took the last purple vial off my shelf and tucked it into the bag, then ran my fingers over my two bulbous Edison vials, watching the blue, swirly liquid moving under my fingers. I'd worked so hard on those, put all my magical energies into them, and they seemed so silly to me now.

I took one and threw it on the ground.

"What the . . . ?" Cain jumped a bit, then turned around and looked down. Slowly, a magical sunflower burst up from the ground, glowing and dancing to the silence.

"Huh," Cain said, his eyes on the sunflower. "You did that?"

I nodded. "Yeah."

"On your own, with no real training?"

I must have looked pretty pathetic, because Cain kept

his opinion on that to himself, although I could see him struggling not to yell at me for taking that kind of risk.

"Pretty impressive," he said after a long pause.

"Yeah. It is." I turned my back on the sunflower. "Lot of good it does me now."

"Hey." Cain put his hand on my arm, and I looked up at him. "Things looked pretty bad this time last year, too. We got through that. We'll get through this."

"We didn't all get through it," I said, and our eyes met as the coldness of Millie's ghost passed through us both. Cain took his hand off my arm and nodded, then went back to clearing the last of the stuff on the workbench.

I knelt down and looked at my sunflower, wishing I could feel the pride and happiness I'd felt the first time I'd gotten it to work. All I could see now was dancing light that was slowly going to fade away into nothing, and the world would go on as if it had never existed in the first place.

"Science, my ass," I said. I stood up, tucking the last sunflower potion into my bag. Whatever I had or didn't have, whether Leo would ever love me or not, I was the girl who made the stupid magic sunflowers. It didn't make me feel much better, but it was all I had, and right now I had to hold on to whatever I could get.

Chapter 17

Leo was awake when we got back to the 'Bago, but he was still looking at me with that dead, muddy expression. I called Liv and we headed over there, claiming we needed her space to put up Cain, but really, I just wanted the comfort of being near my best friend. And the guy who could kill Desmond with a look if he decided to screw with us again.

I left Leo with Tobias and Cain in the living room, and went out back with Liv to sit in the Adirondack chairs by her mother's garden. Her mother's urn and Millie's sat side by side in the corner of the garden, surrounded by flowers and the occasional ceramic frog, which, prior to today, had always made me smile. The girl had a bunny made from a mug, but the ceramics that were actually made to like real critters were just decoration.

"How are you doing?" she asked.

"I don't know," I said, taking a sip from the iced tea she'd given me. "I think bad. Mostly, I'm numb. Kind of hollow. I think maybe that's because it's not over. Once it's over, I'll fall apart."

"Yep." She took a sip of her own drink and we sat in silence for a while. More than anyone in the world, Liv understood what I was going through. "If there's anything I can do—"

"You're doing it," I said. "Just giving us a place to stay for a few days, so I can figure this out. It really helps."

She let out a little laugh. "Power doesn't count for much, does it?"

I looked at her. "What do you mean?"

"I mean, here I am, right? I have evolving magic, magic I can control and strengthen. Magic so rare that someone tried to kill me to steal it from me. I have both day and night magic. I'm a freaking unicorn and . . ." She shrugged. "What can I do? I can make you a fish out of a keychain. I can't help. I can't make Desmond give you the cure. I can't fix you, or your mom, or Ms. Troudt, or Clementine. It's frustrating."

"I know," I said. "I can make a potion that will make you fart rainbows, but I can't make Leo love me again. How stupid is that?"

"Oh, baby." She reached out and put her hand over mine. "He'll come back to you."

"Yeah?" I swiped at my face. "How do you know that?"

She gave me a sad smile. "Because he's Leo, and that's what he does. Sometimes it takes a while, but he comes back."

Just then, we heard steps behind us. I shifted in my seat and there was Leo, looking a little haggard, but standing on his own power, which was good.

Liv hopped up out of her seat. "Sit down, Leo. I'll go get you something to drink. Water? Iced tea?"

"Water'd be great," he said, his voice scratchy.

"Here," she said, and handed him her iced tea. "Take this for now, if that doesn't gross you out."

He let out a short laugh. "I used to drink wine from a glass with a thousand people every Sunday." He held up the iced tea and smiled at her. "Thanks."

I watched him as he watched her go, his face full of warmth and affection. And then he looked at me, and the light in his eyes went out. I must have reacted to it, because he said, "Damnit," and sat down heavily in Liv's vacant chair.

"It's okay," I said. "I have something you can take. It'll be okay. It'll bring you back."

He shook his head. "You have one dose. You can't use it on me."

"I've made the decision, Leo."

He shook his head. "It's not your decision to make. I won't take it."

"That's easy for you to say," I said, my throat tightening. "You don't feel anything when you look at me. You're numb. I'm the one who's hurting."

"You think I don't feel this?" He stared at me. "I remember all of it. I remember every night I was away, how I forgot every detail of this town and everyone in it, but I saw your face, clear as a bell. I remember talking to a parishioner who had married his high school sweetheart and being so envious I wanted to hit him. I remember everything we did together, everything we are to each other, and when I look at you, it's like this big, black chasm. The only happiness in my life was just taken away from me."

I leaned forward, shifting closer to him. "So, take the potion, Leo. Just take it. I don't know if it's going to work on Desmond anyway, but I figured this much out. I'll figure something else out. I'm smart, and I can—"

"It's your best chance of getting through to him, of saving not just yourself, but your mother. Ms. Troudt. Clementine. Stacy, that kid's seventeen."

"You think I don't know that?" I thought about Clementine, her sweetness and vulnerability, and then shook my head against it. I was Stacy Easter, and I did what I wanted, and to hell with everyone else. If that was who I was, then there had to be an upside, and saving Leo at the expense of everything else . . .

I took in a deep breath as my stomach roiled.

"Look," I said desperately, "this might not even work on Desmond. Who's to say he's not naturally a sociopath to begin with? This is all guesswork, Leo, and I have no friggin' idea what I'm doing here."

"Which is why you've got to try everything you have," he said. "Including that potion."

I sighed. "I gave one of the purple vials to Cain to try to figure out what's in it. That means I've got one left. Assuming that none of us uses our powers, that might buy us another day or two. I can figure something out. There's time."

"Maybe," he said. "You're relying on a lot of ifs."

"I know," I said. "Worse comes to worst, I'll just go with Desmond and be his guinea pig until I figure out something to fix all this. But I can't . . . I can't live the rest of my life looking at you and seeing . . ."

I crumbled over, weeping into my hands, and Leo was immediately at my side. He pulled me up into his arms and held me, and for a moment, it all felt better.

Until I pulled back and our eyes met, and there was nothing there.

"We can still get married," he said. "Maybe . . . maybe I can fall in love with you all over again."

"Maybe," I said, my breath catching in my chest. "Maybe not. But this . . ." I motioned toward him. "This is worse than dying, worse than going with Desmond. My heart breaks every time I look at you. I can't live a lifetime like that."

He lowered his eyes. "No. I guess not."

I took both his hands in mine. "Please, Leo. Please, *please*. Just take it. I can't do any of this without you. I used to be able to function without you, but you came back and you ruined that and you can't leave me now."

"I'm not going anywhere," he said softly.

I looked at him, the sight of him blurring through my tears. "You're already gone."

"You have to focus on Desmond," he said. "We'll deal with me afterward, but right now you've got to stay on task."

"I can't focus on anything else while you're like this," I said, crying so hard I could barely get the words out. "I can't do it, Leo. I can't."

"Hey, shhh," he said, drawing me back into his arms. I wept onto his shirt, and he held me, comforting me. I pressed my face to his chest, trying to pretend he was still there, that when I pulled back and looked into his eyes it wouldn't stab me through the heart.

"Okay," he said finally, his voice almost a whisper.

"Okay, what?" I asked, sniffling.

"I'll take the potion."

I stepped back, my heart racing. "You will? You mean it?"

He looked at me with dead eyes. "I believe in you. You're so smart. You can fix this, and I know you will."

I threw my arms around him, hugging him tight. "It's just inside, in my messenger bag. I'll be back in a couple of seconds. I don't have a hypodermic needle, but Cain said it can go through the skin, as long as you don't wash it off." I kept my eyes closed and kissed him. He kissed me back, and it was a little cold, a little removed, but I didn't care. Leo would be back with me in just a little while; I could hold on until then.

I started for the back door, only turning when I heard Leo call my name.

"What?" I said, swiping at my face and sniffling through my smile. "You can't take it back now. No changing your mind."

He smiled, although it didn't quite reach his eyes. "I love you. I may not feel it right now, but I know it. I want you to know it, too. I'm doing this because I know that I love you."

I nodded, but couldn't say anything, not while he was looking at me with that dead expression. Not when the spark would be back in a little while. I ran inside to the living room, grabbed my messenger bag, and rushed back out.

Leo was gone. I glanced around, twirling in circles until I heard the old familiar rattle of Nick's truck starting up. My heart sank to the pit of my stomach, and I ran down the alley between Liv's and Peach's houses just in time to see Nick's truck take the corner onto Main.

Nick, however, was standing on the porch, staring off after it.

"Nick?" I said.

He turned to me, and his expression went from confusion to compassion. "Stace." In that one word was everything. Sorrow. Pity. Bad news on the horizon.

I forced my leaden feet to move. Nick came down the porch to meet me.

"He made me promise I wouldn't let you follow him." Nick took my arm and led me to the porch steps, where I sat with a *thud,* staring down the empty street. Even the faint rattle of Nick's crappy muffler was gone.

"He told me to tell you that everything he said was true, and that's why he had to go. I don't know what that means, but . . ."

He trailed off, sitting next to me on the stoop. I couldn't

even get up the energy to sob, or breathe. Tears just welled and dripped down my face as I stared off into the distance.

"Hey." Nick put his arm around my shoulders. "He'll come back."

"No," I said. "He won't."

"You don't know that. Leo's a good guy. Whatever happened between you two, he'll do right by you."

"I know." I tried to smile, but my lips just trembled. "That's why he's not coming back."

"Oh." He tightened his grip around my shoulders. "I'm sorry."

I sniffed and swiped at my face. "Yeah. Me, too."

We sat there, watching the empty street where Leo had gone, my big brother once again with his arm around me, trying to protect me from the world. Even when he was mad at me, he always loved me first, and the thought made me cry even harder. In response, Nick held me tighter, letting me get tears all over his shirt.

After a while, I pulled myself together enough to look at him. "I'm sorry I broke the Widow and ruined your honeymoon."

"Hey." He gave a dismissive wave. "She was broken when we got her. I shouldn't have yelled at you. I was just pissed because I was getting a lot of sex in Spain, and then there's Mom, staying with us . . . well." He shrugged. "It put kind of a spanner in the works, if you know what I mean."

"Ew," I said, and swatted at him, then I remembered that Leo was gone and a fresh wave of grief hit me. My eyes filled with tears and I crumpled against my big brother again. He held me there for a while, patting my back, only speaking again once I'd calmed down a bit.

"Hey, you want a steak? Peach took Mom to get some more things from the house, so it's just you and me. It'll be like old times, when I used to cook dinner for us. Come on. You know I hate eating alone. Let me fix you a steak."

Despite myself, I laughed. Nick was like an Italian mother that way. There was no problem so bad that food couldn't fix it. At the moment, eating was the last thing on my mind. My stomach was a mess, and I wasn't even sure I'd be able to keep anything down. But Nick showed his love through food, and there was nothing else he could do to make me feel better, so I should at least let him feed me.

"I don't know," I said. "Can I put ketchup on it?"

"No," he said, standing up and holding his hand out to me. "What are you? A savage?"

I let him pull me up to standing. "A1 Sauce? Something?"

"You put sauce on crap." He put his arm around my shoulders and led me up to the porch. "You don't put sauce on a good steak. You think I would feed you a bad steak?"

"I like the sauce," I said, then sniffled and wiped my eyes with the back of my hand, the way I did when we were little.

"I am going to make you a steak so good, you'll never want sauce again."

"But I *like* the sauce."

Nick opened the front door and looked down at me, and his expression softened.

"Okay," he said quietly. "You can have the sauce."

I couldn't eat much of the steak, but Nick was happy with a few bites, and once I'd stopped the breathless hiccuping that followed my sob fest, he walked me back to Liv's. By the time I crawled into Liv's guest bedroom, I was almost too exhausted to hurt much anymore. I knew it would come, that there would be days of unbearable pain in my near future, but for the moment, I could sleep.

When my cell phone rang, I was a little disoriented. It

was light outside, but I wasn't sure if it was still light because the sun doesn't go down until nine thirty in June, or if it was morning. I was still trying to figure that out when I answered the phone.

"Yeah?" I grumbled.

"Stacy?" It was Peach. I glanced at the clock: eight thirty.

"Is it night, or morning?" I asked, blinking.

"Night," she said. "You okay?"

"No," I said. "What's up?"

"It's your mother. We brought her out here to her house to pick up some of her things, and then a whole bunch of people came by and she started in on a sermon, talking about some kind of ultimate sacrifice or whatever, and now . . . well, she's glowing."

"Fuck." I sat up straight and shook my head to help wake myself up. I stuffed my feet into my sneakers and grabbed for my messenger bag. "Fuck, fuck, fuck."

"Yeah," Peach said. "It's pretty bad."

"I'm on my way."

I ran down the stairs two at a time. Liv and Tobias and Cain must have been out back, because I didn't see them, and I didn't take the time to find them to explain where I was going. I got in the Bug and zipped through town until I pulled up in front of my mother's. The lawn was full of people, and the Widow was on the porch, her arms outstretched.

"It is through sacrifice that God showed His love for us," she said, "and through my sacrifice, I will show my love for you."

"Oh, Christ," I said, and a woman near me turned around and said, "Amen," and then looked back at my mother.

Peach met me at the side of the house.

"Please tell me she doesn't have any sharp objects up there with her," I said. "This sacrifice talk is making me nervous. There's no chance there's a goat staked out back or anything, is there?"

"No sharp objects," Peach said, "but no goat, either. I have no idea what the hell she's talking about."

"Yeah, well if it's any comfort, I don't think she does, either."

Peach touched my arm. "I'm so sorry. I didn't know what to do. It just happened, and all of a sudden it was out of control."

"None of this is your fault," I said. "Go back home, be with Nick, and stand by the phone. If we're in the hospital again tonight, I'll call you. If we're not in the hospital tonight, I'm gonna kill her, and you don't want to be an accomplice."

"Okay." She grabbed my hand and squeezed it. "We are going to have a lot of drinks when this is over."

"It's a date," I said. Peach left and I pushed my way through the crowd to get to the porch. I touched the Widow's arm.

She looked at me, smiling. "Stacy," she said warmly. "I'm so glad you're here."

"Turn off the lights, Widow," I said under my breath, and then I turned to look at the crowd. "Show's over, people! Go home!"

The Widow closed her eyes and shut down the glow. The crowd began to grumble with disappointment, but the Widow waved her hand and silenced them.

"You may stay," she said. "The time for my sacrifice is now, and there must be witnesses."

"Widow," I said, but just then the crowd parted and there was Desmond, walking through the throng carrying a wicker basket full of little purple vials.

"For my lady," he said loudly, making a show, "I bring my offering."

He lifted the basket up above his head and she took the handle, fawning over it as though it were flowers.

"Thank you so much, Desmond," she said. "I'm ready to make my sacrifice."

My heart pounded as I finally understood what she was talking about. I grabbed her arm.

"I don't want to be the one to discourage you from doing something unselfish," I said. "Everyone should have every experience at least once, but . . . you're not going with him."

She set the basket of vials on the bench behind us and put her hands on either side of my face.

"This may be hard for you to understand," she said, "but it's what I must do. It's the only answer."

Desmond moved closer, and I put out a warning hand, letting all of my emotion flow, and the air around my palm started to dance with heat.

"Don't you move," I growled. "She's not in her right mind, and if you take one step closer, I swear, I'll set you on fire." I looked back at my mother. "Go inside. Lie down. You're not going with him."

"No," the Widow said. "I'm not."

For a moment, just a moment, I was relieved. And then, I looked again at the basket of vials in her hand. Purple vials. Not the cure, but the continuation, the stuff that would keep the magic going. I lowered my hand, not because I was releasing my threat on Desmond, but because the shock made it impossible for me to hold up my arm on my own power.

"Mom?" I said, my voice warbling.

She smiled at me, her eyes filling with tears. When she spoke, she spoke loudly, so that everyone within a country mile could hear my mother betray me.

"For God so loved the world that He gave His one and

only Son," she said. "And I so love you all, that I give my one and only . . . *daughter."*

She motioned for Desmond to move closer, and he did. I just stared at her.

"What are you doing?"

"Desmond and I have talked," she said, "and he's promised me that I can continue my ministry, my work, my sacred calling. He'll keep me stocked with all the potions I need, and I can make sure that Ms. Troudt and the little checkout girl get what they need, too. In return, all he wants is you."

I heard Desmond's footsteps coming closer behind me, but I didn't even bother to look at him. I just stared at *her.*

"I'm a grown woman. You can't give me away to someone. It doesn't work like that."

"Well, one of us has to go," she said, "or he won't give us the formula. Isn't that right, Desmond?"

"That's about it, yes," he said.

"See?" She focused back on me. "Deidre Troudt and that checkout girl don't have the kind of power we have, so it must be one of us. And it can't be me. I have my flock." She motioned out at the crowd, all of whom were still watching.

I motioned to my face. "Do you see this? Just last night, this guy hit me in the face. He split my lip."

"Oh, darling." She reached up and gently touched the bruised side of my face. "Do you expect me to believe you didn't provoke him?"

It took me a moment to realize that she'd actually said what I thought she just said, but still, all I could choke out was a raspy, "Excuse me?"

"Oh, come on. You know how you get when you're angry."

I knew what was coming. I knew it. And yet, I couldn't

stop myself. "No, Widow," I said, my voice thick. "How do I get?"

She blinked twice as though shocked I would even have to ask, and then she said, "You're ugly. Vicious. Mean. Maybe Desmond can help you with that. The good Lord knows I couldn't, but we all have our failures."

How that could take the breath out of me, how that simple statement I'd heard a thousand times before could break the last of my will, I'll probably never understand. But it did. I could feel it. All the fight just drained out of me. I'd been fighting so hard to change things, to make them different, to save my mother, to keep Leo . . . and none of it mattered. Nothing ever changed. There was no winning.

It was over. Leo was gone, and he wasn't coming back. My mother was hateful, selfish, and incapable of loving anyone, and she was never going to change. I'd miss Liv and Peach and Nick and Tobias, but they had one another; they'd be okay without me. And if I went with Desmond, he'd give the cure to Deidre and Clementine. I could see to that much, at least. I wasn't needed here anymore. I could just . . . go.

It was insane how comforting that was, that act of just letting go. As awful as everything was, the idea of not having to fight anymore was so welcome. Acceptance flowed through me, and suddenly my stomach was calm, my shoulders unclenched. This was it; this was my life.

I didn't have to fight anymore.

I turned to look at Desmond. "I won't go with you until you've given the cure and the formula to make more to my friend Cain. You have to give him both."

There was a flash of surprise on Desmond's face, as if he hadn't been expecting it to be so easy, and then he looked from the Widow to me, and there was almost an expression of compassion there.

"Of course," he said.

I nodded, then turned to the Widow.

"Well," I said. "This is it."

She smiled. "Don't be so maudlin. It's just for a little while, until Desmond gets his proof published. We'll see each other again."

"No," I said. "We won't."

I turned to Desmond. "You ready?"

He pushed up off the railing and held out his arm, motioning for me to go first. I started down the porch steps, keeping a few steps ahead of him, my eyes focused on his silver car. About halfway down my mother's walk, he took my elbow to guide me.

I allowed it.

I stared out the window at the darkening sky as Desmond drove. He had the good sense to remain silent for most of the trip, until we pulled up at the B&B.

"Did you need to go home, get some things?" he asked as he pulled my door open for me. "We'll be leaving tonight."

"Nope." I got out and patted my messenger bag. "What I don't have in here you can buy me on the road."

Desmond raised a brow, but wisely didn't say anything else. On numb legs, I followed him into the B&B, feeling somewhat out of my own body. The day had been so full of loss and pain and betrayal that it was like my entire soul was bruised beyond the point where I could feel anything. I followed Desmond mutely through the back entrance, the kitchen, up the stairs, to the hallway . . .

Past the half-moon table in the hallway. I stopped and stared down at it, blinking as though coming out of a fog.

"Everything all right?" Desmond asked, stopping at his bedroom door.

"Mmm?" I glanced up at him. "Oh. Yeah. I'll wait out here."

He skillfully lowered his eyes, approximating an affect of shame he didn't feel at all, although I had to wonder why he bothered. He took a few steps toward me, and I took a step back.

"I am truly sorry," he said. "I get . . . difficult when I'm thwarted. But now that we're working together, of our own free will, I'm hoping we can put that unpleasantness behind us and be . . . well . . . if not friends, then friendly."

I pretended to think about that for a bit, and then I lied. "Yeah. I'd like that."

He smiled. "Excellent. I'll just be a moment."

I waited until he was inside the room, and then I carefully picked up the letter opener and slid it under the lid of the half-moon table the way I'd seen Addie do when we were here before. The hidden drawer popped open, and I carefully put item by item into my messenger bag until I got to the tranq gun. I took the needle out and examined it for a minute, amused by the puffy red ball at the end. I had no idea what that was about, but I figured, the people who made these things knew what they were doing, right? With shaking hands, I pushed the plunger on the dart until all the tranquilizer liquid was spit out into the drawer, and then I pulled out my little hamster-sized Samsonite. I got the top off the tiny vial and inserted the tip of the needle, pulling the plunger back until it sucked up every last bit of the potion inside. I had just gotten the dart back into the tranquilizer gun when Desmond walked out of the room.

"We'll have to make one more stop on the way out of town. I've kept the cure in a safe place, as I'm sure you can understand."

That's when Desmond looked at me, and registered the dart gun in my hand.

"Well, hello," he said.

"Hello." I held the gun out and pulled the trigger. It clicked. Nothing happened.

"Shit," I said. I pulled the trigger again.

Click. Nothing.

"Shit."

"What are you doing?"

I sighed. "Nothing. You know me. I can't help myself. I just never give the fuck up, you know?" I held up the gun. "Tranquilizer gun. Addie's probably never used it, and apparently, it doesn't even work." I set the stupid thing on the table and shook my head at it.

He laughed. "And what was your plan? You'd knock me out and get away? How would that have helped you or your friends?"

"You're right. I didn't think it through. I'm just stubborn, you know? It would be so much easier if I would just give up. Why do I have to make things so hard on myself? Why can't I just give up?"

He angled his head in a carefully contrived look of sympathy. "I understand. I'm the same way. I mean, look at all the mayhem I've caused here, all in the single-minded pursuit of one thing. I'm quite lucky, in that I don't feel the consequences of it as much as you do." He hesitated a moment and then said, "You know, I do have an idea that might make things easier for you."

"Yeah?"

"You feel things very deeply, Stacy. You try to pretend that you don't, but even I can see it, and I have hardly any emotions left at all. It just seems that all this might go a bit easier on you if you didn't have to struggle so with all of that. After the way your mother betrayed you, and with Leo unable to love you anymore—"

Anger flared hot inside me. "Don't you ever say his name to me," I growled.

"Of course," he said, reminding me of the polite, reserved Desmond I thought I had known. "My apologies."

"Fuck you," I said.

"Fair enough." He lowered his head, faking sensitivity. "At any rate, I do have some more of the Anwei Xing root. If you'd like, before we leave, we can stop by your charming little garden shed and I can mix something up to help you release all of this and move forward."

I gave a bitter chuckle. "Oh, yeah. Two sociopaths making their way through the American countryside. What could possibly go wrong?"

Desmond laughed, too. "Yes. Well. It is possible to be a functioning member of polite society."

"Until there's something you want and you get all single-minded about it," I said.

He shrugged. "It was just a thought."

"Keep your thought," I said. "I'm going to pass."

"All right," he said, then looked pointedly down at the tranq gun on the table. "I will have to ask you to step back while I retrieve that gun. Better safe than sorry, you know."

I looked down at it, the stupid, pointless weapon on the table, and that's when I saw the little orange switch on the back of the handle.

"Huh," I said numbly.

"I'm sorry?"

I looked at him, wondering what the chances were that I would be able to grab the gun, flip the switch, and shoot him before he got to me. Even in my stunned and emotionally battered state, I could think clearly enough to know I'd need a distraction. I reached into my messenger bag, and Desmond started toward me.

"I do wish you'd stop this, Stacy," he said. "It's not going to be any easier on you if you keep—"

The Edison vial smashed at his feet, and he stopped, stunned. While he was looking down at the puddle of blue liquid at his feet, I reached out and quietly flipped the safety on the tranq gun, but was unable to grab it before he looked back at me.

"I'm sorry," he said. "I'm not certain of your intent here. Are you hoping I'll slip on this?"

"No," I said.

"Then what . . . ?" He stopped speaking as the sunflower began to sprout. He knelt down and examined it closer.

"Did you do this?" he asked, a hint of genuine wonder in his voice. Apparently all his emotions weren't dead.

"Yes," I said simply.

Desmond smiled up at me. "And you've had no formal training?"

"Nope."

"Well, I had no idea you were so good, Stacy." He pushed on his knees and stood up. "That's quite impressive."

"Well," I said, "I'm an impressive girl."

And then I grabbed the gun and shot him in the stomach.

Chapter 18

Desmond looked down at his middle and laughed, although I think it was mostly out of shock.

"You shot me," he said. "You bloody bitch."

He pulled the dart out, the red bobbin at the end bouncing with the movement. I could see from where I stood that the plunger had gone all the way down; every last drop of that potion was inside Desmond.

I stood where I was, not sure what to do now. Should I run? Maybe not. I hadn't disabled him, and I kinda thought that if I ran, he might kill me before the potion took full effect. *If* it took effect. If he didn't just kill me where I stood. But the fact was, I wasn't letting that bastard out of my sight until my mother, my friends, and I were safe and non-magical again. If that meant I needed to handcuff myself to the son of a bitch, that's what I would do.

I really hoped it wouldn't come to that.

"Wow," I said. "I didn't think this through. How are you feeling?"

Desmond straightened, evaluating. "I'm all right." He moved his head, looked around. "Not even dizzy. What kind of tranquilizer is that?" He barely got the words out before his face contorted in pain and he doubled over.

"Yeah, that first hit is pretty tough," I said, remembering how it was for me at the wedding when the potion wore off. That was with a potion brewed from just the leaves of Anwei Xing; I couldn't even imagine how Desmond was feeling. "You might want to sit down."

"What did you . . ." He gasped in pain, then tried again. "What did you do?"

"It counteracts the Anwei Xing," I said. "Welcome back to the world of guilt and remorse and shame, Desmond."

"Oh, Jesus." He leaned over, one arm on the wall, propping himself up. His breathing became ragged, and he cursed a few more times. I stayed where I was, feet braced, ready to ride out the storm.

"Oh, my God," he whimpered and slowly crumpled to the floor. "Oh, Christ, what have I done?"

I moved closer, squatting down next to him. "You fucked with the wrong girl, that's what you did. Now tell me, where is the cure?"

He started to sob and I nudged him with my knee.

"Look, dude, I'll feel sorry for you later. Right now I want an answer. Where is it?"

"It's in . . . a safe place," he said, breathing hard.

My heart started to pound with the first real emotion I'd felt in hours: excitement. "Take me there. Now."

He nodded, slowly and with a lot of pain, but it was definitely a nod.

"Let's go then." I grabbed his arm to pull him up. In a moment, he whipped me around by my shoulders and slammed me against the wall so hard I felt the impact zinging in my teeth.

"What . . . the fuck . . . did you do to me?" he screamed, his eyes red-rimmed and wild with emotion: fear, grief, anger, remorse. Which, in the moment, made perfect

sense: The emotion doesn't cease to exist, it stores up, and once the potion wears off, it all comes slamming into you at once. Desmond was experiencing five years' worth of emotional pain all at once.

"Oh, I *really* did not think this through," I groaned.

He pulled me forward and slammed me against the wall again, my head hitting hard enough to make me see stars for a minute. He let me go and, ears ringing, I slid down the wall to the ground, my legs crumpling under me like toothpicks.

"I have to . . . to . . . undo it." He took two steps toward the bedroom, then one back toward me in the hallway, then back toward his room. I wondered absently if he was looking for something to disembowel me with. I tried to clear my head and move my legs, but for the moment I couldn't. All I could do was breathe and hope he didn't bash my head in with the hall mirror before I could get my legs working again. The room spun around me, and I blinked hard to keep the darkness at the edge of my vision from taking over.

He held out his hands; they were shaking violently. "I can't . . . I can't . . . I can't make the Anwei Xing potion like this." He moved over to me and grabbed me, hauling me up. "You'll make it."

"Okay," I said, thinking, *If he needs me, he can't kill me.* "Okay. I'll make it. But you can't hit me again or I'm going to—"

Then I pitched forward, vomited on his shoes, and fell into darkness.

When I woke up, I had a sharp pain in my stomach, my hands were bound behind my back, and the whole world was pitching under me in an irregular rhythm. I could smell earth and trees and leaves, which wasn't a clue that helped me out a whole lot. I managed to open my eyes but all I could see in the dim moonlight was the blurred cotton of the back of a man's shirt. I raised my head a little to try to see more of my surroundings and the darkness threatened to take me again, so I closed my eyes and breathed. Once my eyes were closed, I was able to put everything together: I was slung over Desmond's shoulder, hurtling through the woods, headed to my garden shed. Desmond, for his part, was playing up the crazy, sniffling and crying and mumbling to himself as he staggered through the wooded path.

"Hey," I said, but my voice was weak and he couldn't hear me over all the crazy.

"Hey!" I said again, shouting as loud as I could with his shoulder in my gut. He stopped roughly, and I almost pitched out of his grip.

"Put me down," I said, "or your pants and your shoes are gonna have something in common."

He set me down, glaring fiery red hatred at me, spittle flying from his lips as he spoke. "You're going to make this potion for me, you fucking cunt, and then I'm going to kill you."

"Okay," I said. "As long as we have a plan."

I staggered forward on the path with Desmond muttering and cursing behind me. He was carrying a briefcase in his hand; apparently, he'd gone to his safe place while I was still knocked out. I stopped and looked at him.

"Is my cure in there?"

"The cure doesn't matter. You're going to make the potion, and I'm going to kill you." Even in the darkness, I could see enough crazy in his eyes to know this was absolutely his plan. I could try to run, but the cure was in that briefcase, and I wasn't going anywhere until I had it.

"At least take these bindings off," I said. "I can't make potions without my hands."

He glared at me. *"Move."*

I let out a huff of frustration and started toward the shed. Once we got there, I stopped at the door.

"You have to pull the generator cord," I said. "I can't work without light."

He cursed but, unable to argue, he pulled the cord. Once, twice . . .

I closed my eyes and tried to ward off my dizziness. It would be tough with my hands bound, but he was weak and disoriented enough that I might be able to knock him over in the dark and take the briefcase. Then I could run, hoping that his disorientation was worse than my own.

Come on, generator, I thought. *You've been threatening to die for ages. Just keep him pulling on the cord, and once the world stops spinning, I'll slam his head against you and . . .*

And that's when the damn thing took. The interior of the shed lit up like Christmas.

Stupid generator.

I opened my eyes and the dizziness was still there, but it was better. There was hope. I just had to get him to unbind my hands.

"I have to get the keys," I said.

"Allow me," he said savagely, then slammed me against the wall and reached into my pockets. He took out my keys, unlocked the door, and pushed me inside. I stumbled a bit and got my footing, and he stepped in behind me and shut the door. He leaned against it, breathing so heavily I thought he might faint. I waited to see if that would happen, as it would simple my day up considerably. He stumbled to the wall and crumpled to the floor, but remained conscious, looking at his hands, which were shaking like nothing I'd ever seen.

"I can't . . . I can't . . ." His voice was so thick with emotion that I almost felt sorry for the son of a bitch.

"Look," I said, trying to keep my voice calm and clear

so he could understand me, "do you want the Anwei Xing potion or not? If you do, just cut me loose and let's get to it."

He didn't respond, just stared at his hands, his mouth opening and shutting like a fish's, gasping for something that wasn't there.

"Okay, fine." I walked over to my workbench, turned my back to it, and fumbled to pull the drawer open. I felt around inside until I located the cold, bulky handle of my X-Acto knife, which I grabbed and slid between my wrists.

"Yeah, there's no way this can go horribly wrong," I muttered, and started sliding it against the plastic of the cable tie. In a moment, I was free, and the damage to my wrists was fairly minor, especially compared with how my head and gut felt. I turned to face Desmond with the knife out, ready to defend myself, but he just sat there, head in his hands. The briefcase, with my cure in it, was on the ground, a good three feet from where he huddled against the wall.

"Well, that's anticlimactic," I said.

And then he dropped his head in his hands and wailed. In all my life, I've never heard anything like it, that sound that wrenched up from his gut and tore through him like a movie alien. As much as I wanted to kill him, his pain was palpable in the room, and I couldn't help but feel it. I sat down, putting myself between him and the briefcase just in case, and awkwardly patted his arm.

"Look, it's gonna be okay," I said, my voice low. "I'm not even sure how much of this is provable in a court of law, anyway. I could press charges on the battery but . . ." I released a huff of disgust. "I'm not really that keen on releasing you back into society, though."

"Alysia," he whispered, almost choking on the name.

"Maybe now's not the time to think about her," I said,

and he turned to me, his eyes still wild, but softer now, as though he couldn't quite focus.

"I'm so sorry, Alysia." He reached out to touch my face and I flinched back. He didn't seem to notice, just reached for me and touched me gently.

"You're so beautiful," he said, smiling through the tears overflowing from his eyes. "I thought I'd never see you again."

It took me a moment to realize he thought *I* was Alysia; the pain and grief had taken him straight from crazy to delirious.

"Oh, wow, I *really* did not think this through," I muttered.

"I don't blame you," he said. "You hate me. Of course, you'd hate me."

I sighed and took a moment, then said, "I don't hate you." I was sure I didn't sound like her, I wasn't even convinced I looked much like her, but I knew he thought I was her, and my heartbreak was too fresh for me not to sympathize with his.

"I didn't know you would suffer," he said. "If I had, I never would have agreed to give it to you."

"It was her idea?" I said.

"I'm so sorry . . . ," he sobbed. "I'm so, so sorry."

The poor pathetic son of a bitch. "I know," I said. "It's . . . it's okay."

"When you died . . . I couldn't . . . it was too hard. I was weak, I . . ." He hung his head. "I can't live with this."

"Yeah, you can," I said.

He looked at me, his eyes red and pathetic, his face awash with tears and crippled by pain. Sure, maybe he deserved it, but that didn't mean I deserved to watch it.

"How?" he said, sobbing.

"You just . . . live with it. People do terrible things every day. It happens. You just have to wake up the next morning and stop doing terrible things. That's all you can do."

"Alysia . . . ," he said.

I couldn't take it anymore. "Desmond, I'm not Alysia."

He raised his head and blinked a few times, trying to focus.

"I'm Stacy," I said, "and you messed with my life really bad. You gave my mother magical powers, you made me accidentally dose my favorite teacher, and you screwed with a seventeen-year-old kid. You physically assaulted me, more than once, and you took the love of my life away from me, and right now, I want to kill you with my bare hands."

He seemed to recognize me then, and his eyes widened as he glanced at the X-Acto knife that was still in my hand. He was lucid; he was coming back.

"But I won't," I said, and tossed the knife away, well out of his reach without having to go through me; I wasn't taking any chances. "The problem is, you're not the same guy who did that stuff. He's gone, and now you're here, and killing you isn't going to make the rest of it any better."

He stared at me, misery emanating from his being. "You should kill me. You'd be doing us both a favor."

"No," I said. "I'd be doing *you* a favor. But I'd have to live with it, and you're not worth that."

And with that, I pulled myself up, picked up the briefcase, and walked out of the garden shed, leaving him alone in his misery.

Chapter 19

I sat across from Deidre Troudt at CCB's two weeks later, and goddamn if that woman didn't want another potion.

"I'm still in training," I said. "I can't make potions for the public until I've finished my apprenticeship, and that takes years."

"Look, I just need it for a little while," she said. "Darius and I can't see each other until the situation has been officially peer-reviewed, or he can lose his license. Something about taking advantage of me in my vulnerable state, *blah blah blah*. Like we haven't been together longer than most married couples, anyway. I just need something to . . . you know," She quirked a brow at me. "Relieve the tension."

"Jesus, Deidre," I said. "There are a lot of ways to do that, and I don't want to help you with any of them."

She blinked in confusion, then gave me a wry look. "I've got that covered, thank you. I'm talking about something to help me with my patience."

"How about developing some patience?"

She narrowed her eyes at me. "Have I told you you're too skinny?"

I smiled at her. "Not today, no."

"Refill?"

I looked up and there was Clementine, holding out a carafe of coffee. She'd gotten new glasses with dark, rectangular frames, and her hair was cut to shoulder length. Her uniform was the standard periwinkle dress that every waitress at CCB's had to wear, but she looked good in it, although that probably had as much to do with being under Deidre's watchful eye. I'd never seen a seventeen-year-old kid stand straighter.

"Well, dig you," I said, holding my mug out for her to fill.

She grinned and pushed up her glasses. "I know."

"How's everything going with your mom at home?" I asked.

Her expression dimmed a little, but she managed a smile and nodded. "Better. She still says things sometimes, but . . ."

"Yeah, and what do you say?" Deidre said, a glint of pride in her eye.

Clementine smiled. "I say, 'I'll listen to what you have to say when you speak to me with respect,' and then I walk away."

"Wow," I said. "That's working?"

Clementine shrugged. "A little. She's not around that much, so . . . it works enough."

"And how are things going with . . . ?" I gave a directed look toward the front counter, where Henry sat on a stool, eating waffles. He'd been showing up at CCB's a lot since Clementine started working there.

Clementine went red, whispered, "Shut up," and scurried off to refill Henry's coffee mug.

"Here's to young love," Deidre said, holding up her coffee mug for a clink. I hesitated, just a second, and then lifted mine.

"Sorry," she said. "Was that insensitive? I know you and North were a thing, and then he kind of disappeared into nowhere. You hear from him?"

The bell on the front door of CCB's jingled, and I looked up to see who had walked in. Deidre looked as well.

"Ugh," she said. "Him."

Desmond glanced around, saw me with Deidre, and headed to a series of empty seats at the far end of the counter. I picked up my purse.

"I gotta go," I said, and dumped a few bills on the table.

"I can't believe you still talk to that guy," she said.

"Yeah, it's complicated," I said. "He owes me a favor."

"All right." She got up from our booth and dumped some more cash on the table. Clementine was getting a hefty tip today. "I guess I'll see you at work pretty soon. When do you start again?"

"August twentieth," I said. "Just enough time to get everything in order before the fall semester starts."

"Great," Deidre said, smirking. "Just what those dumb high school boys need, a goddamned sexy librarian."

I laughed, waved good-bye, and walked over to where Desmond was sitting. I took the stool next to his, and I could feel him tense up next to me. He always did that, and while I should be comforted at the sign that his guilt was actively keeping him in check, it made me tense, too.

"Hey," I said.

"Hello," he said.

"Any luck?"

There was a long pause, and then he said, "I'm sorry. Has your friend Cain found another source?"

"Nope. His went off to Africa and disappeared into the ether."

Desmond nodded. "And what of your search for Leo?"

I shook my head. "No joy. He might have gone to Africa, too, for all I know."

"I'm sorry," Desmond said.

"Eh, you know." I shrugged and forced a smile. "Better to have loved and lost and all that, right?" I didn't mean it. I'd fallen asleep crying every night for the last two weeks, but no way was I going to let Desmond see that.

"I . . . I don't know what to say." Desmond looked at me, his eyes full of pain and regret.

"Don't say anything," I said, "and knock it off."

"I'm sorry? Knock what off?"

"If you give me that sad-sack look one more time, I swear, I'll kill you with this spoon."

He smiled. It didn't quite make it all the way to his eyes, but the emptiness was gone. He was racked with guilt and shame, and would be for a long time, probably forever, which he deserved, I guessed. I just didn't like watching it.

I pushed up from the counter, started to walk away, but then turned back to face him.

"Look, if it helps at all . . . you did me a favor."

He let out a small, bitter laugh. "Indeed? And what was that?"

"Because of you, I'm okay with my mother."

He looked confused. "What did I have to do with that?"

"I accept her for who she is now, and it doesn't bother me anymore. I don't question what's wrong with me that my mother doesn't love me. It's not me, it's her. She's just broken, and it's not my fault." I shrugged. "That was good information to have. So . . . thanks, I guess."

"You're . . . um . . . you're welcome," he said awkwardly. "How is she, anyway?"

"Nick says she's fine," I said. "She's so mad at me for making her drink the cure potion that she won't talk to me. One day she'll start again, and act like nothing ever happened."

He raised a brow at me. "And you'll forgive her?"

"Someday, maybe," I said, "but if I do, it'll be for my benefit, not hers. And I think that's a good thing."

Desmond watched me for a bit, then said, "I don't understand. Why are you trying to make me feel better about all of this?"

I stared at him for a moment, then shook my head.

"Because I'm a good person," I said with disgust, then walked out of CCB's and headed home.

I had never been much of an exerciser. Peach, she ran for something ridiculous, like five miles a day. That's insane. Me, I was always more a sit-on-the-couch kind of girl. Exert as little as possible. But ever since all of this happened, I hadn't been able to sit still. I couldn't watch television. I couldn't read. I couldn't go on the Internet. I would be still for a moment, and I'd think about Leo, and that never got any easier.

So, I walked. I walked from my house to the middle of town, ten miles round-trip, every day. Sometimes twice. I couldn't make potions anymore, not until I heard back from the conjuring trainer Cain hooked me up with, and I didn't start work at the high school library for another few weeks, so there was nothing to do but walk. Usually, I worked my way through town, visited Liv or Peach and Nick, then headed back. On that Saturday, one month to the day since Leo left, I just couldn't go near their street. I didn't know why; maybe it was because it was *that* day, and I didn't want to be at the last place I'd seen Leo. Maybe it was because it was almost sunset and I didn't want to interrupt dinner or whatever by dropping in unannounced. Almost on autopilot, I walked over to the swing set, sat down, and just watched the town go about its business as the sun laid out a pinkish glow over Nodaway.

"Is this seat taken?"

My heart jumped, the voice sounded so much like Leo's,

and when I looked up and saw that it was Leo, it took me
a moment to react. I hadn't exactly been hallucinating,
but the nightly dreams I'd been having of him returning
to me had been strangely vivid, and who the hell knew? It
was possible I was losing my mind. Stranger things had
happened, and many of them had happened to me.

He smiled, and the spark in his eye as he looked at me
made my heart sink. It had to be my imagination; the real
Leo wouldn't look at me like that now.

"Cat got your tongue?" he asked.

I still didn't respond, half certain he was going to fade
away if I so much as breathed, afraid he'd be swallowed
up by the same traitorous part of my imagination that had
spawned him in the first place.

"Kind of a strange idiom," he said, taking the swing
next to mine. "*Cat got your tongue.* You gotta wonder
about the kind of mind that thought that up."

He was close enough now that I could smell the special
whatever-it-was that made him smell like Leo. No matter
how vivid the dream, I'd never smelled him before. Still,
that wasn't proof, and I was too scared to reach out and
get that proof. I just kept staring at him, willing him to go
away on his own if he wasn't real.

He didn't go anywhere.

"You're not going to say anything?" He shrugged.
"Okay. I'll start." He looked me in the eye, the way he used
to, the way he did from the time we were kids: with love.
My heart jumped painfully in my chest and I wanted to
reach out and touch him, but I couldn't. If I was crazy now
and hallucinating, at least I was going to enjoy it. I wasn't
going to do anything that might send him away.

"I left," he said. "I know that was hard on you, but I
thought it was the only way. If I had taken that potion,
you might have died, and I couldn't allow that. So, I left."
He looked at me. "You were there for that."

"Yeah." I spoke in barely more than a whisper, afraid speaking would make him go up in a puff of smoke.

There was no puff.

"Well, let me fill you in on the stuff you missed," he said. "I went as far as I could, trying to find someplace you couldn't track me down, at least not before you had to use the potion on Desmond. It was the right thing to do, and I knew that, so I went. And for the first few days, it was okay. I didn't feel anything. I didn't miss you. It didn't hurt. But . . ." He shook his head and looked at me. "Then I remembered you."

"You did?"

He smiled. "Yeah. He wiped out my feelings, but he didn't wipe out my memories. Every day, I remembered you, and finally, I was in a truck stop in Memphis—"

"You went to Memphis?" I said. "Really?"

"Graceland, baby. Home of the King."

"You hate Elvis," I said.

"Exactly. That's why you wouldn't look for me there." He grinned at me, pleased with his own cleverness. "Anyway, I was in this truck stop and I remembered that time when we were in junior high, and you wanted to go out with me and Nick and the guys to the football game, and Nick didn't want you to go." He laughed, engaged in the memory. "And you followed us, about thirty paces away, ducking behind trees if Nick looked back. And there was this one moment when I looked back and you caught me looking back and instead of hiding, you touched your fingers to your lips and blew me a little kiss-my-ass kiss."

"Huh," I said. "I don't remember that."

"I do," he said. "I fell in love with you that day. I remember it so clearly, how that felt, and when I remembered it that day in Memphis . . . I fell in love with you again."

It all hit me in one big painful blast of hope, and I

froze on the swing as it occurred to me, for the first moment, that I might actually not be hallucinating.

"You what?"

He nodded, his eyes red-rimmed and happy. "So I got a motel room and I started writing down everything I could remember about you. The way you laughed. The things you did. The things you said. The way the left side of your mouth quirks up a little bit more than the right when you smile—"

I touched the left side of my mouth. "It does not."

"—and I fell in love with you again, and again, and again. Every day, I woke up and I remembered and I fell in love with you again. I didn't want to come back until I was sure, until I knew for sure that I could look at you and you would see . . ."

He trailed off, his voice cracking as his chin quivered.

"Can you see it, Stacy?"

I got up and walked over to stand in front of him. Slowly, I reached out and put my hands on either side of his face, looking deep into his eyes.

"Yeah," I said. "I see it."

He pushed up off the swing and pulled me into his arms, one hand caressing the back of my head as he held me tight. I laughed and kissed his cheek and squeezed him. My love. My Leo. He was real and he was back and he was mine.

Just the way it was always meant to be.

Do you love fiction with a supernatural twist?

Want the chance to hear news about your favourite
authors (and the chance to win free books)?

Keri Arthur
S. G. Browne
P.C. Cast
Christine Feehan
Jacquelyn Frank
Thea Harrison
Larissa Ione
Darynda Jones
Sherrilyn Kenyon
Jackie Kessler
Jayne Ann Krentz and Jayne Castle
Martin Millar
Kat Richardson
J.R. Ward
David Wellington
Laura Wright

Then visit the Piatkus website and blog
www.piatkus.co.uk | www.piatkusbooks.net

And follow us on Facebook and Twitter
www.facebook.com/piatkusfiction | www.twitter.com/piatkusbooks

piatkus